Praise for Hugo Charteris and Marching with April

Hugo Charteris' novel is a flight of ironic fancy employing all the darts and stings of caricature, burlesque and satire.

The Scotsman

...the book is good, savage farce, the fun has an edge, because Mr Charteris really cares about the things he is talking about, and hence is funnier than mere fooling can ever be...with whatever mixture of pain or pleasure, *Marching with April* is a book that the reader will long remember.

Observer

Immense, civilized, almost metaphysical, too.

Yorkshire Post

extremely funny...

Sunday Telegraph

Mr Charteris is witty and original, gay and gloomy together in a way I find rather exhilarating, like the smiles of a gentle and lugubrious undertaker... His characters [popping] out gargoyle-like are masterly.

Spectator

...the most original, quirky, stimulating, odd and enjoyable novel that has come my way for a very long time.

Daily Telegraph

Half-farce, half-comedy, the book is exuberantly funny and rich in invention.
Edinburgh Evening Dispatch

Mr Charteris gives grim situations a witty twist; farce has a note of fury. He is not only one of the most brilliant but one of the most incalculable of our postwar novelists...I should call him a romantic anti-romantic. *Marching with April* offers high entertainment – you may also find that this book bites deep.
Elizabeth Bowen, Tatler

Involved, bitter and very funny, Hugo Charteris is a newcomer to ~~ growing school of satirists.

Satire in a glorious broad sweep is joined in the author's narrative gift here… a delight to read. [Mr Charteris] takes over our tired old words as a chef might take a wilting lettuce and, by his art, produce a temptingly crisp salad. So does Mr Charteris, by his art, produce a freshness that is stimulating. He has a gift for a stick-in-the-mind phrase…The result is a book that will make you read and appreciate words again instead of merely skimming their sense.

Manchester Evening News

With *Marching with April* Hugo Charteris triumphantly clears the hurdle of the second novel that trips so many authors of promising firsts…It is funny in a rather frightening, obsessed way…Mr Charteris is highly observant and excels at physical description, at recording mannerisms of speech and gesture.

Francis Wyndham

MARCHING WITH APRIL

MARCHING WITH APRIL

APRIL

by

HUGO CHARTERIS

introduced by

FREDERIC RAPHAEL

with a review by

ELIZABETH BOWEN

ADELAIDE
MICHAEL WALMER
2017

141436

Marching with April first published 1956
© The Estate of Hugo Charteris

Introduction first published in this edition
© Volatic Limited 2017
Review first published in *The Tatler*, June 20, 1956
© Elizabeth Bowen 1956

Published by

Michael Walmer
49 Second Street
Gawler South
South Australia 5118

ISBN 978-0-6480233-2-6 paperback

INTRODUCTION

Hugo Charteris' first novel, *A Share of the World,* was published in 1953. Its leading character, John Grant, is heavily marked by the trauma of war. A year later, Charteris' contemporary Kingsley Amis (both were born in 1922) served notice, with *Lucky Jim*, that literary airs and rueful graces belonged to yesterday. Amis too had done National Service during the war, but he had never been under fire and won no medals. His alter ego Jim Dixon was a decidedly peacetime, lower middle-class figure, an academic arriviste made stroppy by his own good luck. Dixon's family scarcely figures in *Lucky Jim*. The progress of an upwardly mobile opportunist announced the advent of what sociologists chose to call meritocracy. The old order was done for, serious fiction and artful allusion with it.

Charteris was twice wounded in the Italian campaign and was awarded the M.C. for outstanding courage. Educated at Eton and (briefly) at Oxford, the grandson of the 11th Earl of Wemyss, he came of a line of "born leaders" on whom the British empire relied to display steadiness under fire. His first, unsmiling novel was of a rare and harsh authenticity. John Grant makes a literally fatal, if understandable, mistake and cannot escape its malign shadow. Charteris' "good war" alerted him, painfully, to the role of chance in khaki circumstances. In his first fiction, he seems to split his personality between John and Christopher, Grant's Etonian chum, whose own "good war" tips him into becoming a furious alcoholic.

Marching with April, Charteris' second novel, takes place in the immediate post-war. The British upper class, however straitened its circumstances, is doing its best to keep up ancestral appearances. Evelyn Waugh, whose *Brideshead Revisited* sentimentalised the old (recusant) aristocracy to which he could never belong, but whose manner - if never its manners - he aped, said of the period of Clement Attlee's Labour government that it was "like living in an occupied country". After Winston Churchill led the Conservatives back into power in 1951, until 1956, when the Suez Affair shattered the fantasy that Britannia could still conduct herself as if she ruled the waves, the British Establishment dared to presume that nothing fundamental had changed. Waugh continued to complain (he said that the Tories failed to "put the clock back by a single minute"), but five years of unrationed peace passed for a return to the Good Old Days.

Lionel Spote, the principal character of *Marching with April*, is treated only a little more indulgently than John Grant. A demobbed captain in, no doubt, a good regiment, he has a private income of £5000 a year (a huge sum in the 1950s). To pass the time, he reads manuscripts for a grand publisher, called Mackintosh, very like my first publishers, Macmillan's, with their panelled offices and air of patrician patronage. We meet Lionel as he strolls down St James's. In his eyes, the palace clock seems to have stopped, as if single-handed, at noon. Where he once had three pips on his shoulder, he now carries a chip or two, for no immediately clear reason.

Why should a toff with a "cushion-margin of money and social position" not like it here at least as well as Kingsley Amis? Is Lionel Spote's febrility – revealed by the uneasy cant of his shoulders – due to his being a "black" Scot, one of those whose families emigrated, however long ago, to brighter prospects south of the border? Until the recent rise of the Scottish Nationalist Party revived separatist ambitions, "Red" Scots, who stayed north of the border, were regarded more as resigned stay-at-homes than as revenant scions of Robert the Bruce. Lionel displays no conscious wish to be anything but a southerner and, it seems, a bachelor.

The accession of the beautiful young Queen Elizabeth, in 1952, was trumpeted in the press as the dawn of a new era. In *Marching with April*, Charteris deputes a pair of minor characters, a journalist and writer called Lizz, and a sour novelist, Fleight, to put royalty in unsentimental perspective:

" 'Once they had a purpose. The best bed. The best escritoire. The most horsemen. Top of a pyramid. Now…they're a sort of coloured balloon attached by a string which anyone can jerk – from the earth below. They're civil servants.'

Fleight said, 'That may be the facts – but it's not the emotion. And why do the remains of the upper class go to such hideous lengths to get them to stay? Is it merely snobbery?'

Lizz said, 'They want to get in on the piece of string. Otherwise they're just smaller balloons without the piece of string.'

Lionel looked from one to the other. He said, 'Isn't it a good thing to have one emotion a Canadian postmistress or a Durham miner can share with an Old Etonian?' "

The chip on Lionel Spote's tailored civilian shoulder has no manifest source, apart from his domineering mother. Hugo Charteris seems to have been possessed by a *cacoethes scribendi*, a rage for writing, that presaged the brevity of his life. By the time he died, of cancer, at the age of forty-eight, in 1970, he had written nine adult novels and a good many television plays, of which the series *Take Three Girls* had the most durable reputation. *Marching with April* is paced in a staccato style which owes something to the abruptness of film and television narrative.

Charteris was only somewhat left behind by the advent of John Osborne's Angry Young Man whose speciality was denouncing the tedium of English life in the 1950s. Anger of a kind fuelled Charteris' scorn, in *Marching with April*, for the localised vanities of the dwindling number of residents in the depopulated Highlands. Lionel's inheritance of his uncle's huge estate is more an embarrassment than a blessing, since it seems to require him to stay in Scotland and play the laird. Archie Mackintosh, Lionel's London employer, basks "in John Buchan's version of the highlands", but when Lionel travels north of the border, reluctantly, he fails to find any kind of Caledonian promised land. The residual inhabitants of the Highlands are a set of provincial grotesques with whom he achieves a measure of solidarity with more resignation than enthusiasm.

Even in the 1960s, when he was publishing one novel after another, Hugo Charteris was never a modish literary figure. His long-lived cousin and contemporary, Francis Wyndham, was one of his few loud admirers. He recalls that Charteris was "a brilliant person – brilliant to meet and talk to, very attractive to women. But nobody really wanted to hear about the war and being an officer in it". Simon Raven is one of the few post-war writers who admitted to shame at being just too young to "go for a soldier", as Dr Johnson put it. Simon joined the post-war army, but was chucked out, for plonking his funds on the horses. He made larky and lucrative literary fun of his own shame and never made the mistake of boring people with upper-class *angst*.

Wyndham recalls that Charteris' sisters, Ann Rothermere (later Ann Fleming) and Laura Dudley were "terrifying – young women who married everyone they wanted to"; and had no lack of lovers whom they did not. The suggestion is that Charteris found that the values for which he thought he was fighting were little respected by those close to him. Did his "good war" leave him resentful of the smugness of those who had survived without a scratch? His sense of justice may well have been outraged by his brother-in-law Ian Fleming's runaway success with the James Bond novels (said to be President Kennedy's favourite reading). Fleming had run no known danger during his wartime career in the navy, yet his hero stood, and stands, for a notion of innate British superiority: Bond saves the sum of things for a well-stirred martini. Never seeming to suffer, even when being tortured, he stands for a new kind of self-made alpha male, to whom the civilian public could depute responsibility for protection from devious megalomaniacs.

Charteris went, with his wife Virginia, to live in the very Highlands which he eventually satirised in *Marching with April*. Why did so talkative and sociable a man as Charteris absent himself from the London scene? His success in television alone argues against any large sense of failure. His books were appreciated by the Happy Few, led by Wyndham, and he revelled in cosmopolitan gossip. Was he perhaps too honourable to take full advantage of his own advantages? Too brave to brag, too scarred to giggle, he wrote as if it mattered to get things right, not least when they had gone wrong.

In the sketchy playfulness of *Marching with April*, Charteris may well have intended to break step with the anguish and solemnity of *A Share of the World*. He certainly parades a lively talent for farcical comedy. Yet his "hero" Lionel bears unsmiling witness to the prancing absurdity of characters who, after the war in which none of them fought, mean to hang onto their petty, parochial privileges. A good part of the pleasure to be found in *Marching with April* lies in the contrast between the follies it advertises and the desperation it implies.

Of much the same vintage as *Marching with April*, Angus Wilson's first novel, *Hemlock and After (1952)*, has a similar sweet-and-sourness. When Evelyn Waugh wrote to congratulate the author on his satirical acumen, he said that he found only one character implausible: the village Madam, who rented rooms to illicit lovers. He therefore guessed (correctly) that she was drawn from life. The targets for Charteris' derisive portraiture seem to have been painfully aware of his accurate arrows. Today's readers can relish the caricatural parade of his now obsolete or extinct familiars. Another of Angus Wilson's titles, *Such Darling Dodos*, might be applied to the kilted Monarchs of the Glen, male or female, whom Charteris nails with such merciless precision.

FREDERIC RAPHAEL

London, March 2017

REVIEW

Marching with April is Hugo Charteris' second novel — his first, *A Share of the World,* attracted attention, and its successor seems likely to do the same. This time, the scene is the Highlands, though our hero's heart decidedly is not there. Lionel Spote, Londoner, is appalled when an uncle's death lands him with the estate of Rossiemurchat: he goes North with but one intention — to sell the place. Only to find himself neck-deep, poor young man, in every possible complication.

Rossiemurchat hits Lionel at a moment when he is already struggling for equilibrium. He is "a case," and knows it — has he not just emerged from a lengthy course of analysis, conducted by a ruthless German lady psychiatrist? He is an ex-prisoner of war, whose return home has landed him back again in the toils of an indefatigable Edwardian mother. (Mrs. Spote is a lady one longs to meet.)

Junior member of a venerable publishing firm, he daily wades through MSS. of neurotic fiction — if he yields to hallucination, who can blame him? Already he is more than half the prey of an ex-Mayfair existentialist spinster novelist. This is Lionel's London. The Highlands, one might have thought, should do much to blow such cobwebs away.

Far from it. Arrived at Rossiemurchat (after a dire journey) Lionel finds his own complexes waiting on the doorstep. Also, the heir is awaited by retainers, neighbours. Mrs. O'Shea, the housekeeper, loses no time in making her personality felt: successions of batty dialogues with this lady are, indeed, high points in *Marching with April.*

"Mrs. O'Shea, when do the *papers* come?"

"Today's, will it be?"

"Well...yes."

"Tomorrow, except Saturdays."

Sir Duncan Fidge, progressive Conservative M. P., hovers over Lionel's first high tea, set on involving him with the Brackenator, which is to further Highland development. An apparently empty Hillman whisks up the avenue, containing tiny but resolute Mr. Huish, factor. Alcoholic Hew Mackay of the cadets and the fanatical Rev. Abigail Skene have ready for the new laird their own private mare's-nests. Most ominous of all is the information that Lionel, at Rossiemurchat, "marches with April." What, or who, is she? What does this involve?

April is no less than Mrs. Gunter-Sykes, six-foot amazon. We are told:

> "Her voice could carry from one end of a grouse-line to another, and even for her prematurely ageing son rang as curt as for pointers. She shot well both scatter and solo, and could lay a salmon line against the wind, with a noise like a sjambok, so that it marked the water strict — a line pencilled along an invisible vast ruler. Annually she moved, like certain tribes of long ago, in the wake of game, her cycles broken only by peaks of the London season such as Lord's or Ascot which she attended with a brazen authority, that shed no deference to the changed atmosphere of England.
>
> She stood now on the Fluach face breast high amid her domestic bracken; weatherbeaten but powdered.....In her hand was a shepherd's crook seven-foot tall and on her head a deerstalker of the same tweed as her plus-eights."

With this lady, Lionel is unfortunate in sharing the River Fluach, and still more so (at a crisis) in falling into it. And even were it not for the Brackenator, to which Sir Duncan wins Lionel over, conflicts over a wide range would be inevitable. Unexpected ally is Laura, April Gunter-Sykes' dumb but lovely, far too disturbing daughter.

Complications multiply. Mrs. Spote arrives at Rossiemurchat with the family lawyer in her pocket, puts a spoke in Lionel's wheel as to selling the place, but looks with sinister favour on the romance. Lizz, the existential novelist, also arrives to stay, but is routed by the pro-Laura faction. *Marching with April* is really an agonizing comedy.

Nor is this novel comedy purely. (Nothing, for instance, could be less like the Compton Mackenzie Highland fun of the *Monarch of the Glen* series.) Mr. Charteris gives grim situations a witty twist; farce has an edge of sombreness, laughter a note of fury. He is not only one of the most brilliant but one of the most incalculable of our postwar novelists — his generation, viewing the postwar scene, have no use for comfortably blinkered humour. I should call him a romantic anti-romantic. *Marching with April* offers high entertainment: you may also find that this book bites deep.

ELIZABETH BOWEN
The Tatler, June 20, 1956

To
Charles & Elizabeth

1

"In destroying the true world we also destroyed the apparent world."

YET APPARENTLY it was twelve a.m.

Lionel Spote, with a fussy little click, pulling outwards the two sides of his moroccan leather watch, checked the correspondence of his own with St. James's Palace time. Noon it was, for there, far down, on the toy fort with its white crenellation, the clock seemed to have but one fat hand so absolutely was it twelve a.m.

He was disproportionately reassured—at the proof.

Unless of course the clock had stopped. For a single second a bottomless uncertainty pained his eyes. Then it vanished and his features formed up, column of advance, with intellectual bugles blowing.

While putting his watch away his eyes remained lifted to the clock face, there, far down over the scaly surface of traffic which had it been cattle would have been lowing mad with boredom. Then he went on.

London, for the Festival of Britain, was trim and coloured as a new denture. The sun shone, the tar-blocks smelt, cotton dresses swept webbily about bare legs and their owners, like the tar-blocks, emanated an essence—which varied with how the woman or the scent won.

7

But Lionel went down to work, without ever noticing which did.

He had five thousand a year unearned, a fact he considered germane even to his bowels and the shape of his nostrils. And, indeed, it lent him an aura.

In 1945 he had voted Socialist but had gone to work with one shoulder higher than the other—giving him the appearance on bad days of a cripple, and on not-so-bad days, of a person who had slept in a shrill draught. In 1947 the difference in levels between his shoulders varied considerably but on some days was nothing. In 1948 it was seldom noticeable. And on the day in question of 1950, a spirit level, placed in turn on each of the spots where he had once temporarily worn captain's pips, and on a line drawn between them, would have shown a perfectly central bubble. And all this in spite or perhaps because of having become richer, by £2,000 a year, earned.

Become, said Hilde Reisenthal, if necessary a postman. He had wetted the couch a little, with tears, at the idea of being so useful. But in the end it had not been necessary. He could have got any job he liked: with Transport House because he was so Public School, with the Central Office because he was so Socialist and with the Foreign Office because he spoke Russian and looked right.

Instead, after a year in Paris, he had gone into Mackintoshes', the most businesslike of publishers.

Meanwhile, gradually his treatment ended. Transference was never attained but he had shed, so to speak, the oppressive bowler and tie of his super-ego and retained its quiet suit, its " impeccable " cut, and acquired, inside it, shoulders level. So that now, after three years, he only saw Hilde occasionally, usually about her boys whom he had offered to educate under covenant, at Eton.

8

He walked on and found himself taking stock with reluctant complacence of his life. A hiker on a rise, he put his rucksack on the milestone of this moment and turned back.

Seven years ago he walked out of an Offlag, learned and well, but within a week of getting home began to go under with a queer delayed reaction. His mother put him to bed in Belgravia as though he were six and said he shouldn't go to his father's office till he was quite better. She had taken his grey flannels out of moth-balls, controlled his food and neutralised his occasional revolts like nine spaced blankets neutralise a rifle bullet. She had even brought him a book about the Spanish Civil War in which, she remembered, he had been deeply interested.

Slowly, fostered by several literary periodicals, a conviction sprouted: the last five years *hadn't happened*. This was worse than if they had.

While Lionel thought of this period a clerk sent out with letters saw his face and skirted him by a yard.

But he did not notice.

There had followed the liver-and-Harley-Street period. Pills. Finally American vitamins, a dollar a lozenge.

Then injections. He had lain in bed till eleven with his knees up to his chin. Friends had visited him. He had stared—with caged apology.

Finally the couch. Jungian, Female. With dermatitis.

In a word: Hilde.

Sometimes he just lay and didn't say anything for days. Often he went to sleep while remembering his dreams which had a snowball effect on the agenda.

But he had risen not only better, that is—able to get up in the mornings, but also with a new vocabulary and influenced generally, about everything. He had let out the bath-water guilt while preserving the twins responsibility. But he did not for a moment pretend that he could yet " take " very much. He depended too often, he knew, on such phrases as " being related " which, clearly, he'd never have harped on had he been " related ".

Such labels constituted important bearings in his cerebral desert. They had, whenever they occurred in his thoughts, a line, so to speak, to themselves—an asterisk as well. Thus:

* The shadow of John Knox was a bottle of Scotch.

He needed such banisters. He needed them most when his shoulders were not level and least, when like this morning, he was reasonably dis-enturbulated and squared off. For instance, he didn't hate that woman for her hat, and think:

* Pétainiste: Mary would do well to remember the Channel.

And so he turned down the cul-de-sac where Jaguars and self-driven Bentleys queued on the pavement like liqueur chocolates with intentions. There among service flats for dukes and film stars, in a building like a Georgian vicarage, stood the publishing house of Mackintosh.

Yes, he could face even the compulsive garrulity of Lucien Milosh—the most paranoid of all Mackintoshes' paranoid authors—with equanimity. " Have an apple, Milosh," he murmured experimentally—and then touched his breast pocket where a rustle reassured him. He had been loose of late and if Milosh wanted him to lunch at his flat it were better to be prepared.

Spote's clothes, at a distance, said he read the *Telegraph* or *The Times*, but seen closer (particularly the shirt which could often be Viyella, or even cricketing flannel) they shouted *Guardian*. In fact he read all the sober papers—and the *Express* for one minute.

He was long-headed, with an almost moorish nose and a certain un-English high colouring and hirsuteness which recalled bum-boats off Marseilles to those who had been there, otherwise pictures in the newspapers of foreigners. He was strikingly clean.

And now, continuing to relate himself, he thought that not only was his job necessary, unlike that of a journalist, from an absolute point of view, but also few people could do it as well as he and nobody *exactly* as he did it. He had his own particular flavour. For instance Milosh and Elizabeth Craik and Lady Hindshead. How many men could tune in like a crystal to expatriate, ex-Marxist Viennese Jew under three psycho-analysts, spinster under thirty existentialist novelist of Mayfair extraction and gaiety girl widow of a peer, whose memoirs had to be pruned from three thousand libellous pages. Like an experienced gardener—he could move from medlar to cactus to hydrangea —and facilitate the growth of each, sympathising with the purposes of succulent decay, desiccation and superabundant mauve fructivity.

Sympathising. His whole technique—in a single word.

The transference never failed. They rang him up sometimes at three in the morning and threatened to strike him as soon as possible.

By the time Lionel reached the scraped door of Mackintosh he was light as a party balloon with euphoria. Milosh apart—the morning's work lured like play.

Craik was coming.

Probably he was the only person she didn't hate in the world. Nothing to boast of, this—his unfailing success with

cerebral females. It merely meant he didn't make them
feel short of something, a slot perhaps. Certainly his penny
was not—*exigeant*. (The French word toned down the
pain.)

Now slightly depressed, he took off his coat in the
incensed fug and moved past the receptionist and switchboard girl—Daphne, two firsts. Mods and English. She
must have read magazine stories about street violinists
considering the way she had posted herself at the entrance
to this Albert Hall. On some mornings he permitted
himself not to look at her or have a few words with her—
but this morning, already on the rebound from euphoria
he decided to take the load.

"Daphne!" he said, surprised, exactly as he might have
done to an attractive cousin in St. James's Street. "You've
got a cold."

Ah, Christ—a pound in her hat, and what a currency.
He floated her out of focus so as not to collect the come-back
—and while she was speaking said, "I feel awful, too. I
think London is bad for one." Then he peered at her with
confiding apprehension:

"Milosh! Hm!—not here yet? I think you ought to
search him always . . . that brief-case."

They smiled together and before moving away his face
relaxed into a hint of helpless apology for going upstairs
for the preferable task of gassing to Milosh and Craik
while she sat draped in wires till she became a modern
female centaur—office stool, from the waist down. He
wished she wouldn't. He—just wished none of them would,
if they possibly couldn't. And yet they were the kind he
sought most. The ones with jobs.

The stair carpet was thick and noiseless; the whole
building " informal ". The rooms suggested those of a

12

reading squire 1880, yet here were vetted books about Arctic Slave Camps and Fission.

Mackintosh *fils*, came out at the first landing. He was an earnest worker, not gifted. He had had books and greatness thrust upon him at six and his nonchalance was as precarious as Spote's relatedness. But he was always pleased to see Lionel who was the admired cushion between him and people like Milosh and Craik.

"Lionel," he said and then with verve because the subject was not a book, "I was most awfully sorry to see about your uncle in *The Times* this morning."

Lionel always missed personal things in the papers. He waited defensively.

"My uncle . . . ?"

"Wasn't Charles Spote your uncle?"

"Has he died?" Lionel found himself smiling as unrelatedly as the drift of an unmoored boat. He might begin laughing. He made a long tightening face and then frowned as though focusing in poor light.

Archie confirmed.

And then Lionel remembered. His head suddenly shot up and he stared sideways cocked like a dog for a strange step. Slowly his eyes moved along the wall and then rested with horror on the bun of a passing secretary who disappeared adjusting it.

Seldom did courtesy or subordination so desert him. He stood bereaved of flow.

He said simply and helplessly, "Rossiemurchat."

Then he took in the senior partner. "Forgive me, Archie—I scarcely knew my uncle. He was young. Absurdly young for this. My shock is for other reasons. You see he was going to leave me a Highland estate . . ." and Lionel suddenly laughed one certifiable peal.

Had he been talking to Elizabeth Craik or Milosh he would have added, "there still are such things," and was about to add some modified equivalent when he intuited that Archie Mackintosh still basked in John Buchan's version of the Highlands.

Indeed Archie's face had taken on a perfectly appropriate Hannay expression. Sober congratulations set in moderate 12 point funereal Gothic with black borders. Also a change. A deference which had always lurked. Now surfacing—almost a diffidence.

"It seems wrong to congratulate you—at such a moment, Lionel."

"It *is* wrong," Lionel said with feeling.

Silence.

Archie said, "I hope you won't be leaving us, Lionel."

"Good heavens *no*."

The words came out like a violent sneeze and were accompanied by a sudden showing of the full circumference of Lionel's pupils. It was momentary—but it happened. Demonic.

Mackintosh *fils* was frightened. Lionel. The infallibly courteous . . .

Lionel collected himself, holding his brow, said the news was rather sudden—and with inadequate apology took to the stairs. One arm hung slack as though broken while the hand of it fumbled, reversed, in thin air.

Mackintosh, staring up after he had disappeared, heard a high disorganised laugh—then Lionel's door—like the lonely crash of suicide.

One of his shoulders, Mackintosh noted, had been high as his ear, the other had melted away bottlewise into the slack arm.

2

LIONEL WAS short with his mother. And by telephone.

The funeral was to be in London. She didn't hold a single card.

"No, Mother—I'm *not* going to stay up there for long. I simply can't see any purpose in your coming at all."

He knew he was, so to speak, twisting her arm. But he continued, because he knew what she was up to.

"I'm simply going for a few days. Find out the form. See the factor—and probably arrange for the whole estate to be auctioned . . . Hallo, hallo."

She was still there . . . Always something terrible about her pauses. Like a bird of prey opening one eye. Calm—and so collected. Fingering one pearl above black, below white, powdered pollinose white.

She said, "Why don't you come over this evening and let's talk about it."

"But what is there to talk about?"

She had learnt some of his weapons and used them recently, to the manner born. "My dear Lionel," she said *psychologically,* "your father died there in my arms, we spent his last summers there during the war—you can't expect me to feel absolutely nothing about the place even though *you would like to.*"

But it was no good. He knew what she was after. Him to live there, get ill—be given 617 instead of 408. Her to be sent for. Then ten years' convalescence in the half-light. Tension about maids. The best herbacious. A smell of antiseptic on the top landing. The occasional tactless construction of a glass case for the replica of a fish that had really been eaten long ago. And she might do it, even now, if he broke his leg at the auction.

" Mother," he said from a high far-off place of dispassion and rubber-gloved sympathy, " I *don't* want you to feel nothing for the place. I don't. I simply don't. But *I* feel nothing for the place and I can't, won't live there. Do *you* want to live there? "

The conversation went on like a maze. Frequently they came face to face through the same thicket as a minute previously. It ended with some verbal cautery from Lionel which left him touching the replaced receiver feeling absolutely meek with inevitability. She deceived herself. Had she been processed at seventeen she might have had a squeak of a chance. As it was—well, he was sorry.

★   ★   ★

The train jiggled his pencil point till he gave up.

A few sessions with the factor, arrangement for auction —visits to the older tenants.

A week—two perhaps, three at most.

He sat alone in a first-class carriage now, looking up with an offended eye at the beginnings of waste land, a vast undulating East Coker with stops at deserted platforms, on trestles.

As the last British proconsuls reconstructed Surrey in the Cameron Highlands of Malaya, where bands of aboriginal men with blowpipes stride in file beneath " Heart of Oak " hanging from olde ironwork brackets on half-timbered inns, all near the first tee—so Lionel took with him an excess of his identity—a whole array of manuscripts, and book trade periodicals.

He needed every one of them. Because although he had defeated his living mother he had been ambushed by his dead father.

The reverend figure, a prelate of shares, had come to the platform at Euston to see him off. He had shaken Lionel warmly by the hand staring into his eyes with religious anxiety—because for him a Hardy's rod had been terebinth and a Purdey gun ampulla, waders surplice of a rooted cult. Alas, only in his seventies had he been ordained—too late to initiate his children. To-day his son took on the purple. Death prevented speech but Lionel had interpreted the agonised doubt of that silent platform figure. It was quite simply this: Who would be there to tell Lionel how to conduct the rites?

When the train moved he had found voice, " Lionel, Lionel—if it's cold—wear two pairs of drawers. *No one will know.*"

The memory of this strange hallucination, as it deepened, gradually wizened Lionel's face, till he looked like an old, old orange seller in Fez. Nothing now Theta-wise—and Christ what was that blackboard?

On stilts in the waste of heather, with white lettering in relief. " The railway here is 1754 feet above sea level."

In front of this statement the train stopped. Lionel opened the window to look out but immediately closed it again. He might have opened the door of a Frigidaire.

After a second look at the hills—their dimensions, uniformity and essential blankness, he turned to the *Listener* —which he considered the best four pennyworth in the world.

Soon his eyes rested on the following paragraph:

" If you condition a dog to expect food when shown a white circle, and an electric shock when shown a black ellipse, and if you gradually make the shape of the ellipse harder and harder to distinguish from the circle, there comes a point at which the dog responds to both circle and ellipse by signs which in human beings we would call a neurosis."

The empathy which Lionel experienced for this passage obliged him to close his eyes a moment and massage them with his fingertips. The sense had been like a roulette ball bouncing delicately from ridge to ridge alighting at last in the 36-1 socket.

That dog's expression! It had only to be referred to barely and objectively—for the picture to become immediately three dimensional and vivid, and *felt*.

Lionel sat back, digesting, and when next he looked out of the window he saw not Dalwhinnie—but the fathers and grandfathers of his own particular circles and ellipses; which led to a feeling of knowledge of his own knowledge. Surely he was in National Post-war Sixth form; or perhaps he was one of the nation's ten million teachers. . . .

The likelihood weighed in until he gently put aside the periodical, and simply sat with added gravity, thinking.

There was really no reason, he thought, why the whole thing should take longer than a week. He could always make another trip later . . .

★   ★   ★

Changing at Inverness, he had tea at the Station Hotel, an experience which disturbed him.

* These people should be stuffed.

An elderly woman with soft red complexion and deer-

18

stalker matted with flies was talking to a man with a shepherd's crook half as high again as his high self. The large amount of floor space between them necessitated raised voices but not such shouts. They were discussing Geordie. Isobel had been over on Saturday and said he was much better.

"I heard he was worse," the man roared with moody aggression.

But the disagreement in no way marred the conversation which slid with ease into "Is Hughie taking Ardgower this year?" At one point the woman caught a hotel porter by the arm and whispered into his ear. He whispered back, cheerfully.

Lionel's distress deepened. Even domestic servants connived, it seemed, in the macabre.

Lionel would not have minded if there had been no more than one or two to be stuffed but as time passed the hall filled up with them and though he detected rifts of doubt in their eyes, when there were lulls in conversation, he was bound to admit their shoulders were levelled off. Their eyes rested on him with calm effrontery and he felt judged. "Tax-collector from Llandudno", "Traveller in fertilisers", and their eyes moved on without flicker to empty chairs, the swing door and wet granite outside.

Was it some premonition of all this that had jerked him into blasphemous discourtesy to Archie—that morning—premonition of more than he could take?

Outside by a monument to the Crimea, the streets had a tempo that disturbed . . . Why? All huts till 1850. Then . . . this. Washed, plum-coloured granite, temperance halls. McColls and Birrells and Woolworths, a smell of sea and space. Seed shops and seed shops. Mowers on the pavement. *A pony cart.* Ennui the spine.

His shoulder had crept up an inch. A dog was asleep on a Zebra crossing.

*   *   *

The branch train stopped often and having stopped no noise of voice or removal of luggage or arrival of passengers accounted for the pause. Motion was only revived by a cry in what might have been Swahili, from the desert of heather or forest. The woodwork wheezed and miaoued and Lionel got quite a frisson when his window was dragged past a stationary face beneath a single gas lamp and advertisement for Mazawatee tea and that—was it Haig saying England wants YOU. Or death on the road . . .

Soon he fell into a trance before the view of "Royal Dornoch", fading brown, with an early motor-car and a waistless cloche-hatted woman forefront.

Even under a week, he thought, if the factor were intelligent.

Narcotic motion; always arriving, never there. Someone whistled a jig in the corridor.

The train often stopped where no station was and it was this which all but undid Lionel. After a hill on which one of the engines had continually slid back with hysterical puffing, the train eased so imperceptibly to a halt he comatosely pictured two men climbing out off the footplate to look underneath after the recent experience. Perhaps fitting a ratchet. Or opening a gate . . .

Then came a cry which, fortuitously, informed.

" ROSSIEMURCHAT."

For a moment he could do nothing. His luggage was never light or single. Even as a P.O.W. he had contrived to keep far more than was allowed. And for this expedition

20

he had based his computations on the advice of a friend who had said in summer it can be arctic—*or* tropical, but is usually somewhere in between. And even farmers dress for dinner.

Experience had already taught the cry was followed by immediate movement. He fumbled like a prude taken short with the window-sash—and got it down. " Hey ..." his voice missed the compromise between force and clarity. A frog had formed since Inverness. The result was the misbegotten protest of a choir boy sacked for adolescence.

But his hand meanwhile had done something which swung him out. And the station master blew twice and shouted. The engine sighed. Lionel was surprised to be upheld by gravel.

" Porter," he said, and then after a little while, " Porter? "

A figure in mufti with flag stood some way off.

The engine hissed. Suddenly a cry came—at him, sharp. " Are ye right? "

He scrambled back, garrulous with whispered obscenities. Some of his luggage was more than he could manage. A ligament in his neck went. He felt it part like one span of trouser-brace.

" Are ye right now? "

Back for his small stuff, a glove, a manuscript, *The Book Window*, the *Listener* he hadn't finished—and then was able to answer—by slamming the door to break it.

" Right, Charlie," shouted the figure and waved.

The train went.

A voice behind him, close, said, " C'n'v yer tucket, please."

A hand received, then a boy receded into a building. A door closed.

The legend "Rossiemurchat" stared at him above half a poster recommending Nottinghamshire with a picture of Robin Hood letting fly, as sample.

"Come to Nottingham, Sherwood Forest. British Railways."

Lionel's head was tilted against the normal slope in order to ease the pain. He stared at Robin Hood's hat for some seconds. Now. Here it came. In the silence; the absence of movement, business of any kind—the sort of sensation he had dedicated his life to avoiding. It had his mother's face on one side and on the other nothing. Nothing. And these days it could leap at you out of a poster.

With the resolution of the irresolute he stepped boldly for the fence. There: a car.

He walked round it officially a few times in deference to it having nothing to do with him. A man examined him from the cab. Finally he paused distrait, looking up the empty road.

Then the man said, " Mr. Spote, is it? " as though mentioning the weather or some other cul-de-sac courtesy, dropping it phlegmatically into the vast bowl of silence.

" Yes," said Lionel with an edge.

" Are you wanting up to the lodge? " The man seemed to be deliberately tantalising him.

" Yes, I am." He replied firmly. He would not beg.

" Well, then."

" Well."

" Well."

*   *   *

When in motion the man said, " Mrs. O'Shea did say but I didn't know, like."

" Oh, she did—good."

" But I didn't know, it was you isn't it? "

" Yes," said Lionel.

" Mrs. Charles Spote's nephew, isn't it? "

" Yes," said Lionel, warming a bit.

A pause then, " He was a guid shot."

This obituary might have come from his own lips. But in the circumstances he found it impertinent. He didn't reply.

They entered a village of low white houses and a few shops. At a pub the car stopped and a woman climbed in without a word, beside the driver. Lionel took note of a pitch-pine drill hall opposite. Before it were parked one private car, a Royal Mail van, a Milk Marketing Board van, an Austin marked " District Nurse " and a midget van with Esso flagrantly inscribed wherever possible.

Lionel said, " A meeting? " He felt a little better at the idea of business being conducted.

" Eh? "

" A lot of cars."

" It's the drumma," said the man.

" The . . .? "

" Drumma."

Lionel calculated for half a mile. He felt lonely. Drummer? T.A., presumably. Taps. A parade with a drum. But why the district nurse?

Then the driver said, " They're doing McBeeth for the golf club annual."

" Is that right? " said the woman.

The driver retreated a bit, made a case for thinking what he just said. " Three acts anyway," he said finally.

They drove on.

" There's Sir Duncan Fidge waiting on you at the lodge," said the driver factually.

" *Who?* " Lionel leant forward, worried, and at once, responsible.

" The Member of Parliament, Sir Duncan Fidge, he's waiting on you at the lodge."

Above all Lionel liked order, relevance, *meaning*. And on the whole he loathed M.P.s.

He would not believe in Fidge. He simply would not believe in him. Fidge, like drummer, would turn out to be something utterly different and in this case more ordinary. The caretaker's dog.

When the taxi arrived before the ugly lodge he saw a Rolls standing some distance from the house and in front of it—a small man in a brilliant kilt.

Lionel dismounted and stood to gaze—in doubt—for the figure made no move.

" Good evening," Lionel shouted with more interrogation than welcome.

The return shout was prompt.

" And good evening *to you* Lionel Spote. But go in, go in. I'm not here."

Lunacy, eccentricity—all forms of unrelatedness, should be treated clinically. Instead they were elected to Parliament.

" Won't you come in? " he shouted exasperated.

The man advanced—and stopped short of him—in admiration.

" Lionel Spote. Welcome. WELcome."

He felt his hand taken by one hand and his upper arm by another. " WELCOME LIONEL SPOTE. Fidge here. Duncan Fidge. This is a great day for the Highlands. Let me say again WELCOME LIONEL SPOTE."

The voice suggested a crowd.

" Good ev . . ."

" Quite unpardonable, the most terrible bad manners. But there's a reason which you shall hear. And I won't come in not if you press me. No, you shall be my guest. While you have dinner I'll wait in my car—and have dinner too (I brought sandwiches, plenty, enough for you if you like) and I'll hope you'll do me the kindness of calling on me after dinner—because it shan't be said Duncan Fidge ever called on a man before he was even in for the first time.

" Don't, don't. I know what you're going to say. Well —let me save you. No. This is business, the business of the Highlands and the well-being of Highlanders which leads me to presumption."

Fidge's head turned this way and that. His voice had a warm timbre which suggested condolence and encouragement, and the urging upon others of a sincerity proportionate to his own.

" Indeed," he continued, " hallo Andrew, HALLO ANDREW MCLEOD, and Mrs. Tawse, HALLO MRS. TAWSE, how are you there——" Suddenly Fidge's voice dropped to the whisper of a confident. " Slow taxi? I knowiknow-iknow, but great people, great people."

Then louder, " And so Lionel I'm going to wait in my car till you've got a moment then I want a few words. A few words. No more. And *you're* going to do the talking. Then I must be off: I've got a meeting in Lewis at ten to-morrow. Steamer at eight. Flying to Mallaig. Own plane. Wick. Now you know the reason. Horrible manners . . . Lionel, I can see you're hungry. Go. Go."

Nothing like it had ever happened to him before. He did now, feel ill. To crown all—there was a wind he scarcely believed possible in May—a little sly stiletto that killed without effort in the neck and which was playing on the side he couldn't lean towards.

With hands plunged in pockets and back turned skewing out a compromise between self-defence, pulled muscle and politeness he blurted out, " But, Sir Duncan, forgive me— but what business can we possibly have together? I don't know *anything* about the Highlands. I'm only here for two days."

Pause.

Then, rallentando. " You're quite right, Lionel. You don't know anything about the Highlands. And it's too late for business. I know I was wrong to make even the attempt. I should have said ' He'll be tired after a long journey. He'll feel he doesn't know anything about it. He'll think Duncan Fidge—Westminster?—ought to be in a looney bin. And if I suggest duty—duty to Highlands —*in extremis*, not a moment to spare, not even at midnight, after a long journey—he'll think Stuff'—no. You're right, I shouldn't have come. Not only bad manners. Folly. Picked the wrong man. After Lewis—America. Can't meet again till October. By then . . . but then what does it matter? You're probably right. Let the Highlands rot. Cut them off. Float them into the void. They're a liability. A sink for subsidies. Let the sons and mothers of the glorious 51st . . ."

" Sir Duncan . . . shall we go in? I don't think I can take this wind another instant."

At the front door as Lionel stood back for Sir Duncan to pass, the little man seized him with bonhomous roughness and thrust him through. " No, indeed no, sir, *your* home-coming. Go through first—and stay long. The Highlands need men like you."

Lionel caught sight of the man in a mirror: His reddish

kilt was centred by a silver-topped sporran and three tippets of fur hanging from its owl face. His hair was grey and his large bronzed face free from the smallest trace of experience. His eyes had the quickness of a chimp's, mingled with the brooding softness of a lemur's, a combination which disturbed unaccountably like lunatic art.

"Mrs. O'Shea, MARGARET O'SHEA," he said taking the hand of the woman who opened the door. "It's great to see you looking so well."

A short square woman of fifty with fortune-telling eyes —a bit Yeatsey, Lionel thought, said, "Well, then isn't it himself?" but just losing the confidence of it as though this time she had gone too far, adding, "Sir Duncan." And then to Lionel as though he were her son, "Mr. Spote, you'll be tired." She went ahead saying, "Well, well—I don't know, I don't know."

As sabres are sometimes crossed over cavalry couples on the eve of their new life—so he found himself advancing into his inheritance with Sir Duncan Fidge under deersheads, snout to snout. They graduated at last to a brown room with a tartan carpet hung with thin water colours of grouse and skylined stags. There, with the courage of pain he turned and said pedagogically, "*Sir Duncan* . . . What can *I* do to help you?"

"Eat, eat. While I stay here. May I write a letter?"

3

Mrs. O'Shea having set broth before Lionel withdrew to a window where she opened a chink of curtain and looked out at the darkening hills with a sigh of second sight.

" And what a starm that was yesterday," she said, giving the key-word a musical, metaphysical prolongation.

And then in a dulcet flirtatious whispy voice, " You've your own uncle's way of eating soup."

Lionel regarded a personal remark as bad taste. There were only about three situations in which it was permissible. One of them he had just let go by. He laid down his spoon.

" Mrs. O'Shea," he said, " I'm afraid I don't know how my uncle ate soup. But perhaps you could tell me this. Was the gentleman next door a great personal friend of my uncle—was he often here? "

" Oh, no," she said, touching her glasses and looking sideways at a huge ready ham.

" They never met? "

" Oh, I think they will."

" But does Sir Duncan often pay calls . . . like this? "

" Oh, I'm only from poor folk. He's a great man Sir Duncan. Isn't he a great man—though when he says there was no hunger he's—well I'll not surprise you with how we talk among ourselves, though it's true we were harpy, putting lugs on seven hundred hooks sometimes and not a fish. I can see my mother with her skirts tucked ha'way up," Mrs. O'Shea chuckled at him, " ha'way up. But not a fish. And ten of us to feed. Now it's wonderful, isn't it. I'm Labour. But you'll be one of the others . . ." and she chuckled again.

Lionel said, " I voted Socialist in 1945."

" Get away with you," she laughed. " Don't be saying such things in case the Lord hears you."

Lionel liked peace at meals at any time. This time his neck was hurting—and she had called him a liar. There was a madman in the sitting-room dressed in a red skirt, waiting for him; and the soup came out of a bottle, disguised by pepper, barley and salt.

He didn't reply. He got the impression that this had the effect of convincing her. For now she was shocked—and slightly affronted.

" And you a gentleman," she said uneasily.

" What I really want to know about is Sir Duncan Fidge, Mrs. O'Shea."

But she was still shocked; studying him.

" And how long will you stay ? " she said.

" Certainly not long," he said, adding politely, " I'm afraid."

" Be quiet," she said humbly. " How can a person know what will happen."

His neck speared him as he reached for butter—he came back without it, and sat for a second with closed eyes. " Then why ask ? " he said, really equably.

" And why not ? " she said. " A cat can look at a king."

He refused to continue. Or even look up when later he heard her say dreamily, " Sir Duncan, well he's excitable —like yourself, isn't it ? "

She said it so warmly, so confidingly—like a compliment. But he couldn't. He was too tired. He soon left—without cheese.

Fortified by food and drink Lionel faced Sir Duncan more as though he owned the place, which after all he did. The M.P. rose with extravagant alacrity from the main desk where he had been writing his letter.

" Sir Duncan, you will of course stay the night . . ." and Lionel frowned slightly, having sought to convey by tone and manner that thus—with time and leisure at their disposal—they could talk in a way which made sense; establish a common language and finally examine the proposition that he, Lionel, could be of use to the Highlands. So much of modern talk, anyhow tended to be like conversation between a driver who doesn't know his way and a policeman on point duty, each under pressure from conflicting streams of traffic, waiting. Here surely this need not be the case . . .

Fidge was amazed. " To-night I travel, Lionel." Then gently, a gesture, which had been an illustration of himself travelling, became a touch and then a sure hold on Lionel's arm just above the elbow.

To be touched, except inevitably as by a barber or tailor, was for Lionel a sort of physical distress. He couldn't think while it was going on.

Sir Duncan, believing the contact he had made with his hands was softening the young man with every passing second into a state of ever more gratified filial receptivity, steered him to where hung a map.

" Now . . . Ever hear of the evictions, Lionel?"

" The Highland Clearances," Lionel said.

" The evictions. A hundred years ago. Crofters turned out to make room for sheep—and deer. Thousands of

Highlanders exiled: Canada, New Zealand, Australia—and d'you know what I get asked about to-day when I hold political meetings. Not the atom bomb. But the evictions. Highland depopulation."

Lionel relaxed slightly. The man was making sense.

" Yes, Sir Duncan," he said encouragingly. " I suppose one can underst . . ."

" The evictions ! " Fidge suddenly struck the empty air to his left and leaned to his right with head averted, towards and nearer to Lionel. Lionel leant away slightly with him. " Aw forget it, I tell them. You'll be wanting reparations from the Romans next. But depopulation . . ." Sir Duncan's voice struck the note of Hi-Fi sincerity, " That's a different matter. That's still with us. The best are going south. Why? Better wages, more scope. And what's the result—fewer people in the Highlands, less ability. More and more subsidies for ever fewer and feebler people. What's the answer ? "

Lionel said, " Shall we sit down ? "

Although parted now by the bulky arms of Victorian arm-chairs, Sir Duncan leaned so far towards Lionel that he was once again able, periodically, to touch him—on the knee.

" The answer is this: bring the opportunities to the Highlands. Make industries here. Find out what can be done with what there is."

Lionel's eyes widened slightly.

· " Ever thought of what could be done with heather," Fidge suddenly said, low and rapid, staring at Lionel with what might have been vacancy or moving sincerity.

Lionel said he had not.

" There you are," Fidge snapped. " There, straight away,

31

is an example. And shall I tell you something: nor has anyone else. And that's why I'm here."

The thread had slipped again. Lionel peered as though the failure had been in his attention.

"*Bracken,*" Fidge whispered, holding Lionel's eyes with a confessor's appeal, passionate dispassion. Sir Duncan pointed sideways. "*Fluach.* A hundred square miles of bracken. Not a soul. Not a house. Not a stag. Not a sheep. Not a grouse. Nothing—but BRACKEN. Below—a village. Fluach village. Two hundred fishers. No boats. No nets. Unemployment. Depopulation. Drift south. Communism. The end. But wait, wait—a very good friend of mine, secret, all secret—along comes the Savette Brackenator. Rope from bracken. Rival the great jute industries south. One obstacle—April Gunter-Sykes."

Lionel propped up his face with curled knuckles. An immense index finger reached his eye.

Fatigue has third and fourth winds. He felt everything now could go on indefinitely. He even roughly understood. The little man rotating, occasionally threw out an arm.

"The great need in the north: *Light Industries.* But what happens: a woman—I'll flatter her, yes I will, I'll flatter her —a woman—refuses to sell—bracken. Says there's plenty more bracken—why pick on mine. So—we explain. Oil well disused at Fluach Mains. Harbour. Trunk road. Height of bracken. Accessibility. Extent. Nothing doing. 'Mrs. Gunter-Sykes is in Norway', 'Mrs. Gunter-Sykes is in Newfoundland, fishing.'"

Fidge looked at his watch. Not briefly—but with pugnacity. He had an argument with it. He browbeat it into a further concession. And then he thrust it from him.

" 'Foundland, fishing," he went on and then suddenly, without leaving his chair, came, wholly, a foot closer. His voice now was that of a different, quiet, stoic person.

" Spote," he appealed. " It's getting on. It's later than you think."

Aware that he was being called on a yet graver plane than hitherto, Lionel made an effort. His eyes opened wider, and saw Fidge's face pregnant with intent.

" Yes—Sir Duncan?"

The whisper came fast and straight.

" Marginal seat! Two hundred. Hm?"

They stared at each other, with wholly different expressions.

Sir Duncan gauging him. Switched.

" Politics a dirty game. No time for 'em? Is that it...? *Then it's men like you we want.* To persuade Mrs. Gunter-Sykes."

" Sir Duncan—how can I possibly help?"

The little eyes of Sir Duncan Fidge rested on him steadily. Lionel felt young, *gauche*.

" Lionel Spote," he said steadily. " You march with April."

Lionel's head sank towards his now raised shoulder and his mouth was lost and shapeless in his face, his skin creased and pale and his eyes purposeless. On these occasions only some obscure schoolmaster within kept him from weeping or laughing hysterically or just simply getting up and going away.

" March?" he said sudden like a belch. Drummer, Fidge, march, starm, lugs. He suddenly hooted quietly. " Ha, ha!" But stopped, sudden, controlling himself, making it like a tummy-rumble: brief and irrelevant.

Sir Duncan fixed him till he felt flippant, trivial.

" Sir Duncan, I'm sorry but you see—I'm not going to be here long."

" You want 'em back? The Socialists? The Vandals? And you want the Highlands to rot."

" Sir Duncan . . ."

" You another Marquess, Spote? Cans. Monty. Croft rents on back-a-rat?"

" Sir Duncan . . ."

Fidge switched. Without any effort at all he looked suddenly very like Ronald Colman as a squadron leader, hearing who was missing. He moved slowly to the window. There was muted kettledrums in the repose of his hands on his kilt top.

Sinking from G major to E flat minor, he said, " Mackintosh. Old Mackintosh—Archie's father. Old friend of mine. One of the very best. Said ' You're in luck, Bodger. Take him to you. Soon as he comes. Sort of man you want. But by God give him back. Or share him. Share him'll do.' So I said—' not his first day.' But Bob said —' if it's urgent. Meet him on the train. Get him out of bed.' ' But it's not right,' I said,—and it isn't. Let a man settle in."

Lionel passed his hand over his face. " Sir Duncan," he said humbly, " if you could just give me *the facts*, I'll do all I can—so long as you realise that will almost certainly be—nothing."

And soon, after a few more details, Sir Duncan took Lionel's hand and held it, without a word. Electrically speaking it was a curious contact. One depended on reason, the other on emotion. Lionel felt weaker and weaker: he would write—to-morrow—and outline the dimensions of

34

the probable gulf.   But now . . . to-night . . . nothing more.

" Lionel Spote," said Sir Duncan, " thank you."

And soon Fidge went into darkness and with a whisper of new tyres vanished as though he had never been.

4

Ever since Hilde Lionel had remained a self-conscious sleeper, aware of many different grades of sleep. In the mornings, he often looked back with the self-critical distance-probing eye of a golfer after driving. Because life—even the descent of the stairs to breakfast—was an act of faith powered by sleep. To sleep badly was to wake up not believing. The libido hung back unsatisfied by the mysterious cookhouse door of the unconscious. Sometimes quite clearly the terrible skinny female hand of an unidentifiable dream could be seen withholding the day's ration. And thus it was this morning as he lay in his uncle's comfortable bed.

Just *what* had it meant?

He had been walking over a landscape such as he had seen all yesterday from the train window—but with this difference: in two steps he passed two horizons. For a time it seemed natural. Then he had realised: he was vast, bigger than Gulliver in Lilliput and moving faster than a jet. But in spite of this, he came to no end of the rounded brown hills, not to any landmark—until suddenly there on the next horizon Elizabeth Craik leant, on one elbow, watching him come.

Speech, the silent kind that occurs in dreaming, at once passed between them.

" Elizabeth—what can I do—this is terrible. These toy moors . . ."

Now for some reason, although Elizabeth was obviously in the same plight as himself, occupying as she did half a whole horizon with the sprawl of her upper arm, he expected her to reassure him, point out that all was as it should be. Perhaps even point out that this was a dream.

Instead she said, " What on earth has happened to you: you're *tiny*."

Then he woke up.

He tried the sometimes successful trick of merely turning it back to front.

I am infinitesimal in a titanic landscape, he tried, closing his eyes. Elizabeth, too, is infinitesimal. The landscape crushes, overwhelms by its size and age. So I compensate . . .

His long nose twitched slightly and he scratched, switching his mind gratefully to the tickle.

So what? Why should he wake as though with an unburst boil—merely because he had gone for a walk as a giant and met a giantess.

He turned over wearily, avoiding the window that led to the view. Besides perhaps that's what he did feel, a giant, here. What should make one feel bigger or more solid than nothing? Hundreds of miles of nothing. A pea in a million cubic miles of empty space would be . . . super colossal, he drowsed; and he smelt his late uncle through the sheets. But why had Elizabeth thought him tiny when he had realised she was vast, also? Why? There was a reason for everything.

*   *   *

Mrs. O'Shea let in the light and then considered him with hands folded across her belly.

"My husband never would take two pillows either," she said. "That and the cross-saw brought us most to disagreement but I shan't take the advantage of saying where the fault lay when he can't answer." She drifted about talking. "Won't you be sick of hearing an old woman's tongue."

"Yes I will," he thought—but said kindly, "I'm sorry to know your husband's dead, Mrs. O'Shea."

"He's in Inverness."

She emphasised archly the place-name—but Lionel risked nothing. Too often he had had his antennae pinched in Mrs. O'Shea's mental machinery.

"Yes," she said, moving toward the door, "that's where William O'Shea is. And when he comes home for a spell I often say to him: Don't you be ashamed William, there's better than you in there. And worse who aren't."

The pointedness of the last words did not escape Lionel. He cocked a brow clinically at such aggression—for how was he to know that this was the normal treatment Mrs. O'Shea meted out to the rich—gave and then regretted, as now with suddenly flooded eyes, leaving an embrace, even with a stranger, as the logical next step.

Lionel, horizontal, made no reciprocal sign. Penitence was all very well.

"I see," he said astringently, "I'm so sorry Mrs. O'Shea," and then her face, a cross between a Pieta and rare steak, unnerved him.

"Haven't your lodge neighbours," she said at the door, "three of them that's known had treatment with . . ." she paused and then slowly, with an outward movement of her hand, that was half sanctification half protest, she said "electricity."

"Really."

38

" Yes," she said, " electricity."

★   ★   ★

Scones, oat-cakes, tea in a cosy, thick marmalade, soupy, salty porridge and two snow-white fried eggs. He began to feel better—and looked forward to business with the factor.

Business. Figures. Facts. He stretched, closing his eyes to the scratch team of his aunt's ancestors on the passage wall. Gone Fidge—faded into the night. Done with. *Brackenator*!

" Mrs. O'Shea when do the *papers* come? "

" To-day's, will it be? "

" Well . . . yes."

" To-morrow, except Saturdays." She was about to go on her way when she turned, struck. " There now— you'll be missing the papers! "—as though he had rickets.

" Mrs. O'Shea. Things are happening in the world. Which concerns us all. You and me. I like to know what they are. That's all, Mrs. O'Shea."

" Yes, yes—things are happening." And she became still as distant moonlit water and raised eyes sideways, seeing the things. " Ai," she said like the first tremor of a medium, " Ai, Ai—happening—everywhere though ask not of knowledge too much. But it's right we should read the papers. They were given the people, a weapon put into their hands. Though I don't like the word weapon. It's my nephew's."

Lionel said, " Which paper do you read, Mrs. O'Shea? "

She gave three names. " But it's all lies, I know," she said defensively, beginning to clear.

" Then why do you say we must read the papers? "

" Oh, we must," she looked at him surprised and formal,

39

surely he could not be making that mistake. " Oh, we must read the papers. I'm surprised at you, Mr. Spote, thinking the contrary."

Had he thought the contrary? She had a confusing effect. It was like looking at things through water.

" Good," he said irrelevantly, " Good," and went—with the odd sensation of yesterday already returning.

For a few minutes he explored the house and was relieved to find a piano.

Then he entered the living-room much as he might enter his office. As a charm against the view of waste land he emphatically got out certain papers, arranged a chair for the factor just as though Milosh or Craik were coming, and clicked open his little moroccan leather watch and looked through the window. He saw an unusual sight.

Coming up the drive was an empty car—an empty Hillman van.

In the rather ceremonious attitude of refobbing his watch, a manner which despite couch, Milosh and all, was his father's, Lionel froze.

The empty Hillman breasted the last slope and turned slap across the face of this ground floor window. Only then did Lionel see what *might*—only might—have been the upper surface of a cap, low down opposite the steering-wheel.

He went to the front door and was in time to see the Hillman door opening and a man slide out, with two eyes. One of the eyes focused on Lionel, the other, with the lion's share of apparent intelligence spied a spot only very little to the left of him, giving Lionel to think that in business it were better to have a large than a slight squint.

" Mr. Huish," Lionel said warmly and advanced with hand outheld, but wondering if it would get a touch.

" Howdyedoo, Mr. Spote."

40

The voice was like a whisper in a cave and came out not from the man's mouth but from all of him.

Huish had no visible neck, yet a huge head, with a long nose that had such a dainty separate tip it looked mobile, as though it could smell sideways without anything else moving.

They went in.

To prise a small hole in the ice, Lionel said lightly, " I've already had a visitor."

" Oh, indeed."

He must stop, now, worrying about this husky conspiratorial, omnivorous whisper. He must.

" Sir Duncan Fidge. A very active M.P. isn't he? "

" Oh, Sir Duncan. Yes, yes. Very active."

" Wanted to enlist my help."

" Oh, indeed."

" He wants to start some sort of factory at . . . Fluach. Is it? Take a seat."

" Thank you. Oh, very interesting. Factory. Good idea."

" Well. That's the point—is it? "

" One would want to know more, would one not, Mr. Spote? "

Lionel paused, with dawning hostility. " You've never heard anything about this before? "

" I've heard about a factory to make cattle-fodder out of heather at Boig, to harness the Corgi, to teach crofters silage, to grow alfalfa on Achnagilt—and I heard talk of bracken."

The slick sibilance had an edge. Was he in some way rabid?

" In other words it's all eyewash? " Lionel said, smiling, *entre nous.*

41

Mr. Huish stirred with dignified criticism of the word. He had silver curls. He smoothed them. He made some sort of patriarchal noise of wounded deference, while examining two divorced spots on the carpet. Then with a cough-like laugh whispered, " Eyewash! Good, very good."

An implied moral criticism from a stranger made Lionel feel there had been no progress in his life from Norland nurse days. At the same time it galvanised his reason into aggressive astringence, the whole involving him in the trip from laugh to grimace.

" Mr. Huish," he said, " all I wanted to know—bluntly— is (a) whether you think I should assist Sir Duncan to acquire the Fluach bracken—for the benefit of the people of Fluach. (b) Whether it is possible to do so, and if so how."

" Mrs. Gunter-Sykes," said Mr. Huish.

" Mrs. Gunter-Sykes . . ."

" A very sporting lady."

" Indeed. You mean she shoots and . . ."

" A champion shot I've heard. She killed three hundred and thirty-two out of three hundred and fifty pigeons."

" Clay ? "

" No—out of cages. At Monte Carlo. 1936."

Lionel loathed her. The date also upset him.

" Does this effect the issue ? "

" And a wonderful fisherwoman. Devoted to the Corgi —your river here. She has the other bank, you have this one. And you have the spawning ground—at the top end. You march with Mrs. Gunter-Sykes, Mr. Spote."

Lionel felt lonely. This phrase kept cropping up. He now understood it but not its relevance. " Mr. Huish," he said, " I want to do what I can while I'm here—in any way—to help. But I think I should make it clear. I hope

42

to sell Rossiemurchat because it won't be possible for me to live here. I feel that if the land is owned privately it should be lived on by the owners, or sold."

Mr. Huish's eyesight parted either side of Lionel, who was made to feel that he had indeed changed the subject.

The whisper came now from even farther away, the sibilant echo from the gulf between them.

" Yes, Mr. Spote, though there's the will."

" The will ? "

" I heard the wording placed restraint on sale."

Lionel's eyes fell, fell forward into those of Huish, falling, falling—without a concrete touch.

" Restraint . . . ? " he said vaguely.

" That is a sort of veto."

" Why on earth wasn't I informed at once? "

" Did you not hear from Salmson, Mr. Spote? "

" I heard nothing."

" Perhaps he just has Mrs. Spote's address."

Huish can have had no idea what he had insinuated.

" Mr. Huish," Lionel said, recovering—and managing a tone of mild mature criticism, " I mentioned to you on the telephone possibility of sale: why didn't you say then . . ."

" Salmson told me he'd be writing you."

Pause, containing condemnation if Huish had ears to hear.

" When may I be allowed to see this will? "

" Would you like Salmson up? The will could be complicated, Mr. Spote."

" Mr. Huish—I should like him up *at once*."

Huish wrote into the palm of his hand, apparently with no pencil and no paper, two squiggles—and finished.

" Yes, Mr. Spote," he whispered, and gave the carpet a long forked stare. He seemed joined by the two late Mr. Spotes, finally by Lionel's mother.

Suddenly he said, " The death duties could be paid by selling Muig—if you wished to keep intact . . ."

Lionel stood up. " Well," he smiled, " that would be *sale!* We'll have to see apparently."

Mr. Huish's hands floated over papers he had got out and they vanished. He said, " The late Mr. Spote was very fond of sport—and the scenery. Might I ask if you share his predilections? "

" No ∴ . . no," said Lionel earnestly and not, oh not merely iconoclastically, " but I *have* fished."

Then Huish closed. " Might I ask how Lady Glenegg is keeping? "

Lionel eyed him. The whisper had never been more cavernously priestlike.

" My aunt—oh, yes—very well I think—did you know her? "

" Yes, yes," he whispered urgently, " beautiful place Glenegg, finest view in Scotland. It was the stronghold of McLeod of Ara."

Lionel waited. Nothing came. If you were really related you were related to everyone—even Huish, even to the view from Glenegg. But nothing came.

" *Really*," his interest was fierce with discipline.

" Is O'Shea suiting you? "

" She seems an excellent woman. Full of information."

" Huh! "

This sudden hard statement from the hitherto viscous Huish was shocking.

Lionel said uneasily, " A good woman, surely."

" A great talker. Mr. Spote. You'll be wanting your lunch. I'll get along, and I'll let you know when Salmson can come. We can't do much till then."

Lionel watched the guided missile grow distant. When

44

he turned, the lodge seemed to have come closer. He took out his watch and opened it; but why? Perhaps to relate the present moment, to at any rate one thing: time.

Because now . . . what now?

★   ★   ★

The piano, for Lionel, was a disenturbulator on casters.

He opened the music desperately as though only just in time. He manipulated his fingers a moment examining the opening bar. *Order.*

Then the telephone rang in the next room.

For some time the instrument eluded him because of its archaic shape.

The voice—a man's—required him, so to speak, if his name were Lionel Spote, to put it there and come up here —with *us.*

" Yes," he said, " Lionel Spote."

" Hallo—Hallo, then. Glad you've arrived. This is April Gunter-Sykes. I knew your mother—and of course, Charles, all m'life. Now when are we going to see you? How long are you up? "

Lionel, hedging, was chopped:

" Any day suits us. Shall we say Thursday lunch? Or name the day. You'll probably be snowed under. Say when."

Intolerable. Perfectly intolerable. Presumption, nothing but presumption—ever since he'd arrived.

" Good then, Mrs. Gunter-Sykes. Good then." Harder and drier each time—" Shall we say Thursday? Good-bye," and he replaced the receiver.

The amputation of the conversation had been due to a rush of blood to the head. Even while committing the social atrocity he desired to modify it—which resulted in

45

his singing the last word or two on different, high, cheery notes. But as the receiver went down he had heard her starting up.

"April," he muttered as he approached the piano. And his tongue popped sideways from his mouth where it remained while he ground out Schubert chords in a manner which would have better served Schoenberg.

5

MAJOR OF Cadets Hew Mackay, Islander, Councillor, Pipe-major, C.Q.M.S. retired Argyll and Sutherland Highlanders, Ack Ack I., T.A., caretaker of the Territorial Association Drill Hall, Secretary of the Corgi Home Guard Miniature Rifle Club, President of the Mod, member of the Education Committee and Secretary of the local Labour Party, stood in the attitude of an emperor humouring a portrait painter. One hand high on his broom handle the other on his hip.

At a distance a small boy sat on a form, lolling right back, his hands deep in his shorts and his legs thrust out importantly with eyes upon them, and not, as seemed desired, on the major.

Every morning the major did the hall in company with a child—under school-age in term time, and under ten in the holidays. It wasn't always the same child and sometimes it was several. He never stooped, hurried, or got dusty and if it was sunny he loitered in silence by the porch looking down the road as though expecting somebody important, though less so.

Afterwards his wife did the hall.

This morning he was more than usually solemn and his presence correspondingly more satisfying to the small boy who was in no hurry for this moment ever to stop. He was included. He could even think about his own legs and still be included.

Since the death of the late Charles Spote the commandantship of the County Cadets had been vacant and in this county there was only one company commander—himself: Major Mackay.

Colonel Mackay . . . a hand strayed to his wisp of grey moustache suggestive of the man on Greys' cigarettes. He cleared his voice as though about to answer some ghost that had addressed him.

If he got the commandantship that would mean three weeks of two thousand a year, i.e., a colonel's pay at camp. About 1,000 nips.

He made a pass like a myopic duchess at a feather. Relented.

" Child had to walk two miles, Colonel Mackay protests." " Corgi should have car park, Colonel Mackay's motion," though he had never yet moved anything. His chest heaved slightly, bringing his whole volume to the point, always promised when he danced reels, of soundless airborne departure till he tapped gently on the ceiling—face down, for it was his chest and protrusive kilt-fostered rump which seemed the main bags of his buoyance.

But this nephew was it who had come. Inverness could be relied upon to make him the commandant. He gave a few disdainful sweeps at an exposed part of floor.

There were three cadets in Corgi, and three in Muig and the three minister's sons in Strathcardale, and a platoon commander for each, making nine cadets and five officers for the county. Nevertheless there were two tons of correspondence dealing with this force and communications both in and out averaged about three a day, most of it being concerned with the three hundred uniforms and the valuable compasses prismatic in store. The screening of new officers, the method of applying for grants and camp capitation, entailed procedure which a newcomer would be lost in. So. Supposing he declined to continue as company commander/clerk unless granted the *triple role*: Colonel/Coy.-Comdr./clerk.

Who could they get to replace him? The only possibility was his predecessor who hadn't yet explained the disappearance of the Welcome Home Fund.

Major Mackay flipped at a bit of paper. It scurried under a chair. He desisted and leant on his broom. Queen Victoria surveyed from close in photogravure, but he was insensitive to the implications of her manner. As also to the etching " Saving the Guns " alongside.

Would they wear it? That was the question.

Supposing he made it quite clear to this young fellow from the outset—he skiffed again at some dust—and took a few steps with the toes well turned out, just supposing, he made it absolutely clear, from the outset to the fellow, that if he wanted the commandantship, then he would have to take the company clerkship too. Mightn't the fellow advise Inverness to promote Major Mackay . . .

He stared at the boy who had taken some chairs from the wall and had begun building a house with them. Normally he would either have at once dictated the construction or treated the boy to a taste of the verbal military discipline—the royal sternness which was a marvellous game they and he never tired of. As it was, he said, like an R.S.M. at a depot:

" Hey—Glen! Is your auntie still at the lodge? "

But the boy had fallen and in falling discovered a new

position on his back, which for some reason arrested his previous plans.

" Is she, boy? "

" I can see the sky," he said, " through the roof."

" You can not," said the Major decisively.

" I can so."

After some time and grudgingly the major raised his eyes to the roof.

The child said quickly, " You canna see it from standing up. Ye have to be right doon here."

The major surveyed his care, the walls and roof with misgiving. So bad was the dry rot in the pine, a decision had been taken just to let the place go on till it collapsed. After storms, strange fungoid ears formed on certain areas and in many places there were seams of coloured specks. And everywhere tiny worm craters. But, still a hole in the roof . . . he craned his neck.

" From *here* then," the boy said savagely, for the lack of contradiction had gone to his head, and he added, " There are things you can see lying down which you can't standing up."

The major's neck was thick and inflexible. After some time and reluctance he got down, flat, on the boards.

" Where, then," he said.

" There," said the boy, now hollowly and without confidence.

" That is a white mark," said the major.

" It's *no* a mark."

" It's a white, white mark."

" I saw a bird through it."

The idea pleased the major, rested him. His wily little eyes stayed suddenly still, in the purple-tinted folds of his huge soft face.

" Was it a big bird? " he said.

" Yes, it was so."

" With two wings? " he asked, almost drowsily.

" Yes.   With two wings."

But even there on the ground the thought stabbed him—of the young fellow getting colonel.

There was for him no position incompatible with pomposity which after all is only make-believe.   " And your Aunt O'Shea," he said in his sternest tones which were those of an upstanding officer and a gentleman because that was the first English outside Gaelic he'd ever heard after leaving the islands, " Is she helping out East—at the lodge? "

" Yes," said the boy dully.

" Mr. Li-onelle Spote? " he experimented.

" Yes."

" And what like is he, boy.   Tell me."

" He wore mittens in the house and he was wanting into the bathroom all night."

So . . . Colonel Mackay.

Colonel Hew Mackay.   He stood up and took the broom. His other hand clasped his hip in the attitude of one about to dance.   Then his chin became slightly elevated and he looked far down the hall.

Perhaps it might happen he would go out East, to the Lodge, to-morrow—or before the back-end, then.

" Glen! " he rapped, transformed.   " Get those chairs back.   Or you'll get a drill to-morrow."

Torn between the desire to obey and the desire to get a drill the boy drifted to the first chair.

The major skiffed a stub under a chair.

" Spote . . ." he tried, tersely, " Mackay here."

51

Then he listened to it, resting on his broom, as though the whisper had been a pebble thrown down a shaft and could be heard bouncing and clanking and also initiating other movement—towards the bottom.

6

APRIL GUNTER-SYKES, six foot in her socks, was breastless and freckled with a forearm for neo-barbaric bangles. An Olympic gold medal was evoked by her buttocks. Her voice could carry from one end of a grouse-line to another and even for her prematurely ageing son rang curt as for pointers. She shot well both scatter and solo, and could lay a salmon line against the wind, with a noise like a sjambok, so that it marked the water strict—a line pencilled along an invisible vast ruler. Annually she moved, like certain tribes of long ago, in the wake of game, her cycles only broken by peaks of the London season such as Lords and Ascot which she attended with a brazen authority, that shed no flake of deference to the changed atmosphere of England.

She stood now on the Fluach face breast high amid her domestic bracken; weatherbeaten but powdered, in deep tweed reefer with baggy pockets for cartridges and a para-military belt with several attachments for slip-leashes, whistles and a heavy plaited whip. In her hand was a shepherd's crook seven foot tall, and on her head a deer-stalker of the same tweed as her plus-eights. She was exhorting a geologist.

He was from Glasgow—and though accustomed to country—had always been left to work in his own time. This morning Mrs. Gunter-Sykes had taken him up the face without pause and had stood over him in the most offensive and impatient manner while he examined the very ordinary gravel.

"Try over there," she said arbitrarily pointing her stick at a patch farther up. "It looks different."

Her son followed, listless, deeply unconcerned, except for the feelings of the geologist, whose generation might yet wring his neck.

"I should chuck it, wouldn't you, mother?"

"If you ask me he hasn't a clue."

"Perhaps there isn't a clue."

"Don't tell *me* Rupert, Duncan Fidge wants to buy this ground for the *bracken*."

It was an exasperating morning for all concerned.

"My good man," she said: "You tell me there's nothing here—but even *I* know there's oil. A crank once started a pump at the bottom. You never mentioned there was oil—so how do I know you mayn't have missed a lot of other things?"

The "little man", as she kept calling him, seemed to have difficulty with his breathing and sweat in his glasses. He said no doubt—in the valley, on the level, there might be evidence of oil. If she wished a drilling to be made through 2,000 feet of solid granite mountain, down to sea-level, then he should have been warned.

They went home. "Shouldn't we ask him to lunch, Mother?"

"The *geologist* . . . ? He's paid."

★   ★   ★

April had compassed herself about with a sanitary girdle. Shambling crofts with zarebas of bedsteads wired together, holed enamel and rubbish dumps roof-high, gave place suddenly to high deer wire, new gates with anti-rabbit grids for cars to pass over, then—after miles of birch and rowan, pink out-houses like chalets, barns with vast Dutch roofs—and animals whose udders, combs, hocks, feather and, let it be said plainly, balls, just suggested not then at genetic perseverance and achievement but sheer flukes as well; at last you came to April's granite and glass casteletto.

Her keepers were commando and paratroop n.c.o.s but they did not stay. Only the butler fortuitously called Stickett, remained. April paid high wages and in return expected obedience—except from her son. From him she expected obedience without high wages, and had sent him to London " to the office." The Gunter-Sykes bacon-cutter had swallowed all the minor bacon-cutters in the 'thirties, and she expected him to represent " your father—on ten times what *he* had when *he* started."

Rupert had complied. Based on Tite Street he sickened slowly and shot rats by torchlight with an air-gun with a friend who owned a wharf. At week-ends he held on by this thread. Sometimes he came home and shot all day, and all night by headlamps. But he had several old copies of *Horizon*, bound, and had read Beauvoir.

★   ★   ★

Having dismissed the geologist April sat upright at her roll-top desk in a room decorated almost exactly as the one at Rossiemurchat except there were fewer stags and more ancestors, all called Coope.

She sat suddenly even bolter upright—achieving extension from what was already rigidly vertical, like an interested hen. There was a figure on the Callach Rock.

" Mother," Rupert said, " I believe Lionel Spote is the Lionel Spote who was in prison with me."

It was the second time he'd told her.

Range 2,000 . . . but probably the shepherd. She relaxed.

" Well, if he comes—just keep my end up for me. I must powder my nose. We've got the Fleights too. I thought it a good opportunity."

Rupert was going through a *Tatler* for the second time and rose mechanically to salute her departure.

April was a stickler for manners.

★   ★   ★

Before mounting the car of his dead uncle, to lunch with April, Lionel breathed deeply once or twice, the clear air.

* People should have bodies.

After driving for five miles he thought how titles by Elizabeth Craik would have here as much purchase as sanskrit. Not a soul here would understand what it felt like to be Elizabeth Craik. Yet Elizabeth was right:

* No intelligent person likes the country to-day.

When the road petered out into a raging torrent he got out slamming the door like a word for the whole expedition. On the far side another road started—almost exactly opposite this one.

If happiness lay in small things then so did unhappiness. Lionel stared, wizened, into the endless passing by of liquid. There was a solemn swollen bit, in the middle, black as ink and heaving with a considerable swell and in its midst a post with a brown bow-wave.

Eventually all his resentment centred on this post, and its presumption.

Unpunctuality in others irritated him; in himself it occasionally induced hysteria. Besides, he had no wish to be at a moral disadvantage with April—on the smallest point.

He began pulling at his long fingers and making the most futile excursions to right and left trying, from heights, to get an impression of depths.

He began to curse the people who had told him the way without mentioning this.

He mounted and backed, with his lower lip between his teeth.

About half an hour later he was back in the same place looking almost ill with irritation. " Kip goin' kip goin' and it's nut at arl dip, na na." Closing his eyes, revving the engine as once taught in the Army, he ploughed in.

He arrived on the far bank without sensible check.

As often happened in times of stress he began to talk to himself and it was thus he caused a first unfortunate impression when, still talking to himself, he drew up before a window from which the hungry lunch party could see his mouth crabbed on the move as he wrenched the brake.

On such occasions Lionel's reputation as " a bit odd " was only balanced, when he appeared close, full length, in the flesh, by his clothes, face and manner, all of which would have supported his canditature for any white-collar job in the world.

When he said " How do you do," he appeared to be asking a question and even pressing for an answer with his eyes—and this did cause a slight stir.

" Mrs. Gunter-Sykes," he said, " I *am* sorry."

Then he took note, like a sentry from behind his courtesy, while the voice of his hostess struck off the names like a bored auctioneer, " Other (an author for you) and Caroline Fleight. Laura Childe, my daughter . . ."

That April Gunter-Sykes should have had issue " as white as snow, as red as blood and as black as ebony " offended at once Lionel's scientific way of thinking. His easy old Etonian manner and even his couch-fostered priest-like courtesy were alike arrested as he conned the youthful Mrs. Childe with a stud stare. A smasher. The reflex, instinctive exusion of mental sepia with which he protected himself on such occasions, fogged her into a murky formula : upper-class extravert with strong sexual orientation. But the heart of his normal manner did miss a beat—and having prepared to go forward and shake her hand, he paused and then compromised with an inclination of his head and a smile which, coupled with wretched disassociated footwork, was all a clear confession.

The fact the girl was laide as well as belle did not help him in the least. Her wide mouth, almost negroid lips and teeth as short almost as those of a hand-saw all seemed to add rather than detract. Immense animated eyes and a black curl modelled and clamped low down to the line of her cheek-bone like a scimitar, and the whole head emerging from a jersey-collar as soft as the inside of a tit's nest—all this by offer of the big eyes was *for* whomever she looked at. Which was now Lionel and the more so because of his displaced reaction.

" You've probably met," April shouted.

Lionel said contemporaneously with Laura. " No— I don't think . . ."

" Of course you have," April interrupted, " dozens of times without knowing it. In London."

She said this as a pushed Customs officer swiftly applies his chalk cross—without investigation, adding, " And Rupert thinks you may have met in the war "—another cross for the writing-case, almost forgotten.

" *Rupert?* " said Lionel, privately as amazed as pleased. They had shared an over-and-under bunk by choice in a room for a hundred. They at once stood side by side saying nothing while Rupert's mother assessed for them the coincidence. She came quite close to Lionel and shouted, " Of course, in the army he always called himself just Sykes, didn't you, Rupert? Shorter on aquittance rolls. Haw, haw. Come on in. Take it with you."

Lionel found himself between April and Mrs. Fleight— a girl whose strenuous idealism shone in her blue face from eyes like oxy-acetylene blow-flares. It was the ford again. Life a *test*. Then he looked across to the husband—a pretty arrogant looking youth rather like a moth-eaten white dervish whose face was redeemed from being insufferable by a certain penitent morbidity in the eyes. Wrote. What? *Fleight*. Lionel cast his ear back to the Spring Novels list —Secker he thought. Gone. No matter.

First came salmon.

" Are you going to live at Rossiemurchat? " It crashed in from the flank. While he was still manœuvring the second shot came.

" Fishing's not your line, is it? "

" I *have* fished, Mrs. . . ."

They tried many approaches to each other. Conscientiously and with patience. She made the running—at last sacrificing herself robustly on his territory. " What *sort* of books? "

" All sorts."

" Do you deal with Dulcie Howard? "

" No—I think she publishes with . . ."

" They tell me she makes thirty thousand a year. Doesn't see *half* of it."

" God send me such hard cheese," said the dervish sourly.

April took this as hostile and attacked back uneasily. " What do you write, novels isn't it? "

The dervish looked with sickly potence at his hostess's hands and with bereaved smugness said, " I try."

" Do you succeed? "

" No," said his wife, laughing.

He smiled at her, privately.

Lionel looked from one to the other dutifully. Very interesting. Well, well. And this far north. Nostalgically he looked across at Rupert, who was demure. Bully-beef in the motley fug had been fleshpots and civilisation to this.

*   *   *

April was showing him tulips, standing back from them. " They could be worse," she bawled. " Tell me, Lionel— I must call you that: I'm old enough to be your mother— as a matter of fact I was at school with her—has Duncan Fidge been after you? "

" He did call, Mrs. Gunter-Sykes."

" Let's make it April, shall we? Now, I'll be frank. He's after my bracken—and I expect he's after yours." Her arms were akimbo, frankly. She even stood back from him, to get squarer.

Lionel seized truth, by the little toe.

" No—he hasn't been after mine."

" Well, well. The plot thickens. Don't tell me Duncan Fidge wants bracken just to make work for the people up here: (a) they won't work; (b) bracken is good for damn all. So he never said anything to you."

" He did mention something about a machine to be used in connection with the bracken "—Lionel browbeat the tulips. " It's all nonsense is it? "

" Making rope out of bracken! He's got to think up

60

something better than that. Well. You're in the dark, like me."

The promise made to Fidge now dislocated Lionel's ease. In vain he disowned it, as extorted, and therefore valueless.

Besides, he simply *could* not try and persuade this woman to sell bracken. He would explain to Sir Duncan . . . his ignorance, his incapacity . . .

"When you know the people up here as I know them . . ." For some minutes she gave a social-economic survey while Lionel continued to clear himself. "Of course," she ended, "the land here's not worth ten bob an acre."

To save his conscience he then blurted, feeling even a stranger could say *this*—a natural *sequitur*. "But if the bracken is worthless—why not sell it?" smoothing it with a polite smile, making it casual.

"Haw, haw—so he has been at you."

Lionel frowned as though she had outwitted him. Which merely proclaimed to her that she had.

"Haw, Haw." She laughed louder.

*   *   *

"*Rupert*," he said with relief.

"Lionel."

Talk had never been the link but this—a harmony of auras. Lionel frowned at far away hills as though in search for a word to celebrate the renewed experience and the interval. Not there. None. His face wrinkled as against great light.

Rupert blew his nose and in the folding away of the handkerchief, like a map, answered.

Later, aloud at last, he said, "Are you up for long? I mean—are you going to live there?"

" No," said Lionel, " I'm not. Rupert, what do *you* do now? Farm, isn't it? "

Rupert was a withered little old man of thirty with a touch of child which a moustache merely emphasised.

He peered up the valley with wan discretion.

" Actually, I don't."

Years ago in the over-and-under bunk Lionel had with care arrived at a label, Linnæan, irrevocable.

*When we get out of here: Rupert must farm.

" *Rupert*," he murmured, turning, " I'm most awfully sorry. Then what *do* you do? "

" I work in the office."

" *The* office . . .? " Lionel whispered, beginning a slight snarl of apprehension.

" The family do."

Lionel spied far off into the brown, heaving desert.

One, two minutes passed.

" But here," he said, " aren't there farms? " And now he was looking close at Rupert's eye-white skin texture, round the eyes, fingernails, position of feet and all those marginal details which might save his friend the breath of autobiography.

" Yes," Rupert said.

Discretion above all. Lionel cleared his throat formally— and their eyes met about seventeen miles away on a hill the shape of a German tin hat.

By making patiently that ocular combined journey, no impediment was admitted to the quiet marriage of their minds.

" I suppose," Rupert said at last, " if we're drawing thousands from it somebody ought to be mixed up in it."

" Are . . . you . . . ' drawing thousands? ' "

" My mother is."

Lionel caught his nose-tip in a little delicate tongs of thumb and index finger, a gesture which, with slightly bowed head, he employed as insulation when mental rape threatened.

He said, " Your mother is."

And then for some minutes they rested. Their eyes on the tin hat. The strain had been considerable. A flow of extraordinary deference and concern dawdled helplessly back and forth between them. At this moment they suggested a daguerreotype of Crimean convalescents. Cast dead-still for ever in an hierarchic woodenness—imposed by the exposure. Rupert chopped at a weed.

Lionel was snarling, silent. Let one thing be clarified. He said:

" Tenants cling on to farms don't they? Quite rightly. But I hear it's impossible for landowners to get hold of one for their sons, hm? "

" Yes, it's difficult."

Lionel felt relief.

Rupert said, " Though my mother has three in hand here."

At that the tin hat was not enough. Lionel's lips pursed. He made a noise that Rupert remembered—like the last sucking evacuation of a distant sink. In Offlag days this noise had followed his own confession. " I suppose I must admit: I don't really *want* to make a tunnel *or* go out with the washing."

Conversation ditched. They were left as often long ago, with nothing but a frail respect for each other's capacity to admit.

" Tell me," said Lionel, " about the man in a kilt. Is he really true? Did you say his name was Otto."

63

" Other. The O is long"

" German ? "

" No. Scotch. A laird's son—but no land."

* And no North West Frontier either—Lionel mused.

" So he writes. *What* does he write? "

" Heavy stuff. Laura knows them. Apparently his heroes always go mad just before the end—then he bleeds from the ears and goes shooting. Then he starts again."

Rupert said it all sadly—but factually. They pretended to be examining the flowers in the vicinity of the Fleights.

Lionel might have known it.

" How do they live? "

" She has something. Also he's ack ack I."

" I beg your pardon? "

" T.A."

He tried to take it all in—by eye. " T.A.," he murmured reminiscently.

But that would be enough of that. " Rupert, why haven't we met till . . ."

Laura Childe came over to them.

" Mother's got seven salmon in the larder—will you ask her to give me one? "

Rupert was ill at ease. The request had had follow-through.

" Will you? " she insisted. Rupert smiled weakly.

But the girl did not persevere. She let the matter drop as though Rupert must, as expected, share with his mother, for different reasons, the blame for her salmon-less departure.

" Good-bye," she said and held out her hand to Lionel.

" Oh—*Good*-bye.".

She went.

Big dogs with bumble-bees are perplexed deeper than

they know. Their faded hunting instincts are *frolé* by the noise and the general zig-zaggery. They look where it no longer is with ears all afloppy gog. And yet the whole adds up to incapacity—finally a few baffled snaps at air, to picking up a stick as a firm change of subject. Thus was Lionel with attractive women.

Unfavourable preconception of April's daughter had been upset if not reversed by a certain winsome barmaid quality, surprising in Rupert's sister.

But then genes were like billiard balls. The most astounding genetic flukes were possible—even by April. For instance—Rupert . . .

" Well," Lionel said vacantly.

Not beautiful, not pretty, yet not ugly. Not merely making the best of a bad job though certainly making the best of *a* job. Definitely self-conscious yet in the pay-off natural. Enough bitch for practical purposes he guessed—which was, alas, more than enough for his.

" I too must go," he said. " What a very charming sister. Does her husband work up here? "

" He was killed in the war."

Lionel was at once deferential to this fact in the way that had earned him love.

" I'm so sorry," he said. And he was. Standing there, for several seconds. He was sorry.

When they reached the house Laura was protesting thanks for a salmon which April was putting in the back of her Landrover.

" Are you *sure* you can spare it, Mother ? " she said with a filial consternation that had no follow-through; and her eye for a second rested on Rupert and then . . . on Lionel. She got in.

April turned on Lionel.

" Now, before you go and while I remember. Can you do the 25th for the S.G.S. ? "

Lionel was aware of Laura Childe staying for his reply, hand on starter, window down. Was he a seal with a ball that she looked at him like that? Her mouth was just open; white teeth; red moist lips.

" The Garden Scheme," Rupert murmured.

April said, " The Garden Scheme. Of course you won't know. But Spence will. Just tell Spence you'll be opening to the public on the 25th and give me a ring if it's O.K. I expect you two have been winning the war again."

Few ex-service men were more sensible than Lionel of having been shut up for the duration.

" Going over it all again I mean. Well, it's been awfully nice, Lionel. First of many, I hope."

" Barking " said his anti-bodies while he said, " Thank you so much Mrs. Gunter-Sykes."

She said, " Can't you make it April? "

Blank, groping—because April was already past.

" For the garden you mean? But . . ."

Then with passion and sincerity, " Oh!—*April*. I'm mad. April. Of course. Good-bye, April."

Laura Childe had taken her hand off the starter and pushed the window wider.

Would he kill a fish with Rupert before Rupert went?

Pause. April, he was still thinking. Rupert said, " You must."

He looked at Rupert. " That would be delightful, thank you." He wasn't quite sure what he had accepted.

Why was the girl still waiting . . . for him to go first? Then let her not be disappointed.

As he drove off he hummed the Offenbach barcarole, swaying slightly from side to side. It had a frivolous lurching, blind, circular and predestined nature which was the sort of thing he was fighting against but which was probably related to his achievements, his progress in total relatedness.

In the driving-mirror the snub green vehicle of Mrs. Childe followed his as persistently and as close as though attached. After a mile he tilted the mirror as for a sudden overtaking headlight, at night. But without knowing he had done it.

7

" A week," Lionel said, " Did you say a *week*? "

Huish rustled at the other mouthpiece: Salmson, he said, was a very busy man.

" But did Salmson suggest ringing me or writing . . . ? " Lionel protested, and then galled by an aftertaste of insinuation added, "And I too, Mr. Huish, am a busy man."

Huish said he understood Salmson *had* written.

Lionel allowed a silence which as it piled up defined itself as a reflection on Huish, Salmson and the Highlands.

Huish, goaded into something like self-defence, said:

" These things aren't simple Mr. Spote. Salmson definitely said there *was* a clause in the will which affected sale."

" But, Mr. Huish," Lionel said, level and quiet, " It's the first time you use the word ' definitely.' And this was what I wanted to know . . ."

No rustle.

" Hallo . . . *Hallo?* "

A rustle. Mr. Huish seemed to remember he'd already told Mr. Spote just this. Repetition, he thought, might have been tedious.

At last Lionel said, " Thank you. I should have rung Salmson myself. It was my fault."

Rustle.

" Good-bye."

Rustle.

Seven days!

Well, at least—he could kill one of them, if not a fish too, with Rupert.

*　　　　*　　　　*

Fly-fishing is an artificial art which has been developed since the middle of the last century with perhaps particular regard to the psychological necessities of the tired professional classes. Whoever has watched for long the weaving cast, the winnowing hand-movement, the slightly bowed devotional attention of those isolated damp doctors and businessmen, and heard, close as they do—the gurgling, guggling impassivity, the monotonous but soothing variety of the passing surface will see the whole thing as a charging of batteries, and like all charging, a long business —one amp going in all the time, and nothing apparently happening.

April was not a typical enthusiast. The whip-scream of her line and the set of her face was in answer to a maw which the several records she held had merely increased. And there were " scenes "—savage competition on her banks. Strong men had determined never to come again. Ghillies, helped by legend to be " characters ", had found their usual leverage of unexpected directness—come off bent in their hand, their humour unappreciated. They were boomed at, chivvied and worst of all—made to feel not priests of their own rite, but skivvies of hers.

Even the prodigal river was corrected by April. In several places by concrete bastions, false pools, accentuated shallows, and casting platforms. Strange, the salmon were not discouraged. The seed in them drove them, regardless, up April's Dnieperpetrovsks. Indeed a few falls, which in the past had eliminated weaklings, now had ladders put into them so that more salmon than ever ran the gauntlet of April Iridescent (her own patent home-tied fly).

*   *   *

She was on the bank. And she greeted him at forty-five yards. "Hallo, there," and leant back and *whiouch*—like a dud 88—she put her line round his head and then out, straight, for fifty feet into the water, the fly alighting later, like a seed with a parachute.

Rupert was not in sight. Nor any ghillie. Only the Landrover and April.

Lionel's shoulder was up.

When the distance was twenty feet April shouted, "Laura killed a nice fish this morning."—*Whiouch*.

When the distance was twelve, "Now let's see what you can do."

Presumably he invited the way this was said. There were places, he would have liked her to know, where he was respected.

"You go on," he said firmly, "I love watching."

"I'd better reel in a bit," she said, and having done so handed him the rod as though he hadn't spoken.

It was either an enjoyment or it was nothing, he fumed, fussing with the handle and line, and so one thing he promised—not to degrade himself by making excuses or even by trying. Because—the very *idea* that it mattered . . .

"It's ten years since . . ." the words faded into a grimace, the line had fouled the wheel-handle.

Yet he had always been able to cast adequately—the first time he ever touched a rod.

He cast. Then again.

He began to derive sour satisfaction from April's silence. She had clearly expected him to catch his ear—or start going

70

forwards while the line was still going forwards from the previous cast.

But no, April, no.

Simply no, he thought, letting out another five yards and laying it fairly straight.

Neither of them thought about catching a fish. They might have been playing with a washing-line in Euston.

April said, " That's not really at all bad."

He tried to scrape off the feeling of gratification—and handed her back the rod.

She said, " No, of course not—you go on."

" Please . . ." he wouldn't say April, " no really. I should like to find Rupert . . ." Let her play washing-line alone.

Hwiauch, behind him, *hwiaouch hwiauch*.

Directed upstream he set off. A screech and then continued screaming turned him about. And there before him was the orgasm of April's existence.

She was into a fish.

The rod and line made an inverted splayed U.

" I . . . think . . . we can do with you," she said with stertorous chumminess to the fish, meaning it was heavy.

The line carved clean through the water downstream. April followed, goat-foot on the rocks.

Should he help? A sense of emergency infected him. He followed rather like a private schoolmaster loping along the touchline, " Oh—good," he called, " excellent."

Suddenly the monster leapt—and Lionel's heart skipped a whole beat while the bloody great bull stood, curved airborne out of its element. Fifty pounds he thought. Perhaps a hundred. Something made him want to cry.

" Can I fetch anything? " he said.

The gaff was in her belt. " Perhaps . . . this . . . one

71

. . . I won't be able to myself . . . when you get the chance . . . take the gaff off me."

Hours it seemed, later resting in a clinch: " Is Murdo in sight?" she said backwards, "I don't want to lose this one."

Lionel was not offended. He wanted Murdo anyone to be in sight. But no one was.

At last it was Lionel who stood curved at the brink with gaff outstretched.

" Wait for him," she panted sharply.

Lionel recoiled.

" Not so big as I thought," she shouted suddenly peaceful, steering the armless, helpless, dozing thing in towards Lionel. Now! He jerked the hook up into it and felt the quiver of heavy life up his arm, turned to celebrate the *mise à mort* with a smile and suddenly found himself in the water, the sort of cold that might equally have been white heat.

Some impulse to keep the fish survived, alongside the instinct of self-preservation. He floundered with one arm taut, uplifted. Skated on slimy boulders and bruised his bones, at last got his balance in four feet of pushing liquid brown ice, fish still gaffed.

Then laughing unrelatedly, only just not hysterically, he waded for the bank.

And again partly disappeared.

Such were the radiations of April's personality that even thus he paid her the sort of coin he thought she must be waiting for. He heard himself from another life:

" I'm so sorry. Thought you'd got away did you."

For years this remark appalled him. It was *he* who had pulled the *fish* back into the water. And then . . . to have tried to put *April* at *her* ease, to apologise to *her* for nearly drowning, fetching her fish—was proof of fragile related-ness.

"I say, Spote," she shouted, "are you all right?" and then at the fish, "You're even blacker than I thought. And not half as big . . ."

He collapsed on the bank.

He wished he wouldn't laugh so amiably. He wished he could stop his occasional amiable laughs, his too frequent deprecation of concern; and he wished he would not examine his shin, as he now proceeded to do, with a lover's tenderness. "Darling," he might have been saying to his shin, "Are you sure—but are you sure . . ." with the triumphant boot of his hostess beside him.

"You'll just about do for the dogs."

He looked up sharply at that—but she was lost in the fish. "Lot of kelts this year," she shouted. "I say, you're pretty wet."

Then a clear voice behind, "What on earth's happened?"

Laura!

Lionel rose with athletic nonchalance.

The stuff of his trousers kissed him clammily on the inside of the thighs but he said "*Good* afternoon" with only the slightest concession to this sensation.

"Shouldn't you take them off?" she laughed, increasing the inferiority of his predicament, on purpose, he perceived.

"Perhaps I should," he said, keeping it academic. "As a matter of fact I think I'll go home."

"Oh, don't go."

She looked at him with *complicity*.

He repudiated it.

Trousers, slippers, shirts, whisky and muffins were pressed upon him if only he would return to Ardstruie Hall. He pictured himself in an IZ tie, wrapped in a

73

Lebanese blanket by a banked peat fire, sipping hot toddy while the eyes of the *famille* Gunter-Sykes strayed to him no oftener than was compatible with keeping a straight face.

" *Tell Rupert*," he said, meaning it strongly, " how most awfully sorry I was to have missed him."

Crimped now, at a strange angle as though from a sharp instrument gently pushed into his side, and mottled like bad peel, with his chin gone black, and his fingers in the snuff-testing attitude below his nose, he faced April and Laura, as he hoped and expected for the last time. Then started towards the car backwards like an ambassador leaving royalty.

Laura faced her mother.

" I think he ought to have the fish."

" It's only a kelt," April rapped. " But he's welcome to it if he wants it."

" D'you want the kelt ? " Laura shouted.

" The fish ? " he was now wizened with apprehensions of grippe, and his courtesy was a lily festering in each eye.

The tweed bitch was on the verge of abandoned laughter. He could see signs of it all over her. Good. *Good.* Laugh. If he had started in the Station Hotel on Monday he would like her to know that he might never have stopped.

" Yes—the fish."

" You can have the fish," he said crisply.

He was smiling, but with not quite enough irony for she said more cheerfully than ever, " I hope you haven't got your death or something."

Or something. By what other kind of people in the world's history had vapidity been cultivated as a sexual lure.

Looking at her suddenly, closely and scientifically, he investigated the fact—and published the findings in his expression—that she did nothing, day after day, from morning till night. Painted parasite. But what now raised his shoulder slightly higher than already, was (*a*) her expression (*b*) her skin. Objectively the Spote commission had to report that both showed every sign of psychosomatic health.

* Give woman security and issue, then she thrives.

" Come some other day . . ." she said, " when my mother isn't fishing." And then she blushed.

Lionel had once known the explanation of blushing but for the moment it escaped him, in a sudden disturbance of the stomach—as though she had made some shocking suggestion.

8

HEW MACKAY wrought with his ladies' nib—a squirl here and a grace-note there. He had worked all night at the pistol he would put to Mr. L. Spote's head. Such entries, vouchers, attendance rolls, receipts and debits, grants as per 2½ per cent attendance and uniforms returnable as U/S after collection of 8 per cent depreciation from a boy living in Cape Wrath yet really gone away to the Merchant Navy last year with his whole kit, the police to be informed. What would the nephew of Rossiemurchat say when told he must take this rough with that smooth? What but neither.

He looked up sharply. " Flossie, that's not nearly it."

She was eight and practising the sword dance between two sabres with silver and plush grips.

" Look then."

He demonstrated—really to let off steam from the foretaste of triumph.

Alone in his dusty office between the 25-pounder boxes stuffed with chaos of deficiencies and the legislature of a weird almost anonymous game, he rotated with a fey buoyance on toe-tip, his little eyes always slightly awash from spirit, stern with the illusion of an immense importance. No caterwauls of simulators—but the ghost of Mcrimmonds, the banshee skirl of Alamein when he had read a comic at B Echelon and sold W/D marmalade to wogs, isn't it. " D'you see now. Be a cat in cutlery. Skifty, airfooted but not looking at arl. Know where it all is."

Long after the purposes of demonstration had been answered he continued. Alone now. Flip-flip-flip—flip-flip-flip—flipper-flip flipper-flip—d-d-dee-di—d-dee-di—aflipper-flip—aflipper-flip.

" Hoy," he suddenly shouted involuntarily.

" Haven't I eyes in my feet? " he said.

" Yes," said Flossie.

" Well, then."

She did not take it as a *non sequitur*. She gave him all he wanted with stay of breath, of life almost.

" Hoy," he said with terrible quietness.

Because it was in the bag.

*   *   *

For many people a small illness is a relief. They enjoy the rest. For a few it is even more—a chance to think in a floating, subjective way that almost merits the term contemplation. These, after looking through the window for an hour like a horse in a stall, think " there—a cloud " and dimly realise it is months, perhaps years, since they actually took a cloud *in*. They may even enjoy the experience until it puts a query to their whole way of life.

No such compensation for Lionel. Illness for him was

* *diminished adaptation*—and
* received as guilt on at any rate some level of consciousness.

He lay in the dressing-room of his dead uncle—surrounded by pictures of grouse-groups, captioned " Over " or " A big pack " or " Right and left.".

Being ill was like anything else, he thought. There was a right way. Which is always the shortest. So he lay admitting—and seeking the flaw in his adaptation.

Facing the half-darkened wall he looked like a French cardinal of two hundred years ago, swathed in a silk dressing-grown and eyes closed like set mouse-traps waiting to snap dead wide on a noise, a movement, a commiseration that vexed him. But by now there was no such attention. Even Mrs. O'Shea had been frozen off by his polysyllabic requests for privacy and tranquillity. He lay tracing the little feelers of fuzziness which Veganin and whisky were developing in his brain. And if there was discipline on his face which could not be traced to methodic illness then it was the determination not to think about April or Laura Gunter-Sykes—particularly the latter, the presumption of that cool come-hither prune-eyed . . . *planner* . . .

His eyes started wide . . . and he stared long at the wall. From the cauldron of fever—a phantom of his own free-assocation, this word "planner" had sprung with spinal impact. It was the *mot* entirely *juste*. And its appointment was with him.

He felt worse.

*   *   *

Lionel practised friendship.

Just as some men detect at first sight and after a few words a girl with whom, all else being equal, bed would be natural, so Lionel sensed straight away the person who might become a friend.

It was thus at once with Dr. Smiley.

He was a small man with a boyish face—a blue-chinned middle-aged twelve-year-old with kind round eyes so disabused as to be saved from apathy only and occasionally by sparks of irony. The shock of having been born still seemed to colour his view on any new matter or person.

" I'm most awfully sorry to bring you here for nothing —probably nothing," Lionel said, bracing up.

" Oh, we can always finish you off," said Smiley quietly from the bed end and having spoken, his face became illuminated with a wry smile, which faded into guilt for the liberty he had taken in speaking what might prove the truth. Penitent, he said quietly, " What's the trouble, then ? "

Lionel described symptoms and probable cause.

Smiley laughed at the fishing incident—a little too suddenly and loudly Lionel thought. And his comment— a single headshake was instead of much, much Lionel would have liked to hear.

" I find it rather a strange part of the world," Lionel said.

Smiley fixed a spot on the wall. He seemed about to cry.

" Where else have you been then ? " he said.

" Several places," Lionel said firmly.

After this show of resistance Smiley, though on the move, sank into a professional trance. Lionel liked the close-up of his conscientious pessimistic face with the stethoscope.

" Ai," Smiley said quietly, then with a spark, " D'ye like fishing then ? "

" I think I *might*."

" Come to see, eh ? D'ye take penicillin ? "

" When it's prescribed."

Smiley's trance lifted. His smile curled round Lionel's dignity, dwelt on it, with reluctant discourtesy. Class, it

seemed to say. So be it. Then slowly, " When it's prescribed, hah ? "

This man was the only good thing that had happened,
Lionel thought, since London.

" Tell me, Doctor Smiley. Is there much unemployment
in Fluach ? "

Smiley eyed him with forlorn curiosity.

" Unemployment? Or the primeval curse d'ye mean ? "

" What's that . . . ? "

" Work."

Lionel was not amused. Had he been mistaken ?

Smiley grew sad after his little sally. " I suppose there
are about six who would if they could."

" Six."

" Or five."

" And how many who wouldn't even if they were able
to ? "

" Three," he said without hesitation.

Six. Five. Three. These were figures clearly which
would take on a sharp human leverage, if you lived here.
You'd know them all. Lionel was impressed.

" Thank you," he said seriously, at which the man looked
at him for the first time medically.

" Are you starting a factory then, like Sir Duncan
Fidge ? " Smiley's face lit over the name as though he
were mentioning a funny film not to be missed. " Rivals,
eh ? The great thing here is—if yer industrial revolution's
a fellure, you'll have no excuse. Just about five billion
wretched guinea-pigs to learn from in the rest of the
world."

Then suddenly—" Well, d'ye want it in yer bum ? "

Lionel would still like him—but it required a face at this
point.

At the door Smiley said, "Take a bathing dress next time. Then you'll expect it. No bad effects then. Psychology, eh?"

With which unwitting personal remark he illuminated Lionel with his smile.

Lionel eyed him. He wished strongly the man were not going.

Smiley's face disintegrated, abandoned itself to the complete pessimism of his private, unstated, total shock of being born and lifelong after-effects. And didn't move; didn't hope. Just stood there taking Lionel's feet in.

"D'ye think," he said at last, "there's a lot in this explanation of illness by psychology?"

He raised his eyes to Lionel sensitively. Was the man in the bed going to laugh at him? The new-born Smiley hoped not.

Lionel eyed him.

They eyed each other.

"I think there wull be," Smiley ventured.

"Doctor *Smiley*," Lionel said, "I'm *extremely* grateful for your visit. We must have a talk some time—we must. We really must. *Of course* what you say is true."

Smiley looked puzzled and embarrassed, shook his head. Then he went.

*   *   *

The only good thing. But *how* good.

Now again—the grouse, the aroma of his dead uncle. He closed his eyes.

With a groan he rolled over. His feet were cold in spite of bottles. He drew them up to his chin. But this position meant a desire to return to the womb. He thrust them down

again. Cold. After a time they came back. Before he fell
asleep he looked foetal and cunning.

★   ★   ★

Mrs. O'Shea by a shaded lamp—with fresh pyjamas and
something hot. On ship. Or the customs at Berne. The
night the guards got them up to march farther west. All
one taste. He was transfigured with sweet courtesy. She
shone with goodness. And so did he. The pyjamas were
divine. The grippe a state with intimations of immortality.
A radiant but peaceful conscientiousness. " Send word,"
he whispered, " I forgot—to the gardener. He's to open
on the 25th." Montcalme. Jena. White rabbits. Brighton.

★   ★   ★

And then never, never would he forget it. Never let
Mrs. O'Shea explain or try to. The significance of cause
perished, as irrelevance, in the finality of such an effect.

It was when he was a bit better—a day later.

There stood his mother.

He just lay. Brutus at Philippi, MacBeth at supper were
more welcoming. Not so endlessly silent.

At last, feeling quite, coldly, ethereally well, he said
normally, " Mother " as though she had forgotten herself
in a way no son could pass over.

She said he wasn't to talk much, she had just popped up
to see he was all right.

This was an emergency. He sat up and in that motion
knew he still had a temperature.

" Mother would you please give me the pills that were
here. I have to take three first thing."

" I've put them out, darling. When I saw Smiley's
writing on them."

He closed his eyes.

"Mother. Listen. Just listen. Will you please go back to London."

"No, darling. You can talk to me like that when you're well. But now it's my turn."

"*Turn*...?" He began to feel weak, began to be certain that he would lose.

She began putting things in order—that is, where she wanted them.

"Perhaps you think I'm going to twiddle my fingers in London while you have pneumonia under horse doctors—who only come up here because they like fishing or bird-watching ten times better than their job. That, or drink got them on the run. Oh, no, Lionel, I know."

That crowing cry—Oh, no, I know. It came repeated out of the primeval infinity of childhood like a medieval *cor de chasse* motif in a modern symphony. His *mise à mort*.

She knew.

He lay quite still, getting used to the fact of her presence, as to bad news.

He was uncomfortable. His pillows wanted rebuilding. But he wouldn't ask her.

"Your pillows aren't right are they?" she said.

As she closed he thought he detected a whiff of anæsthetic. He felt himself shunted into a cooler, more supine position.

He heard the blind go down and his eyelids darkened. He could see her pale face turned back like a portrait photographer getting it just right. A cast-iron technique. Now all was the colour of her own clothes.

"I've got Spence to send up some flowers. And I've telephoned to Dr. Wingate. An Englishman in Aberdeen. I've told O'Shea to cancel Smiley."

He opened his eyes and fixed her.

" You what . . .? You will now telephone to Doctor Smiley *again* Mother—and re-engage him, on the National Health emergency visitors basis."

" On the *what* dear ? " she said strikingly, casually, at the weak link.

" You know what I mean. Now please, do as I ask."

" There now, just leave . . ."

With a savage whipping movement he threw back the bedclothes and stood up, shakily and drably in his silk pyjamas. While he was fumbling with his dressing-gown she gave in.

As often in the past he half hoped he might die while engaged in protest against her. Angina while reaching for his Jaeger dressing-gown in order to by-pass her. At the inquest a pause would come in the coroner's voice while he gravely and significantly murmured the word Misadventure —meaning of course murder.

" Thank you," he said—and regaining his bed cut her by the position he adopted in it.

A knock came. Mrs. O'Shea put her head in.

" Mrs. Gunter-Sykes is here now, madam."

Gunter-Sykes? *Madam?*—Lionel opened an eye on Mrs. O'Shea in absolute reproof.

She wilted as though to look at a dying kitten.

" His first time here," she said to Mrs. Spote. " What a terrible place he'll think. Well, one thing's sure, Madam —he'll have to stay there, till you tell him he can get up."

Mightn't he have guessed her socialism was merely womb-talk for Great Wars and Unemployed. Breast-politics. They were in league. Mothering.

A few minutes later, muted by floorboards, pile carpets

and distance, a faint vibration, sometimes sound, reached him. April was talking, below. To his mother. April and his mother in *his* house.

How much later he didn't know or care—the door opened—and Mrs. O'Shea came in, conniving now, with him.

" Your own mother," she said.

" I know," he said with his eyes closed.

" And now a mannie to see you, Mr. Spote—will I send him away? He says it's argent."

" Who is he? "

" He comes from out west," she said archly. " What a great man he is," she mused.

Did she mean this? It was always impossible to tell.

Suddenly April penetrated tonally. Her laughter followed.

Lionel said, " *Yes.* I will see him—send him up."

" Won't I get the sack from your mother," she whispered, now conniving.

" *Mrs. O'Shea . . .*"

She went.

★   ★   ★

" Glen. Get in there."

The boy moved to it. Sharp. Stationed himself square on the square inch indicated by the Pipe Major's index finger. Behind the tree.

The Councillor walked back five paces. " Get in yet."

The boy shifted inwards obscuring himself farther from the house. But could not refrain from peering round.

" Yet. Yet. Yet," hissed the Secretary. " Isn't one eye more than enough for a sentry to see with? "

When there was only an eye and a margin of head the

Pipe Major said, " That's your post. If you're wanting out for a pee resist the temptation."

He turned about.

Even in the town—from the Drill Hall to pub and back —historic bugles sounded his approach—or skirling pipes. Lucknow women caught their breath and looked up from rat-stew, in premonition of his air-footed, white-gaitered, tread.

To-day something more.

He had three ledgers under his arm and his kilt swirled about his grey knees, far far from them, because the suspension was at belly height, and thence, sheer.

To-day he was also on a white horse at the same time as marching across burning sands. And he was tacit with weight of understanding . . . capitation grants, the issue of ammunition to yourself when you expended it taking the empties on charge by weight and transposing the vanished powder as a permissible deficiency from then on. The audit of controlled stores, each with its Part Number— two letters, four figures and sextuplet pages for even a foresight. Personal contacts for buckshee sellables, built up over years. Medals. Ten campaign medals, one of them for two days in the Ritz, Brussels.

He felt eyes upon him—back and front. The drums thickened. Still he came.

" Well, if it isn't himself," said Mrs. O'Shea when she could find her tongue. " And are you wanting in? "

He didn't know her.

" I wish to speak to Mr. Spote. Would you give him word? " and then like a ventriloquist tailing off into his own voice he added, " be telling him, Margaret O'Shea."

" But he's taken a cold. He's not up."

Relief. Even a sort of initial triumph. So. He would spin out the duration of his foothold. He became larger. The youth was running away.

"Kindly ask when I might have word with him."

The door shut on him.

The indignity of not being asked to wait inside was made more painful by the knowledge they had a girl now in the kitchen, the windows of it being behind him.

He strayed casually a few steps to a view of the garden, in which he evinced disappointment, long, long disappointment.

"He'll see you in his room, Mr. Mackay."

For a moment he stood stock still. Then he began moving again, sailing. After her up the stairs and into the sick-room.

He had to become larger all the way.

The warmth of welcome from the sick bed hardened him—which was needed.

He started too soon, before any howdyedo and in a voice he did not know as his: "And how are you liking it here . . ." and leaving the last word in the air, and following it with a twitch, of nose and lips, which was a sublimation, into silence, of the word " Sir."

The man in bed had probably a million nips downstairs, in a cellar, and here a bedroom where no neighbours would get to know of she-visitors and what did he do, why lie in it white, and still, and peering, like a collie seeing a thing where it isn't. . . .

"Howd'you do," Lionel said.

"Not at all," said the major, "but you don't look too good," and his little eyes leaked with the effort of otherness, and the strange speech.

"I've got a chill. My stomach makes the most awful noise."

Lionel offered the intimacy like a boat-hook, so they could come together. He added an appealing smile.

It was all rejected—and had an opposite affect. The major swelled and burst out sternly "*Is trom geum ba air a h-aineoul*," and when Lionel merely looked stuffed with astonishment, translated brusquely, "Deep is the lowing of the cow on unfamiliar land."

After a moment Lionel said, "Might I know your name?" and then "Well, Major Mackay, what can I do for you?"

"It's the cadets," said the islander.

"The *cadets*." Lionel went blank. Was the man drunk? A whiff of proof had reached him.

"Ai, the cadets, Mr. Spote."

"Well—what about them, Major Mackay? Indeed, what *are* they? Perhaps we should dispose of that first."

Major Mackay blinked at the complexity of the man's sentence. But it was nothing. He'd walk through it—and he did, coming out the other side. "The cadets, Mr. Spote," he repeated dourly, suddenly petrified by the position in which he had put himself.

Lionel measured things.

"Major Mackay—are you confusing me with my uncle?"

"I'm confusing you with no one, Mr. Spote."

Sheer aggression. Lionel began gauging psychologically.

"Major Mackay—now that I'm up here I want to help—as far as a complete stranger can. For instance—I want to help the cadets . . ."

The Pipe Major stiffened—at last smiled—from the other end of years of experience—and war, sands, camels and

88

final field rank—at a youth in bed. He swayed slightly. Smiling. The room was hot after outside.

" You can*not*," he said.

Seconds passed. Lionel, deciding he was deaf, shouted, " I should like to take on what I can—in the time available."

" Then you'll do without me," bawled back the major.

Lionel frowned. " I think we must be talking at cross purposes. I . . ."

" Not at arl," the major whispered suddenly in reckless, hysterical disdain of long loyalty spurned. " But I thought ye should know. It's both or nothing." His voice leapt. " Y'can take both—or nothing."

And he stood up—uncertainly. He had known a dozen Lionel Spotes—put his finger on the pay-roll at every bloody place they had to sign.

He confided his whole feelings to a long stare from his little, now suddenly malicious, eyes: so let him then, just let him. " You'll be needing these isn't that right?" he said, putting the ledgers down.

Lionel lay back—laughed, or was it sobbed, a few notes. Screening his frontal sinuses and eyes with one hand.

So the man was drunk. So they let a drunk up. His mother, April Gunter-Sykes and his mother when he was ill, let a drunk up.

" Major Mackay," he said, " I've enjoyed your visit very much—but one thing I do insist is that you take away with you now, those public ledgers. Because I won't be responsible for them. I won't."

Major Mackay swayed. His jaw clamped. At last he said, " I'll take them away with me. But this is not the end of this. So don't think it. The cadets have a right to be consulted. It's a voluntary organisation and so I shall write."

Tears stood out in his eyes. The malice all drowned in *tears*.

In the terribly controlled voice which he reserved for his mother Lionel said, " Would you mind leaving. Because I can't stand this any longer."

" It would be a pleasure," said the major, now weeping properly—and he played himself out, head back rigid through a broken tooth to a lament: Ronaldsay. Not touching if it wasn't for his feet. And O'Shea a flunkey.

★   ★   ★

When he got to the tree he said sideways without pausing, " Fall in. Follow on."

The boy followed the imperial flounce; he ran this side and that for a statement, and got none. He dimly felt he was in the presence of one who had lost a battle—but would win the war; but it took him a hundred yards to learn that silence was appropriate.

★   ★   ★

There were more things in heaven and earth Lionel thought, than . . . Suddenly he sensed his mother moving round his head.

She drew up a chair to the bedside. She had a pale face but she made it more so with powder and black clothes. She always sat in stylised positions. Her voice was low and velvety but bore in on one formal Edwardian note. She listened, even to experts, on remote subjects with the shut calm of total preconception. But once she got talking herself she did a hypnotist act with her eyes—projecting a domineering norn-like metaphysicality, even for the most banal statement, such as:

"It's silly to blame April like people do," she said. "April is and always was just stupid. But she can't fool me."

Lionel used his illness as a barrier. With eyes closed he lay with head turned slightly from her. What hell-brew he thought had those two concocted in an hour and why had they fallen out?

"If her son is so ' good in the country '—why doesn't she let him live here? She kept on saying you were the sort of person who was probably ' happier in London.'"

"Well, I am," he groaned.

"As though it might not have happened to anybody: falling in like that. Might have happened to her. No April I said—quite nat'rally—no—don't go on like that. Ever since he was two Lionel has been very good on his feet and won the High Jump at Eton. That quite took her back. What year she said. 1938, April, I said. And then she got quite moody, she said her Laura will soon be marrying again—Lord Manchester. I didn't know there was one, did you? Apparently he's got a castle in Spain. I congratulated her: he'll need it, I said. She says he's always pesterin' Laura, Lionel, are you comfortable like that—always following her. And Laura won't make her mind up. Of course she loved the other one (Charlie told me)—a *doctor*, (but with money), killed at Arnhem. Rash I expect—they were both under twenty. She's got a child— probably the engagement ring. I wonder if the doctor had been treating her. The one she married. April was funny about it . . . Fancy a doctor having money of his own . . . in fact a fortune. Money goes to money."

"Mother. Mother . . ."

"Yes, dear, I'm here." And some time later, because he didn't answer, she said:

"And now I'm here, I'll be able to help with the lawyer. I get the impression from Huish you'll be glad of a little help."

"D'you think I might be allowed to sleep?" he said, "in total dark."

9

THE DRILL HALL at Kreevie was a by-product of Queen Victoria's Jubilee. It has cousins all over the world—a mission seat in Togoland shade, a tram shelter in Singapore, a drinking-cup in Hyderabad. None of them can have looked more out of its element when first set down.

At the time of Lionel's inheritance the Kreevie community had almost ceased to exist. Only six out of fifty-odd crofts were still worked. The rest stood roofless in ramshackle webs of walls. Scraggy descendants of long-ago potato, turnip and corn survived in ditches and odd corners, as flowers; but the people had gone. To America, Canada, Australia, Slough and Uxbridge.

It was a wild night Major Mackay got for his parade there.

And difficult because it was his first taste of the winding road since being appointed company commander three years ago; and also his first experience at the wheel of the cadet truck.

He would never have got major if he hadn't said he could drive so he said that, and was certain many months would pass before an emergency would put him to the test. A commercial traveller in popular silks—a Sikh—had done all the ferrying of uniforms necessary and *gratis* being dependent on the Council, of which Mackay was a member, for certain permits.

To-night the emergency had come.

*　　　　*　　　　*

A naked gas jet, with small bulb of incandescent muslin, stuck out sideways and lighted three youths, one in a battle-dress like an adjustment of two sacks, and the other two in gum-boots, grey flannel trousers and battledress top. At a little distance stood a middle-aged man whose turn-out was as smart as battledress can be, elegance and style being concentrated in creases, fit, folds over anklets and pressing of bright medal ribbons. He carried a little leather stick and consulted his watch. A beret sat his head chic enough for a poster: you're someone to-day in the Army.

The youth in the largest gum-boots had his head low between them and his elbows on his gaping knees as though straddling a hole in the floor and staring into it for ever because of a preferable monotony down there. He was smoking though the cigarette was mostly invisible in his cupped, reversed palm. He broke at last into a whistle and the catchiest fragment of a tune, top of the list on the Light. The hiss of the gas and this whistle were for quarter of an hour the only events.

Then the lieutenant called out, "Is yer father still off work, Johnny?"

Like a plug in the lips the question stopped the whistle.

"Ay," said the boy—and then didn't resume whistling but gave himself up utterly to the hole beneath him and the stub of smouldering tobacco which he held lightly in the nerveless callosities of his huge fingers.

Later the whirring of a clutch in difficulties stirred their attention. Again and again the urgent, pining, unmistakable hysteria of a 15 cwt. in trouble came to them from not very far.

" He's stuck, isn't it? " the lieutenant said.

But then silence suggested all might be well—and indeed soon the door did open and Major Mackay entered, kilt, silver-topped sporran, dirk, two decks of medals and ledgers. His little chimp's eyes which made endless reckonings, without disturbing the position of his head, alone marred a vice-regal, levee presence.

" Good evening, Lieutenant Mackay! " he said taking the salute of his namesake. " Have you all your men on parade? "

And then in a tone which suggested what he had just been through, " I can't spare you long—no. So get cracking."

Lt. Mackay again saluted, with his stick horizontal under his left oxter.

Then he turned on his men.

" Get on—P'RIDE." In the R.A.F. Regiment they had had cockney instructors.

When the cadets were ready, standing stiffly awry, and moving more than for the last half hour, Major Mackay, followed by his cousin, walked round them with cold, critical deliberation.

The Major stopped, opposite a face he knew.

" You—Watson—what's yer name? "

" Watson."

" Well, then—where's your trousers? "

" They've been condemned," said the lieutenant sharply as though the boy hadn't really got a right to the excuse. Watson had used them for ploughing till they were U/S

95

and knew that Lt. Mackay knew this, so his jaw sagged. He was out of his depth.

"Stand them at ease and easy," said the major—and he walked to a central place where he could address them.

"No. 3 Platoon, Kinnairdshire cadets," he said and his voice was pulpit solemn, his chest so full that the miracle was he didn't float. "Does your voluntary membership of this force—dependinlargemeasure—upon the way in which it is conducted and upon its present leadership?"

He had got the words by heart and as a result telescoped some.

Now at last they were still. Foxed in the very kernel of consciousness. Like intrigued poultry they stared, all pupil, and doubt. Then they stirred uncomfortably in the vacuum where comprehension should have been.

Lt. Mackay—with whom it had all been arranged—came to their rescue. "Well, boys—I'm a volunteer like you—so shall I answer for us all? Well, then, I'll answer Major Mackay simply—yes, sir."

There had been no room for inhalation—but the Major inhaled. "Thank you, boys," he said. "Thank you. I shall endeavour to deserve the confidence you have placed in me."

When they saluted to the front and slow marched, Major Mackay fell them out and left with Lt. Mackay. The boys sat down and waited, listening to the high whirring of the clutch.

"What brought thon?" one said at last.

But the big cadet was staring down into his hole smoking and the third was soft. His brother, was his father.

After an hour they went home passing, on the way, the cold black shape of the Cadet Force 15 cwt. It had a nasty cant. There was no one near. The wheels on one side were deeply grooved in the last midden Kreevie possessed.

On the front seat, wrapped in two army blankets, the child Glen lay asleep—and from a croft on the hillside, there came fitful singing, sounding out over the deserted land of his ancestors.

10

Lionel left his sick-bed and the first thing he saw was his mother's signature—writ large in the passage.

It hung limp in rows like skins. Skins of whole torsos, trunks, calves, busts, feet and hands. The units of it hung so thick they concealed what they hung on. And in the heat of the darkened passage they imparted to the air moisture and a tired whiff of expended washing soap.

She had started.

If he hadn't seen them in time, he might have stumbled into their clammy, wrapping touch, and so started his first day up with an incident which would have defeated his desire to treat her presence objectively.

He skirted them with an expression of mature disapproval, suppressing ruthlessly the power of their associations; went downstairs with decision and stepped straight to the letters as though to the sole relevance.

Work was beginning to emerge as a narcotic he couldn't live without.

He opened first the letter from the office, recognising it by the crossed purple quills on the back.

From Mackintosh *père*:

Dear Lionel,

This morning I heard from my old friend Duncan

Fidge. He exhorted me not to hurry you back! He says no one in the south knows of the desperate need in the Highlands for men like yourself, and much else that must have made your ears burn. What did you do— take him out fishing? I told him we could spare you till next month. Will this do? Perhaps you've decided to take the plunge. I would certainly understand if you did ... Many's the good day I've had on the rumpty tumpty tum."

The sack ...? Lionel looked coldly at the paper, and put it by.

He picked up the second envelope. An unknown hand. Female, sixteen.

DEAR LIONEL,

I heard my mother give you the 25th as your day for opening the Garden Scheme. It's a Sunday. You probably don't know that if you open your garden to the public here on a Sunday you'll have poisoned meat thrown to your pointers—or worse.

Just thought I'd tell you, in case you didn't know!! Hope the chill hasn't gone to your chest. You couldn't have looked colder!

Yours sincerely,

LAURA CHILDE

P.S. Perhaps you'd better get some pointers!"

One of Lionel's thumb nails twitched spasmodically at a bit of rough skin.

The daughter ...

He started the letter again.

He caught his nose at the bridge and closed his eyes. Decency where none had been expected, moved him.

He walked to the window with it. He read it again.

He smiled complacently: April's daughter was on his side.

He had his kittenish moments when his voice became quite unnatural and so did he.

"Good. *Good*," he said aloud—like a schoolmaster who's going to make it all fun this morning. "Let's take the Highlands on. Let's scupper this April. I'll invite Craik—and Milosh. Smiley."

Then he began to brood. April had tried to trap him into offending a whole neighbourhood. Or perhaps to use him as a guinea-pig.

He suddenly snorted, meaning to laugh but sounding angry. And he started the letter again.

"The toad," he whispered at last. "The original toad." And then the daughter: a casual handwriting. But no uprights like banners or tees crossed with lightning or paranoiac capitals like bus-shelters, or firm ascendant underlining—or creepy sacrifice of letter-formation in the name of emphasis. But round, round. A procession of alternate wombs and money-bags going to town. Without asking the way.

Good luck to her. Laura. He tried it again. Laura.

He began to sing. Like his playing his singing was without feeling. But he felt that the noise was *about* feeling —and this engendered a proxy glow which increased his disenturbulation.

Schubert—he somehow rendered as consonants on the right note—till suddenly the sight of Huish's robot Hillman stopped him like a lifted pick-up arm.

The car was receding . . . soon—now—gone.

★　　　★　　　★

"Mother," he said, interrupting her expostulations at the sight of him dressed, "was anyone here—I saw a car——"

"Visitors?" said his mother falsely. "Fancy that. *I* haven't been entertaining."

He fixed her. "Mother. Huish—was he here?"

"Oh, *Huish*—yes, he's been here. I thought you meant visitors . . ."

"What did he want?"

"Oh, he was just payin' his respects. He heard I was here."

"I see. Was that all? Why, didn't he stay? I wanted to see him."

"I told him on *no* account . . ."

"Well, Mother—I wish you'd . . ." No, no—not necessary. That sort of thing belonged to the past—the sterilised past.

Kindly he said, "Mother, when I was in bed you mentioned the will. Huish told me Salmson might have written to you in London. He has never written to me or even shown willingness to do so. It occurs to me you may know far more about this will than I do."

To a sensitive person his tone would have said quite plainly: did you help write it?

Gwendoline remained calm. As with Fidge, her falsities were the accepted girders of her integration.

"There you go," she said, "imagining as usual," and she counted stitches.

"Mother, I insist you answer. Has Salmson ever communicated with you about the will?"

"George Salmson is a very old friend. He took a rod four years running on the Oykell with Edward. Of course, when Charles was dying . . ." She had to count back a bit a recount; her lips moved soundlessly. And she added sleepily, in a different tone, because she felt his eyes prising into her. " Naturally he communicated with me. To ask for your address." She concluded firmly, switching suddenly:

" I take it you said Singapore."

" My dear Lionel—if Salmson didn't reach you by post it must have been because you came rushing away from your address."

This word " address " relieved her more and more. She had, in fact, recovered tactically.

He considered her. She remained engrossed in her knitting. On some occasions she could turn the heel of a sock without ever dropping her eyes from those of an equally prurient colleague. Now she was in a trance of concentration for plain.

" Uncle Charles wouldn't have placed any restraint on sale, would he, Mother?" Lionel said coolly, giving her the stare of a chairman of a selection board, a stare almost insolently personal and complacent in its right to judge.

" Seven, eight, nine, ten," she whispered. " *Such* a wise man Charles was. *Wise*, darling, not intellectual. In fact, almost *slow*. But wise."

" You've simply disregarded my question," he hooted with helpless petulance. " I might not have spoken."

Gwendoline did not contradict this. But after some time she said:

" If you think George Salmson's the kind of man to betray a confidential document—then there you go again—picking holes in someone you've never even met."

" And whom, pray, was I picking holes in before? "

" Charles," she said firmly.

... The circles and ellipses. Now his lip quivered crookedly—saving itself at last in tired disdain.

*　　*　　*

Lionel withdrew to the room which he had made into his office, and sat down with the intention of writing letters. But it was some time before he could rid himself of the subtle psychological problem posed by his mother's presence and her intentions.

To ask her to go would be a sort of failure, a return to adolescent rebellion; it would also be unkind. But to let her remain would be a risk. Something always played into her hands. He had seen it happen again and again. He supposed he didn't really believe in " luck "—yet his mother's life certainly posed certain supra-rational problems. She had something of the fortune-teller about her—and every so often when most desired, she produced a rabbit out of some unspeakable hat. Her marriage to, and subsequent " occupation " of his father, had probably, to enlightened contemporaries—seemed just such a rabbit.

" Urrgh," he groaned apprehensively at last, and bestirred himself to correspondence which he took seriously, being one of the last letter-writers.

There was Leonard in U.N.O., and Jackie disintegrating in Washington, and Henry for the *Guardian* in Berlin, and poor George in Moscow hating it, and Jean-Paul in Johannesburg and Vladislav in Addis—and all of them becoming, as he saw whenever he met them in the flesh, less and less substantial because of living at hubs.

He wrote two of them long serious accounts of his political-economic reaction to the Highlands, interspersed with curt generalisations such as:

103

"The only English here are all canasta swine—sheer sepsis," and typing "L. G. S." under his signature.

And then—last—he came to Laura's letter.

A fussy incipient snarl—or was it smile—disturbed his mouth as he handled it . . . and as he went through it again.

For some reason the answer did not flow from his pen; he wanted to get it right. Short. Very short.

But each attempt expanded—till it lay crushed with its predecessors.

At last he wrote, "Dear Mrs. Childe, that was extremely considerate—and *most* necessary. But haven't you taken a great risk!

I do hope we may have the pleasure of meeting again, before I return to London."

This last statement cost labour. Would she understand the extent to which it forsook formality?

He hoped she would.

He headed all the envelopes PERSONAL and Laura's —CONFIDENTIAL—as well, because even for her he unconsciously visualised an In-tray.

11

Two, THREE, days later . . . ? It was the day after Salmson again postponed his arrival by four days. About the time that time began to lose definition and wear his mother's face; when he began to worry why Elizabeth Craik hadn't answered his invitation, and to wonder if he might not ask Laura over to dinner.

Lionel stood at one of the sitting-room windows, one shoulder slightly higher than the other, a position which was becoming permanent.

His mother had just refused to return to London for the third time.

The frown which, of late, frequented his brow, now accentuated, and enabled him to focus a helicopter without change of expression.

It disappeared behind a near rise.

The unaccountable always distressed him but he was usually saved by never noticing it. On this occasion there was no escape. Nothing else was happening.

He went into the kitchen and questioned Mrs. O'Shea.

She had two gears in her vocabulary—one Socialist-Daily Expressese for the theoretical world—and the other Biblical for the phenomenal.

Her eyes widened and deepened at the information. And she adjusted her glasses with an octave-span as though putting on second sight. She looked out of the window.

" And a great plane with a wheel has come out of the sky . . ." she said, trying it.

" But *why?* Mrs. O'Shea. Is it normal? "

And then she suddenly appropriated the incident, as though it were her own new hat.

" And don't you think we're all mad, Mr. Spote, up here? Now don't be saying you don't. Aeroplanes. Autogyros is it. And no papers till they're old." She went back to her pots, chuckling, stirring complacently and sidling into anecdote if he'd just let things be and sit down and take a cup, and not always be *after* something . . .

" Mother—did *you* see an autogyro come down just then? "

" No, dear." She was reading a biography with a book-marker. She was always reading a biography by somebody who spoke her language. There were dozens of them available every month. She was disinterested now merely because the event didn't concern *her.*

"An autogyro," he said irritably, "doesn't land in the garden every day."

His shoulder was higher and he went from window to window—eventually mounting to cold deserted nursery regions where the altitude afforded insight into depressions.

" Most odd," he said aloud—and only with difficulty resisted the temptation to walk out and investigate. No— yet why not—no—he must work. Two manuscripts had arrived that morning.

With great difficulty he gave them his attention.

The presence of his mother under the same roof made it daily harder to concentrate. It was fully five minutes before he could get comfortable at the desk and then it was only to discover his Biro was in his other coat.

During the journey to fetch it he trod officially and with a face that discouraged accosting.

He had just begun to relax and take in what he was reading—when the wrench bell of the front door distracted with its always disproportionate alarm.

Far away he heard a faintly familiar male voice mingling firmly with the flurried incantation of Mrs. O'Shea.

Lionel applied a protective cap to his Biro.

As he opened the door to let himself into the passage —someone came at him out of the dark with hand outstretched.

"Lionel!"

One of Sir Duncan's hands took and clasped, the other covered Lionel's.

He appeared to be dressed for ski-ing. But his grey eyes rested on Lionel's very solemn and still, with the confidence of the friend who would be there fifteen years later, at the gate, when they let him out.

"LIONEL SPOTE," he said with the timbre that stroked the entrails. "Unpardonable. Quite unpardonable. You were working. And ye've been keeping poorly. Yer first day back in harness—and who turns up? Fidge. Yer a scholar: know what a professor once called me? Sisyphus Fidge. Chap who never lets go."

A weather-beaten face, a forward-leaning stance, a Eureka stare gave Fidge, whom Lionel had never before seen by daylight, the look of one who had suffered for the truth in general, and you in particular. He would not take a seat —or a drink; the offers fell flat, frivolous.

But nor would he release Lionel's hand. He leant close— whispered, "Liking it? Great people . . .?"

Lionel began to *préciser* . . .

" Good, good—knew you'd say so. Now, look. Got five men you'd be proud to know . . . outside. Outside, now. Lionel: they want to see you. There's something they want you to know."

Lionel said " barking " to himself all the way down the passage. Five labourers stood in a row, suggesting the burghers of Calais. Two of them had the faces of worthy eminent Victorians, faces worthy of Chairs of Humanities. Two looked criminal, the fifth was nondescript.

" Lionel Spote—Mr. Spote—meet Sydney Johnson, graveller."

Like the Duke of Edinburgh on a news film, Lionel found himself moving down the line shaking hands.

" How old are you, Sydney? " Fidge said touching him, also acting as translator for Lionel—forty-two. How many bairns? Four. Wife in the infirmary. Graveller. Job— gone. Thinking of going south? If you could get a house. Sydney Johnson—what would the bracken-plant mean to you? "

On this occasion Fidge did not translate. He compèred the reply turning as the man spoke towards his audience with a glance of utter meaning.

" A luvving," said the man.

" George McManus Mackay . . ." called Sir Duncan.

And so it was with the other four. What would the brackenator mean to them? A new deal. A break.

Leaning a little towards them, showing no sign of having been blackmailed into a sympathy which for all he knew might be unnecessary, these men being possibly five secretaries of local Conservative associations, Lionel was earnestly pleased to meet them even though it involved him in an Americanism, for brevity's sake.

108

"Good," he said, "Good . . ." and finally smiled at Fidge with purposed cool formality intended to be criticism of the method by which the whole situation had been perpetrated.

Finally, he said:

"Won't you all come in and have a drink?"

"A dram," translated Sir Duncan, "ye won't say no to that."

Fidge's voice, Lionel noticed, had acquired a Highland lilt in their presence.

They trooped in.

Coming face to face with his mother in the passage, Lionel took her hand in his and said, very sternly—separating the words—as for a child that is being warned for the last time, "MOTHER—I HAVE SOME FRIENDS COMING IN FOR A DRINK."

"How are you, Johnson?" said his mother in clear Edwardian, ignoring her son.

A guttural murmur greeted his mother and two forelocks were touched. A third was jocular with, satirical of her. Lionel uncertain whether *gêne* or *détente* had developed, moved ahead until rooted by his mother rapping out, "Well, Duncan Fidge, what are you up to?"

Fidge held her at arm's length for without seeing—there would have been no believing. "GWENDOLINE SPOTE—time does nothing to you, nothing." The timbre had increased to a buzz within the note, like music on a comb. "Time, where is thy harrow?"

Lionel came back. One of his shoulders was extremely high.

"Of course," he said, maddened to be at a disadvantage with lunatics. "You will all know each other."

Still addressing Mrs. Spote, Fidge said, "Gwendoline—

I've come to kidnap him. Are ye going to let me have him?"

"I want to know what you're up to."

Fidge switched. Suddenly siding with Lionel—physically, too. He confided in his ear, "Yer mother and I are old pals. It was Gwendoline Spote and I who sowed the seeds of the Inveruchie Hydro project. We each got one side of Ted Howard when he was opening the Dornoch Spitfire week —and we said, Ted—see that water there. What's it doing? Nothing. NOTHING. What could it be doing, Ted?" Fidge came unhygenically close.

"A lot," he whispered.

"Isn't that right, Gwendoline Spote?"

Lionel found himself part of a group larger than the passage would permit, impelled centrally by Sir Duncan, and flanked by his mother and himself.

"Like a trip to Belgium, Lionel? You know what, Mrs. Spote—your son's a true Scotsman. He doesn't believe a thing till he barks his shin on it. Quite right, too. Spine of a great race. Engineers. Well, to-day I'm going to show him the Brackenator. He's going to take a bundle of bracken and put it in one end—and then he's going to play a hand of canasta (Sir Duncan pronounced it canarsta) with me while the brackenator works—then we're going round to collect the rope the other end. And we'll be back for supper. Unless you'd like a skid round Liége, to-night."

These last words, sideways, must have been inaudible to his mother and were accompanied by a sudden slight prurient increase of pressure from the hand which imprisoned Lionel's upper arm.

His mother said, "And how d'you think you're going to get to Belgium and back by supper-time?"

"Y'know where Belgium is to-day, Gwendoline Spote.

At your elbow. And d'you know where Tokio is, to-day?
In the same place. Air-sick?" he finished, fast sideways.

"Occasionally," Lionel said.

"Not in a heli," Fidge contradicted. "Nobody's sick in Jessy."

Lionel remembered the flavour of a game called Monopoly. His C.O. had made them all play it during the phony war in Hazebrouck. But the flavour of the game had been there before that. Now Fidge succeeded in imparting it to all life—even, he had to admit, to the probably laudable object of preventing Highland depopulation—and getting use out of a weed.

"Sir Duncan," he said in his most responsible tone, and smiling to modify what *had* to be said. "At first I used to think, I was dreaming whenever you spoke—or appeared. Now . . ." he paused, almost bowing in humility to atone for such rudeness—"I see how wrong I was. I've heard what a lot you get done. But as far as I'm concerned—I DON'T—go to Belgium for tea. I'm not READY to. I've no PASSPORT or . . ."

The face of Fidge kindled remotely on behalf of innocence; where, it seemed to say, did Lionel live, who mix with—to be so profoundly out of touch. *Passport . . .!*

"Lionel," he said, thickening his timbre so that tears and false egg formed at the throat arch, "We can't have it all back. We cannot have it. We've got to move, live, go forward (the sofa had become a well-attended meeting, and it was applauding for Fidge had raised his voice in order to still be heard)—and you're the sort of person we want—need—you're not going to be like April Gunter-Sykes—play into the hands of the vandals who want to destroy our Highland heritage, just for a piece of . . . b-b . . . *bracken*." Fidge paused—because the meeting,

III

sick with empathy, twirled its hats on to the rostrum and broke spontaneously into the welling rhythm of " For he's a jolly good fellow."

The five labourers raised their whiskies. " *Slange*," they murmured, with a suggestion of claustrophobia.

" *Slange*," Fidge said. " Are you . . . ? "

Lionel had always known he could not take very much, but he had thought that should some person intrude— who simply *didn't exist*—that person would have had no leverage. The little soft eyes were upon him now—for one tenth of a second of real sight.

Taking in victory.

" Thanks, Lionel." Fidge squeezed his arm, and put at Lionel's disposal the full perspective of his grey eyes— corridors down which you could march, unimpeded, right into the Essential Fidge.

Little chips of mirage—thought Lionel—towards which I break into a parched lope, giggling and apologising. *Merde alors.*

Fidge leant closer and whispered, " And those men won't forget you." His hand had strayed back pointing brashly at the unemployed.

Lionel, turning, took the Highlanders in. They were examining him with the uncensorious stare of experienced beachcombers : he might come in handy.

*　　*　　*

His mother took several rugs to the helicopter and a hot-water bottle. When she had finished with him he looked like a bird in the second week of hard weather—imprisoned, hunched in a Cellophane casket. With Fidge and a Eurasian pilot.

Breaking the law anyhow made him feel physically ill;

flying frightened him stiff. Nothing Sir Duncan had said convinced him the journey was legal or safe. He distrusted the piece of paper Sir Duncan had shown him. Every day company directors and M.P.s were in the dock for homosexuality or this sort of thing.

Could this be a case of both? He swallowed.

And there was something about his mother's face which suddenly made him feel that this was *her* pleasure, that she was winning again. He knew that peacefulness. It sat her like a sunbeam.

Behind her the labourers smiled. They had been bribed, he supposed. One raised a thumb to encourage him.

What now? It was like reaching the altar with a girl you didn't love. How many ever had the courage to turn back once at the door. He caught his nether lip in a dogtooth. Certainly not him. He laughed aloud one mad laugh—and then pushed something away that was tickling his right ear.

It was his shoulder.

12

SOARING ABOVE the North Sea, Fidge yelled, " I started on five bob a week, Spote."

Lionel shouted, " What? " three times before he heard.

In dreams you don't hear anything at all   He massaged one ear—and with justice for on landing he discovered a draught must have played on it, and also to a lesser extent on its fellow, leaving both of them solid and dull as after a local anæsthetic, and deaf save to their own moony hum.

That day, therefore, he saw people's mouths move, saw them obliged by heavy machinery to communicate with full lungs in each other's ears but he scarcely heard a squeak. He sank deeper into himself.   A sense of hallucination gradually spread till it dove-tailed, retrospectively, with the haze of M. & B., Veganin and whisky.   And then beyond that to the icy shock of April's river.

Yet this—he had to admit—was reality.   This, all this, was the stuff of Fidge's existence.   He looked at the man.

* In Fidge's brain there could be no link between front and rear lobes—thus preserving the latter, and hence his health.

They were met at the airport by an American car fifty feet long with co-respondent tyres.   Their small and only luggage, disappeared without formality, into a four-sided escutcheon for a type of delicatessen.

Lionel's eye dwelt on rev. counters and speedometers like television sets. German jazz—which would have affected him like a cardinal telling a dirty story—welled up from under the steering column while Fidge talked sideways and backwards. All lost. He smiled with the inane conviviality of the totally deaf.

*   *   *

The Brackenator stood on a hillside. From afar it was like a great louse. It could move as it ate—but only slowly. Near it, Lionel felt the ground shudder. With its head it harvested and begot, on the instant, rope, out of a hole at the back.

The principle was pressure. Bracken stalks were pounded into a stringy fibre and then processed internally. How? Lionel prided himself on his French and he leant towards yelling technicians, but the terms he did hear made deafness seem no loss.

Several photographers were kneeling to catch it at striking angles but they were not allowed close—a fact which Fidge dwelt on with satisfaction, assuming his most *entre nous* expression, as he guided Lionel forward past the limit where the photographers had to stay.

When addressed in French, even abstrusely and technically, Fidge responded by taking the speaker's arm, putting his ear close and then allowing his constituency face to crease into a slow dawn of appreciation—smiling astonishment, ending with a head shake which might have suited difficulty had that been the burden, but equally triumph.

There was a lunch and speeches, that went on and on. Everything had " Savette " on it. The menu, the plates, the cars—even a silk woman's handkerchief with a Brackenator motif—all had Savette.

115

Fidge made the longest speech.

The little man seemed to suffer from being unable to touch the people he referred to—and certainly he referred to everyone, and to the man on his right in particular, who grew larger, as though Fidge had a secret pump underfoot, attached to him.

Once Fidge referred to Lionel. Surely. The hand pointed and Lionel saw a lot of faces take him in for the first time, acclaim with smiles that were work. Sheer breadwinning. It was all work. Lionel would respect it as that. In spite of pain.

The wives had corsages of orchids swaddled in tinfoil. He found himself counting the teeth of one. This was like Soviet art—and cemetery statues. It was possible he would scream.

But why not the Brackenator—*why not*? What right had he—a professed democrat, sometimes even a republican —to feel snooty about Fidge—who whatever his motives took the trouble to find out the latest knowledge on a subject relevant to his constituency? If you applied a toothcomb to motives—who'd escape whipping?

He drank a lot of wine. The autogyro continued to pulse in his ears. Why not the brackenator—why not? And if not the brackenator then might he please ask— What?

But to be particular: this, Fidge's brackenator needed, first of all, bracken.

April, thought of in Belgium, appeared merely mad. But he scowled, seeing her. And that daughter: that limousine of a barmaid. Laura!

"Monsieur Spoot—*on vous parle . . .*"

While he was confined by circumstances beyond his control, to the north, he would assist, then, Fidge—to . . .

" *Alors*, Monsieur Spote . . ."

Sir Duncan was speaking to him—and to a certain extent the whole table was aware of his absence of mind. Sir Duncan was drawing his attention to a rostrum at the end of the room, curtained off. Lionel had taken it for a disused band-stand.

" Good . . ." he said.

Apparently he shouldn't have spoken.

The biggest man present, whose front, chins, breasts and stomachs descended in easily imaginable tiers like a baker's fantasy in dough, smote a bell—and with a whisk the rostrum curtain parted.

A sigh or was it a silence, as when a rocket has rushed and parted in far stars falling, affirmed a common emotion.

For there, apparently airborne—apparently levitated without tangible agent—stood midway between floor and ceiling—the anchor of perhaps a battleship.

The eye insisting, discovered—a strand, taut, vertical, connecting the dead tonnage to a transverse girder.

A murmur as of disturbed bees spread through the room.

The Gallic gasp—and chatter—to be the first to put the matter concisely with all due superlatives . . .

" Ah—*mais c'est inouï. Une toute petite corde comme ça . . . une ficelle, quoi . . .*"

Fidge leant across three guests and hissed, heraldic.

" Lionel Spote . . . ! "

In the face of advertisement Lionel's emotional cut-out began to operate. His suggestibility sank to nil. But now something was slipping. A sort of glee as once long ago for a Meccano crane budded. Power.

" I say," he said, " that really is something."

Now Pernod.

117

Two hands alighted on his shoulders; lips closed on his ear.

Fidge had come round. His whisper came fast. " Think of the braes of Fluach. Brown with the stuff. Bracken? —No. Brown with rope. Is that all? No—thread: silk stockings, high durability sacking. A noo deal, Lionel, for those boys of yours hanging about at the corner, scanning the adverts in southern papers. What's stopping us?

" A woman . . ."

Fidge weighed the K.O. carefully—measuring the verbal distance to Lionel's chin, " a woman *with whom you share a river.*"

The blow apparently missed. Now the upper-cut.

He did a little waltz first, and a feint.

" What's that you say? Nothing. Right, nothing—for most women. But with April *that's more than sharing her bed.*"

What followed was really no more than helping Lionel to his feet and the dressing-room.

" You're with us? "

Lionel thought afterwards Fidge kissed him. He remembered going round the anchor with everyone and the fat man rotating it, with his index finger, while the phutting flashes of the cameras, periodically froze the tin-foil orchids and the countable teeth into a sudden shadowless sheet of pasty lightning.

The same faces recurred later in a huge table littered with champagne in buckets, in the dark, half the company looking backwards into the source of light, where ten girls saved from nakedness by the smallest ornaments of commissionaires and toffee-box soldiers, executed drill movements of sexless impudicity with indifference.

"They shouldn't look so determined," Lionel said and then loudly with reverence, " A bottom." But no.

" In Paris," he said, to explain, " they give you a bottom for your money. I suppose we're in the Calvinist belt here."

He was left to laugh by himself. So he said defiantly, " The Calvinist corset. Oh, dear," in somebody else's voice to cover up his repulse, his total disassociation.

Fidge came to him in the dark and spoke of what he had done and would do in the Highlands. He prevented dialogue by providing it, in a parenthesis, himself, and during these parentheses he tightened his grip on Lionel's upper arm, like a brake, to prevent interruption.

The next day they flew home—probably to make rope by hand, he thought, in the Scrubs, for unlawful entry, until 1967.

Fidge set him down in a field near the house.

Lionel shouted up, " When do I see you again? "

Fidge shouted, " Leave the council to me. I leave April to you."

" But when do I see you again? " Lionel roared.

" At the Brackenator Opening." Sir Duncan waved encouragingly and raised one thumb in the air.

Lionel frowned helplessly. The hatch closed. Fidge waved again from inside his Cellophane casket and Jessy began to mount vertically.

As long as she remained in sight Lionel watched her—and believed.

Afterwards—not.

13

Mrs. Spote saw her son standing at the door. She said, "So you're back. Where's Fidge?" as though they had been for a walk round the garden.

At the third repetition she was able to make him hear. He said, coolly:

"He went off again at once. I gathered he was already overdue in Glasgow."

"I think he might have looked in," she said crustily. "It is usual, isn't it?"

Usual...? Lionel paused in his movement, staring. He was unable to answer.

She talked at him in questions. He said he had lost his hearing.

He took a book and went to bed without even throwing a crumb to her ravenous—finally resentful, curiosity.

Later she found his door locked.

"Don't you want me to do something for your ears?" she shouted.

"No thank you, Mother."

*   *   *

"But," she said next day, "what *happened*?"

For apparently something had happened. He was so distrait. She hadn't seen him so distrait since the day he left her for Mackintoshes.

He paced and mused and fobbed her off. She nagged. At last he took her in—not as his mother and an interruption —but as relevant, suddenly highly and unexpectedly relevant.

His eyes rested on her as though she were a symbol for decision.

" Lionel," she continued, unwittingly, " You can't have eaten lunch all day. What else happened? "

His eyes rested on her.

" Mother," he said, " I have to do some telephoning."

. . . " Well, go on—telephone."

" Mother, there's a fire in the other room."

He took the skin at the bridge of his nose and closed his eyes as though listening to the ticks of a second-hand and then, because she hadn't moved, opened them imperiously full upon her.

Mrs. Spote merely put his birth certificate into her eyes: to Gwendoline Mary, a son.

Rising, he said quietly, " So, Mother . . ." and offered to hand her up from the sofa.

She got up. " I don't need your hand, thank you."

*   *   *

Lionel's voice, now, as he rang April would not have been amiss in a head summoning a new and inadequate assistant master.

Her behaviour over the garden opening was the sort of smallness that made him feel fatherly, therapeutic and moderate. Indeed he had forgotten it, as he now soberly requested, " a small business talk."

She tried to backslap it verbally into " a drink, then— say to-morrow."

Which obliged him to redefine his request, " Mrs. Gunter-

Sykes . . . really rather important . . . as I think you will agree "—all in a manner that conceded nothing to hers. Not a laugh, not an irrelevance—in fact only thanking her when she suggested a time. 12.30. " Good! " Even April couldn't tinker with 12.30. " Excellent," he gave her *alpha* plus for that one remark; let her achieve the same standard with others. 12.30.

He replaced the receiver and went to the window—taking in the landscape with a new eye. Perhaps there *was* hope for it. He was wearing his publisher's face. Discrimination. Relatedness. And one hand hovered fussily about a waistcoat pouch—restrained against temptation, to consult the watch.

" Was that April, dear? "

He frowned. His eyes narrowed and he didn't turn. Perhaps she opened letters, too.

" Yes, Mother. That was April."

" You rang her . . . "

It was partly because she wanted it so much that he wouldn't, he simply wouldn't.

" Yes—I rang her."

" Lord Manchester came the day you went abroad."

" Really, Mother."

For some reason he said nothing, although he felt something.

" You had finished, hadn't you? "

" For the moment."

" Are you seeing Huish to-day? "

" I see no point in seeing him till Salmson comes."

" Huish's all right. But he never got on with April."

Round and round. Wrong again.

" Lionel. Forgive me for saying this—but I think you

ought to be firm with April if it's anything about the river. Remember. You've got the whip hand of her. She only shares up to the bothy. After that it's yours—including the spawning ground."

The whip hand. He walked a little. To another window. "Mother," he said at last, "I think I'll invite Elizabeth Craik. We both need—some other faces."

The desire to say it bitterly and the desire not to, and then the repentance for having said it at all, scrambled his face into a leering sweet smile and obliged him to take his mother's hands with helpless apology. How could he tell her what it was like to feel; the quaggy loss of momentum, everything going dead like a glimpse of an old newspaper or a thirties' poem, which her presence under the same roof gave him?

Holding her flesh loosened him a bit. His face softened, and an iron vertical line, from nose-bridge to mid-forehead, disappeared.

"Mother, if you want to know, I'm going to see April about some bracken. Sir Duncan is offering her a partnership in that Belgian machine; either that, or a fair price for land. He spoke to her from Liége. But she still won't see him. So *I* must persuade her."

She drank it in. He could almost hear it being digested. Into what, he wondered, with a sudden twinge of envy. Because if she could make something of it—some deep sense—some meaning—then he admired her; he took off his hat to her—from a considerable distance.

$\star$ $\qquad$ $\star$ $\qquad$ $\star$

About then—in May—Rossiemurchat stood knee-deep in daffodils. You could not tread between them.

On the following day Lionel noticed them. By stages:

Yellow. Flowers. Daffodils. They really were rather . . .
He began inhaling.

   * People should live in sight of flowers and leaves.

An unattached eagerness was disturbing him. Some gland
over-stimulated. Rossiemurchat was high. Perhaps the
pines contained Benzedrine.

He began opening and shutting his watch—waiting for
the moment to start. Towards April.

And Laura.

The thought was like stepping on a stair that is missing. A sudden thrill—bringing him up short, in a different
place.

He stopped quite still, where he was, looking down over
the daffodils towards the line of the river, and began to
snarl as for a too bright light; though the sun was in.

Laura.

He frowned. Became official. Drove off.

But the feeling, which he simply didn't want, became
arbitrarily worse when he came in sight of April's front
door and saw no visiting car there.

Apparently he had expected one.

He had, of course, merely wanted to thank her again—
properly—for that letter.

* * *

April welcomed him boisterously. How she could even
look him between the eyes he did not know.

He made his first point by addressing her as Mrs. Gunter-
Sykes, then after severe but tactful preliminaries, like an
intro. to a leader on Highland Development, he came to
the word " bracken."

Like a thing trodden on she went for him.

124

"Look, Lionel—tell Duncan Fidge from me that if he wants to buy my bracken—there's nothing doing. I want bracken, too. I know you don't mean any harm, Lionel—but that man has made tools and fools of older and wiser men than you."

Who was to be the parent of whom? They stared at each other like quarrelling psychiatrists.

It was some time before he could bring himself to speak and by then she was talking about what a friend of hers who had known Fidge in business had said about him.

Referring her back with critical solemnity he said, " But about the bracken—are those your last words? "

" Yes—my dear Lionel—I'm afraid they are. Ha, ha. I know you meant no harm. Let's have a drink. Had a go at the river, yet? "

" But if a light industry could be made of it . . .? "

" You know, Lionel: you're saying all the things I used to say when I first came here."

" Mrs. Gunter-Sykes—it may interest you to know I went to Belgium to investigate."

" I knew, I knew. It was probably all round the village before you got there. Tell me how did it work? Last year it was Duncan's Seaweed Combine which was going to bring prosperity to the western isles. He's so rich these flops don't touch him. They come out of tax. ' Improvement '—rebate. They may even pay him. Dry or medium? Or whisky . . .? "

" Dry, please."

" Were you at Russell's? "

" I beg your pardon."

" Rupert was at Russell's. I thought you were in the same house."

" No—we never knew each other at Eton."

" Did you know Harry Manchester? He's courting my daughter. Up here now."

" No—I don't think I did."

" Not as Soames major? "

" No."

" He's going to live in half Botton. Did you ever go there? "

" Botton—no."

" If he'd take a pull he could get her to-morrow. He can't see she doesn't like racing. Personally, I don't know what she likes—except that child."

" Which child? "

" *Her* child. What other child? "

" No other: I see now."

" The poor suitor told me he'd never yet seen her without it. She lets it join them after dinner in its pyjamas."

" She's not interested? " Lionel managed, moistening his lips. Intimacies with his intimates cost him dear, with an alien stranger they were insupportable; and about Laura ... the total feeling was new, indescribable.

April said quietly with rocklike empiric confidence: " Oh, yes—she'll see sense. He opened Botton for a ball last year. That's where they met."

" I *thought* I'd heard the name; the great jewel robbery, wasn't it? "

" Yes. Here *is* Laura. What on earth does she want? "

April put down her glass and marched out. The gravel soughed. Lionel turned away.

They came back together—Laura saying, nettled, as she entered.

" Can't I pay a call? We're neighbours, Mummy," smiling as she spoke straight at Lionel as though she'd known him ten years. " Hallo."

126

It was like the lift that goes down too quick.

" Why didn't you bring Harry with you? " April groused.

" He's gone back."

" Back ? "

" To London."

April said, with difficulty in view of Lionel's presence, but had to say: " Why ? "

Laura made herself elaborately comfortable in a chair.

" Could I have a drink? Maddening of him: *I* wanted to get on that train." She laughed—rather drunkenly.

Lionel did the offices. He handed her the glass and she looked up without any shame of any kind. Black provocation.

" Have you been fishing again? "

" No," he said coldly.

" I've never seen anyone wetter. Are you doing business with Ma? "

" Well . . . How did you guess? "

" By your face." She laughed involuntarily as though in surprise at herself—at how far she had gone.

Then reflectively, toughly, almost insolently, " And my mother's face."

An elephant, touched on leather hock with dandelions' puff of pistils, would be more put out than April teased. She said:

" I don't see why Harry went off like that . . ."

" Like what? "

Lionel feared she was going to accuse her daughter there and then—of jilting Botton—or should he say half Botton. Meanwhile she projected so strongly the view that he wasn't there—that he did begin to feel, partly absent.

" But Laura . . ." April shouted, coaxingly.

"I'm here, Mother."

"I think," said Lionel, "I ought to be getting along."

Laura said to him, "Did you get my letter?"

This, in front of her mother, was either showing off—or bad taste. Or was it a rebuke for the slightness of his reply? Very seriously, indeed, he said, "I did. I did. And I wrote to say—Thank you, Laura, *thank you*. I was going to ring up—I was whistled off to Belgium in a helicopter the day before yesterday—and yesterday I spent . . . trying to admit that this had really happened."

He made such an odd angry face saying this—as though still pained by doubt that it *had* happened, that she laughed, and then had nothing to say, which in her adroit case, was a compliment which stirred him.

He found himself staying.

His glass was filled reluctantly by his hostess.

Then it became conspicuously late for lunch—and Laura threw them both on her mother's mercy, in such a way that a double invitation was extracted, like a tooth.

After the flurry of his refusal and their insistence had subsided, he said, with approval.

"So you wanted to go to London, to-day?"

"Yes."

"I want to go to London, too."

"I want to see *Slap It Around*."

"Ah . . ." he said, and there was silence as after a plate falling. He was disappointed.

Yet at lunch he was funny about the trip to Belgium. He felt liquescent, shimmering. Only half-way through it came to him that everything he said was Japanese to April.

"April," he said penitently, and suddenly feeling confidence, in the new atmosphere, to return to the attack,

" I *like* Sir Duncan. He seems to me the only hope for a place like this."

" The more you do for them up here—the less they'll do in return. *I know.*"

The spectacle of April as a jilted heartbroken benefactor kept Lionel leaning towards her in his last warm alcoholic attitude of personal approach—but with a waning grin which evolved at last vacancy tinged with nausea.

" They're hopeless, are they ? "

" Worse than hopeless."

" Corrupt," he ventured—still in the same attitude, with a slow, sprouting desire to display—for the girl opposite.

April peppered her salmon vigorously, straddling the target all along. " I wouldn't trust many of them."

" Oh, dear," he said, " then we'll never get the bracken from you for the Brackenator, will we ? "

" Ha, ha—never Lionel. Not till I'm in the grave— and you and Sir Duncan may be there before me by the look of you. Ha, ha. No harm."

He caught Laura—laughing. *At* or *with* . . .? He believed—yes, he believed it was *at*.

He switched sharply, his eye accused her, with slightly drunk familiarity.

Was it . . . really . . . so very funny ? He had trusted at least *her* to understand that he had made light of the Brackenator only in deference to the setting, the meal. He felt an odd sadness. Good-bye—said his glazed eyes: it was always likely you would turn out to be mother's daughter. Yes. It had quite certainly been *at*. And for the rest of the meal his libido went into itself like a snail before two blackbirds.

When he said good-bye he bowed over their hands surely for the last time.

He said, "But do let me know if you change your mind"—and then to the daughter.

"I do hope you soon get to *Slap It Around*."

"Don't worry," she said, "I will."

Shocked by the confidence of her reaction he studied the question, standing there—when he should have been leaving. *Was* he supercilious, patronising?

"Good," he said at last. The pause had been vacancy due to feelings of ingratitude, of inferiority—desire too late to recoup. He wanted to say he had much enjoyed *Annie Get Your Gun*—that friendship with a tart and a teddy-boy might enlarge him—but it was too late.

And he drove away like one desirous of feeling power. Through bracken. Bracken. Bracken and rabbits. Bracken and rabbits. Bracken and rabbits.

But before he got home he was crestfallen and sober. "Elizabeth Craik," he said, "Come quick."

14

HISTORY HAS a habit of leaving in its wake little pockets that hold out, sometimes for centuries, against the tide of events. They often ambush people like Lionel.

It has been well written (and Lionel had read it) that even in mid-twentieth century there are millions whose " conflicts are capable of a medieval solution."

One of these was the Reverend Abigail Skene, Vice-Convener of the Kinnairdshire County Council, scribe and member for the fishing village of Hackster.

If Lionel's conflicts had been capable of a twentieth century solution then it is to be supposed that he would —in any vital difference of opinion with Skene—have fought, so to speak, a home match, with the wind and slope always in his favour.

But such was not probably the case, neither for him, nor for his century.

Fortunately for Lionel no really naked encounter occurred: his canoe shot the iron black rocks of the Skene rapids while he sat believing the bottom was sandy. The cushion-margin of money and social position, though turbulent and fluid, was still considerable.

He never knew what might have happened to him; he never knew how the Brackenator was all but splintered into a thousand pieces on a single protruding inch of the Middle Ages.

At this point a historical digression is necessary—for without it the power of the Reverend Abigail Skene would lack a dimension, and the authority and confidence of his opposition to the Brackenator, credibility.

In A.D. 1900 the whole of Kinnairdshire belonged to the Marquis of Kinnaird. He was a fairly benevolent despot but his son Coonie fell among press barons in youth and did look curiously like the last Czar, even achieving by faith a certain princely aura, and preserving it well into the thirties, even when physically and psychologically debilitated to a degree which passed him, publically speaking, from a political to a medical category.

In 1938 Coonie was an Under-Secretary at the War Office and also Convener of the Kinnairdshire County Council. He patronised both offices seldom, even with signatures, but was sacked eventually from the first because at a sudden crisis he was discovered to be shooting wolves from a plane in Canada without letting anyone know.

From this reverse came others. And the one that concerns this story: he was not re-elected Covener of the County Council. When he heard the news he resigned—by post from Hudson Bay in a tangled scrawl of grandiloquent abuse—and was thereafter seldom seen again in his native land. Sea birds eventually mistook his castle for an inland Bass Rock and bred in its deserted battlements by the thousand.

The county which had been a squat pyramidical structure, with only a very small and uncertain *bourgeoisie* next the top and an immense shifting base of crofters, fishers and woodmen, suddenly became a political vacuum. The Marquis sold from afar even faster than from near. April and others like her, completed their colonisation of the straths and appeared mainly in autumn—and August.

They brought employment and money. But they did not effect the natives much—even when they employed them. For with a few exceptions—they made no real contact, even though often they fancied themselves loved and served as never in England. But this was just the result of a sometimes lyrical Highland courtesy.

During the war a number of native butchers and sheep farmers became capitalists on a considerable scale—the former providing the old universities with the meat (that was never rationed in Kinnairdshire) and the latter drawing immense subsidies for uncheckable sheep.

But these new rich and newly powerful whose grandfathers had sometimes hoarded coins in socks, kept to themselves as though money that had so dropped out of the sky might denounce them, might bounce back again where it came from if it were noticed, which of course it would be if they entered public life. These new rich therefore, either took shoots in Perthshire or bought aeroplanes to go where no one knew them, or the less lettered among them even kept their cheques in tin boxes and never cashed them on account of vague fears connected with the size of the amount.

Who then "ran things" in Kinnairdshire? Who dominated local government? Not April. Not Pipe Major Mackay—even though a councillor.

Till the war the council had been a junior branch of the Kinnairdshire Estate Office. Coonie's factor had ordained roads. But now at the time of Lionel's inheritance a new situation prevailed.

Local Government had fallen into the hands—not as in English counties of retired officers, land agents, civil servants and farmers—but into the hands of crofters and above all of Free Presbyterian Ministers—the Jesuits of the Scottish church, known locally as the " Wee Free."

Here and there—in certain coastal villages where Gaelic was still the *lingua franca*—and in remote scatterings of crofts in the bleak interior, little pockets of sabbatarianism lingered on breaking surface to the outer world only when Princess Margaret went to a night club and was still there on Sunday, or when the Duke of Edinburgh made news of the Sabbath—with four chukkas.

In such places a minister still had the considerable power of the parent magician. Power for many of these ministers had become the point.

How could they preserve it?

The old leverages, the old stipends were failing. The Gaelic sermons of the Rev. Abigail Skene were cold gravy to the returning soldiers. The few young men who preferred fishing to lorry-driving no longer required his blessing for their nets. The mesh was what counted.

Suddenly, like a dammed river—he went sideways—into local government.

And at that moment his face, and in particular his eyes reached a curious affinity with the eyes of the People's Dictators in Europe. They were formidable, grey cyphers without anything in them to which a person could appeal; thus suggesting his conflicts were capable of a twentieth century as well as of a medieval solution.

Sometimes he raved, over the appointment of a clerk, or the site of a sign, till foam edged his lips.

And it was never really necessary for him to rave.

He had advantages, in Council, enjoyed by no other councillor, except minister-councillors. He had all the week and three-quarters of each Sunday to devote himself to the complex mass of legislation, procedure and precedent without which a councillor was at the mercy of permanent staff such as County Clerk, Drains Officer or County Architect or Accountant.

After ten years of such advantage he had achieved a dominating role in the council. Even decisions taken in his absence by overwhelming majority votes were reversed—by equally overwhelming majorities, when he returned if he so desired. For he always understood, and interpreted procedure just a little bit more deeply—that is to say creatively.

Only in one way was Dingey Dick—as most people helplessly called him—ever baulked. That was over an obvious, purely political issue. Many of the councillors were Conservative or Liberal and if an issue were clearly and acutely political—they would vote so, firmly—without speech or any other such risk—they would simply vote—against the Reverend Abigail . . .

But they were in a minority of one and therefore could only win if a Socialist were absent.

Upon this fact depended now the Brackenator's future and also the Reverend Abigail's manner, in the back of the tailor's shop at Fluach, where tight issues were discussed—and decided—beforehand.

His supporters—seven in all—sat around, eyeing him with the rather blank manner of those who have long ago submitted.

" From Sir Duncan Fidge," he said, raising the letters, " and . . . from," he swung slowly before the surrounding faces, preparing them for the *immonde* concept that was coming, " Meester . . . Li-onel, Li-onelle . . . *Spoot.*"

His neck didn't fill his rim of white collar but came out stringy and long with a suggestion of garrottedness which bulbous, funereal, mucousy eyes did not dispel.

" Chentlemen," he said—and his deprecatory long mouth

uncoiled itself into relish and contempt. "The Flue-ach
... Bracken-hm-ator company—requests right of way
through the land lately requisitioned for the new council
houses.

"The Flue-ach . . ." apparently it got worse each time—
more contemptibly unpronounceable. "Bracken . . ." he
sniffed the last syllables out of existence "Company has
for Directors—Sir Duncan Fidge, M.P.—and Meester"—
they were ready for it this time . . . he unfurled it with
rubber gloves leaning back—"Lionel Spoot."

There was a buzz. It had been beautifully done.

Councillor Pipe Major Mackay turned to a crony and
sniffled once.

The Rev. Abigail let the ripples spread.

In the sea-saw English lately weaned from crossed Norse
and Gaelic, comments flowed.

"Duncan Fidge wants more votes, isn't it?"

"Or divvies."

"Bracken I wouldn't give my pig."

The minister called for silence and continued reading
out the letter. "—In fiew of the need to make work in the
Highlands and to stop the depopulation, which for years
has been the bane of our country."

A hush fell. They recognised the publicity crowbar.

And tacitly they now approved and understood the
nature of this meeting.

No one said anything—even here it had to be done—
differently.

The deprecatory eyes dwelt on them.

"It would be an efen vote wouldn't it?" said the
minister. "Wouldn't our friends who aren't here, *approve*
. . .?" and bang—he had rapped the letter and stood
struck, still—"approve this letter."

Somebody said "Don't put it on the agenda. Put it small, isn't it—'Other business'—then they might not come."

There was laughter which died away guiltily. The minister had not heard the suggestion.

"Chentlemen," he said quietly so the hairs of their necks crept tickling up them, "the site . . ."

The hairs stiffened; he had his hand out, pointing sideways, ". . . of the new school—with its playground—and need for silence—has not been decided."

He was perfectly straight faced. His grey pub-shut eyes roved, accusing them, even his allies. Suddenly he shouted, roared at them, " AND I FOR ONE—NEVER HAD ANY DOUBT —NEVER A DOUBT AT ARL—THAT AT THE NEXT MEETING WE WOULD HAVE TO CHANGE THE LOCATION OF THE NEW COUNCIL HOUSES AND PUT THE SCHOOL THERE. BECAUSE CHILDREN SHALL HAVE AIR—AND LIGHT—AND QUIET—AND SHALL BE REMOVED A LITTLE ON A GREEN HILL. AND NO ONE SHALL STOP THEM. AND NO ONE SHALL HAVE LORRIES PUTTING ASH ON THEM—NOR COMING AT THEM AS THEY CAME OUT OF THE PLAYGROUND. BECAUSE BAIRNS HAVE A RIGHT . . . A RIGHT HAVEN'T THEY . . . ? "

He was joined, sustained, by a murmur. No one could have listened unmoved (unless they had studied his eyes).

No one but Lucifer.

Unfortunately he was present.

One person had had a dream, like a gift, of his own advantage. He dropped his eyes in case the parental stare of the reverend minister should spot it. Pipe Major Mackay. He even blew his nose, and was long behind his handkerchief. The Lord had put into his hands the means; surely it had been sent—after all he had been through, not sleeping —or eating much. His eyes watered a little—as usual with a vision; there he went—up that drive again, armed now with—a vote. A casting vote.

Wouldn't he come down a Colonel?

He would so.

Ignorant of the apostate thought the Rev. Abigail still stood, struck still, with his arm out indicating the road to the oil well, without use of which no Brackenator lorry could function; his arm out indicating—and barring.

And not a hair on a neck nape subsided, till Abigail's arm sank.

The Pipe Major wiped his brow.

15

THE LAWYER came just in time.

Lionel's eyes had begun to look like watering holes for crows. Feetmarks milled the edges during the night and the skin around them seemed filled with smoke. Why? Was work, his related work, merely a narcotic—which he had failed to take with him?

For his own—for Hilde's sake, he could not admit it.

Reporting failure over April—to Fidge—had elicited a storm of trunk-calls, despatches from the House, and jerky letters. Lionel must not give up. The Brackenator was already shipped.

" Shall *I* try April? " said his Mother.

The voice from the shadows. The patient vulture, in black, its naked neck encompassed by a royal blue velvet riband had been played out as a symbol of maternity since years. He would not permit its revival. Yet . . . you thought the room was empty—except for just yourself, with your failure—and there she was in the corner, looking at you.

He arranged with Huish he would meet Salmson off the evening train. But in the morning Huish rang and said " Salmson's here Mr. Spote. He came by the early train . . . after all."

" I'm afraid I don't understand: was there ever any question of him coming by the early train? "

" Oh yes, Mr. Spote," Huish rustled.

Lionel administered a severe pause.

" I should like to have met him—whatever train he came by."

Silence. " Hallo," said Lionel.

" Hallo, Mr. Spote."

" I should like to have met him."

Behind him his mother said with satisfaction, " Well, he's here, Lionel—surely that's the main thing."

" Did you meet him? " Lionel said down the wire.

" Of course not," his mother said—whereupon Lionel covering the mouthpiece, turned on her and said " *Mother!*" —in a tone she could not disregard.

" I thought I'd save you breath," she said.

He was bound to reply and she to reply to his reply. It was fully a minute before he said into the mouthpiece.

" Forgive me, Mr. Huish, hallo . . . hallo . . . *hallo.*"

Huish had gone.

Lionel left the room, with his mother in it.

Later Huish brought Salmson up. He was a large fat man who used geniality, Lionel thought, as caterpillars use colour. He fitted in so as not to be eaten—or even located.

All day Lionel prevented his mother from getting the lawyer alone—but in the evening he was defeated: he had to meet Elizabeth.

She had forgotten to book a sleeper and so had slept a little in her clothes, but that did not radically alter them or her. The purposely colourless face looked out upon the world as usual as upon a vacant and rain-swept platform, and for once reality, answered her view of it, photographically. The sleet was such the Rossiemurchat stationmaster required the train to continue by extending his flag from his office window.

She got out, swearing once with drab, staccato effect.

Then Lionel came twisted out of the murk—radiating pleasure.

"Elizabeth—you got here."

"Yes, I'm here, hun," she said. "It would be swell if you took this case—it's got books in it."

"You don't know what you're coming means to me."

"I can guess. Does that train just go on and on? I mean after one gets out—does it still just go on and on? It would be interesting to stay on it and see. Or does it come back? I got so I didn't care. You look older."

After a time in the car she said, "It's extraordinary to think that people live here, isn't it? Is there much rape?"

This was better. He smiled at her with private welcome, instead of answering.

"Just of sheep after church," she added beginning her trick of screwing hair round one index finger, and looking truly, like a dead cod with the pathos of yet being a human being. "How's the estate?"

"I can't get rid of it. There's a legal hitch."

"There's always that train isn't there?"

"As a matter of fact—it's not as bad as I thought. A little dé-merdification and . . ."

"I'll see," she said.

At the bottom of the stairs Lionel said, "D'you want to go in and see my mother . . .?"

"I think I'd rather come to it, hun."

He felt renewed, fortified.

"Lizz," he said, with serious concern at the first opportunity, "How's it going?"

"Like hell."

But this was how she had her books. He would never understand—but at least he could honour suffering.

141

And she lay on the bed and looked at him—very like a woman between labour contractions. Looking out of something—some sort of vehicle that made her temporarily different in kind.

And he stood beside the bed—his fingers in his fob. For others his fee could be three hundred—for her—ten—when she could.

He said, " There was a bigger room—but this had a table to type on . . ."

" Thanks, hun. I'm glad there's a table."

And a bucket in the corner and guards in the passage he wondered, before saying:

" I expect you'd like to rest."

She lay on the bed without replying. Charged lethargy. The relaxation of the limbs seemed a very carefully chosen only alternative.

He went to the door.

" Tootle-oo," she said. " Tell Mother Spote I'll be right down."

*   *   *

In the sitting-room the telephone was ringing. " Hallo," he said as though it were two a.m. and he'd been enjoying sleep.

" Lionel ? "

" This is Lionel Spote—Who's speaking ? "

" It's Laura."

" Laura ! " The explosion was nondescript. He sat down.

" Would you mind if I had a day on your bank of the Corgi ? My mother's got two admirals out her side."

" Of course—*of course*," he had forgotten he had a river. " Two—yes, that's right. I can sue her if she puts up more than two rods, can't I ? "

" Yes."

" Well—then do. Yes. Of course. I hope you catch something."

Pause.

" Thanks so much. Good-bye then."

Pause.

He caught his nose and closed his eyes tight.

" I've got an awful lot to do," he said.

Surprise was registered—for the *non sequitur.* " Oh . . . well . . . don't overdo things."

" I mean having a guest on one's river . . ."

" Having a guest on one's river ? " she echoed.

Lionel said, " Look—I'd like to come down—if I may— and see how it's done."

" I sometimes give up quite soon."

" I'd like to take a walk down there, anyhow. So may I ? "

" Well . . . don't let me stop you," she said, suggesting delicately he need not disguise the favour which he seemed to think he conferred.

He became wizened. She turned everything you said into giving yourself airs. Which it was, of course.

" 'Bye . . ." she said in American.

" Good-bye, Laura "—tutorial. And he set down the receiver. And remained seated for some time.

He went to Lizz's door and knocked. She said, " Come in," but then she always did, so he opened it cautiously and addressed the carpet.

" Lizz," he said, " Somebody has planted themselves on my river. I've got to put in an appearance."

" I don't follow, hun," she said. " But you do that thing. I'm fine here. I think I could sleep."

143

A smell of shoes and gin was already taking root.

*   *   *

It was sunny.

In a Latin way—he achieved a rather rural appearance that morning—some forgotten count in the Dordogne—with long legs and boots. A knowledge of old miniatures, a friend of the priest. Two swords of Jena crossed beneath a furious *pompier*, his great-great-grandfather.

He came upon a ghillie trying on a fly with a salmon at his feet—and then from a bush she said sleepily, " Hallo."

" Well done," he said impressed.

" Not mine."

She put by her novel.

" May I sit down ? "

" Do."

They exchanged their views on the weather.

He put grass in his mouth. " The lawyer's come," he said.

" So you'll be going soon."

" I thought you were going."

" I decided not to."

They gazed to their front, eyes narrowed in the sun.

He hummed; then sat up cross-legged, silent, and peered at the view much as though it were fog—which he would give a lot to get *through*.

" Of course, it's quite lovely here," he said didactically, and bared his teeth, in the extremity of his alienation.

She laughed.

She wouldn't, he thought watching the ghillie's exertions, kill herself, in any circumstances. But then if she didn't fish why had she come?

He sat mock-confidently a yard from her body which in

144

deference to his arrival had adopted the position of a question mark, in his direction.

He had thought, he said, she was longing to go to London.

" Can't one change one's mind? "

" Why not? " he said reluctantly.

Then strictly against the rules of normal social intercourse she said flat and steady and quiet so that he thanked God, at once, he wasn't looking at her, " D'you really want my mother's bracken? "

He knew the larval note in a woman's voice and it prompted him merely to some modern equivalent of climbing a tree, which didn't always exist. You were left, pretending the sun was in your eyes—hence justifying a snarl, pulling the peak of your cap low and simply waiting.

He had been about to thank her properly for her warning letter—that little delicate boathook with which she had steered him clear. Now she had sent across a boarding party.

" Laura," he said in his piercingly lucid manner, " *The Bracken.*" (Headline of an economic report which scarcely concerned either of them.) " I'm a mere catspaw. Fidge convinced me . . ."

" But do you want it? "

" *I* don't want bracken, *any* bracken, but . . ."

" You approve of this rope idea? "

" In so far as . . ."

" You do. Well—I can get it for you."

He kept perfectly silent, and switched on his asdic for dealing with stomach personalities. The findings were usually unbearable—but he must face it.

* She loathed her mother. This was revenge.

" Laura—couldn't we talk about *Slap It Around*? "

He smiled to soften the extent of the patronage. His smile perished, impaled—on eyes like black wet rocks of contempt. And now yes—he remembered yesterday—he had resented frivolity at the Brackenator's expense.

She said, " I didn't know you were just playing with the scheme," and one of her feet waggled, like the sudden switch of a cat's tail.

He went crimped and bleak, descrying far statistics on the horizon.

Playing. The word simply winded him.

" Laura . . ."

" I simply asked. Do you want it?—or don't you? What could be simpler? "

" Yes. Of course—the *company* . . ."

" The directors? "

" If you wish."

" Well, then—you can have it."

" But it's not yours to give."

" I can get it."

He couldn't take much. He never pretended he could. Disassociation set in. The verge of insane giggles—a noise that he would hear coming out of his chest while he wished he was absent. Because of the set-up of her. The power—like the sweating side of a locomotive or a crowd.

* Women are collective.

The inferiority. Oh, Lord—save him. What did she propose: blackmail, arsenic? At last he sighed. The moment had passed. He faced her—with iron reason.

" Good, then. *Good*. Do please get it for us, Laura. But *how*? "

" I need a little help. Not much."

146

Her voice had changed. Guilt. His nose never missed it. He stared at her.

"*What help?*" he said sharply.

Her foot waggled again—for some other reason. Self-consciousness. Her eyes had gone. She was smiling—making it all a joke.

"This. If my mother accuses you of something—by letter or telephone. Don't deny—or admit. But just say that you don't know what she's talking about. But *don't deny it* . . . See?"

"*It*," said Lionel, rigidly. "Will you please explain *it*."

The foot waggled—and then she looked up. It was shocking really what he saw: he felt himself being slowly pickled from head to foot in contempt. A quarter-plate label was being sewn on to his lapel. LIONEL SPOTE— 6 YRS. OLD.

Laura said, "You *won't* know what she's talking about. Does it go against your principles" (she dawdled slightly with the word) to "say so. The truth and nothing more?"

He stared. It was coming now. What he'd fought against. The breakdown of relatedness. "The Bracken-ator," he said weakly. "Ha, ha—ho, ho. Hee, hee, oh dear, forgive me."

His giggles took the form of cries interspersed with the apologies of an elderly clergyman for hiccups.

"HAH," he tried to void it all in one sound and then stop. Pigeons exploded from a far tree. "Most delightful, oh, most—you'll do it. Of course you will. Thus reducing my status in this one matter which I've undertaken since arriving—to its true worth: a foreign body in the Gunter-Sykes—Fidge *bouillabaisse-en-merde*. Forgive me. But, really . . ."

While in the grip of this inferior behaviour he was aware

147

of astonishment almost overcoming contempt in the girl's eyes.

" Are you quite all right? " she said dryly.

Perfectly still and quiet now he said, " I do that sometimes."

Neither spoke.

" Very well, Laura," he said, " I'll do what you ask. Better men that I have done a stretch in the Scrubs (he was almost off again)—but may I *wait* till I say ' Thank you.'? "

She was staring again. The label was being added to.

Lionel Spote—6 yrs. old. Wordy, nervy, bony and obsessionally inferior,—except when rational. No wonder he was always rational.

He got up and bent his brows on her. Himself again. He said—how much he had enjoyed their meeting; would she be kind enough to consider—hysteria a substitute for facing . . . facts, and he smiled the word down at her with jaded humility.

The speech was really a preamble to asking her to dinner —which he had suddenly decided to do.

But in spite of a very odd face he made now, for half a minute's silence, downstream, the invitation never hatched.

He said vaguely, " A big one jumped just then."

And she smiled at him—for this obvious miscarriage of his expression.

" Well . . . " he said briskly.

" Good-bye," she said, not detaining in the least.

" Good-bye," he agreed.

And went, jauntily.

16

INSTEAD OF LAURA he invited Dr. Smiley and the Fleights.

" I must," he told Lizz, " take a social purge after the will-reading with Salmson and my mother."

The mere fact that Mr. Salmson and Mrs. Spote had met in this very house during his uncle's lifetime filled Lionel with misgiving. Why should they have met? Fishing, she said. Oh, he could just imagine the sort of thing his mother would mix with the fishing—what eight-footed three-headed plot she'd hatch under the rowans in the most casual, velvety tones. Her jollity had always depressed him. To-day he took it as proof of her and Salmson's connivance.

The moment of the will-reading approached. Lionel kept the snuff-testing attitude, pinched fingers below the nose, restive as a child with a full bladder, over solicitous yet tetchy for open doors, for the oversights of O'Shea and her bland acceptance of even breakfast dishes, nicely heated —with nothing in them.

" Isn't that like me, now? "

" Oh, excellent," he hooted in the affected manner which meant he was disorganised, " and now, Mrs. O'Shea, could we have something in them? "

Only Elizabeth rested him. For her the will-reading in some way endorsed her life-attitude. " *Pourriture—grande marque*," Lionel whispered to her, divining her thoughts, as she buttered her toast with the terrible lethargy of one who handles not roasted bread but carbohydrate soon to be sewage.

And then the moment came.

There was the most extraordinary fuss about chairs. Lionel insisted they were inadequate for the purpose—while his mother purred over the superfluity of places to sit. Lionel took snuff in five places, before chairs too heavy to move, and peered into rooms that he had never yet seen—as though looking for someone without whom they could not start. There was really no reason why his mother should be present. Or had she a right?

" Won't you come? " he said aggressively, frivolously to Elizabeth.

" I'd love to, hun," and she would—but then his sense of responsibility asserted itself—with a slight raising of an already high shoulder. " No. I think my mother might stage some frightful scene."

Mr. Salmson discovered a gnu's foot made into an ashtray. He thought it charming.

* Lawyers—the most expendable of all expendable middlemen.

" Mr. Salmson—I think we could start. Mother—are you quite comfortable? " and he leant towards her with minatory solicitude, his brows beetling, meaning since I'm too weak to ask you to leave—perhaps you'll volunteer . . .

" I've been perfectly comfortable all along—now you'll just have to take all those chairs back! "

Intolerable. He addressed his attention to Salmson—persuading him to begin, which he did.

First the preamble, then the money—Lionel closed his eyes at the remote names of the shares—tin, rubber, distillers' stocks, and fiddled with skin at the bridge of his nose, thinking possibly you could not have too much money. Should he start a clinic in Delhi—then:

" And in addition to the other provisions in favour of my said nephew above written I also leave and bequeath to him my land and estate of Rossiemurchat in the county of Kinnairdshire . . . together with the whole parts, pertinents privileges and above all, *obligations thereof.*"

Mr. Salmson cleared his throat. Lionel opened one eye at the carpet. Mrs. Spote mused like a cat on the hob.

Obligations?

" For with reference to the last mentioned bequest I express the hope, nay confidence, that my said nephew (if he have not done so by the time of my death) discontinue all his interest in, association with and participation in " psychological " (this word is in quotes, said Mr. Salmson diffidently) cults dependent upon the fostering of intro-spection and lethargy as a cure for ordinary dumps."

" Is that in quotation marks? " said Lionel weakly.

" No—ha, ha—I see what you mean—no," said Mr. Salmson—and he cleared his throat.

" This is obscene," Lionel whispered.

" And that so far as his business concerns permit he will reside on the aforesaid estate, fulfilling the aforementioned obligations to all those good souls, dear neighbours of my evening years, who are feu-ed to him; that he live there a landed proprietor; for which station the means left him under this document will make him suited. With a view of making the said property . . ."

Lionel slid off. It wasn't really happening. It was a projection of his mother's after crème de menthe and throat lozenges.

" . . . and that he apply to the court of the Lord Lyon for a grant of arms suitable," Salmson cleared again,

" suitable to his station as proprietor of said estate, under which grant he and his successors therein would be entitled to be designated as of:

ROSSIEMURCHAT

" Finally that he attend to the council of my dear sister Gwendoline—until his zenith outmatch her declension of wisdom, for old age is not to be glossed as else but a return, in some part, to that feebleness beguiled by dreams, in which we begun."

There was a piece of thread on the carpet. Lionel bent assiduously and removed it, placing it in his outer breast pocket. He was aware, sideways, of his mother with her handkerchief out.

" Does this," he said using vim to his own unction but half crippled with deference to the validity of the last paragraph and in a way to its dignity, "mean that I am legally bound not to sell—Rossiemurchat?"

" I should say it did, dear." Her speed was what offended. He merely kept his eyes on the man he had addressed.

The portly man was all too ready for it—he leant back spinning his spectacles, and washing his face with one hand, opening and shutting his eyes, and playing a most tedious cadenza on the word legal—which of all words, Lionel thought, he should have been best able to dispose of.

Sometimes the man boomed, after a period of almost private unintelligibility, on a single word. This was still, usually, " legal "—but also sometimes " moral," which hoisted Lionel's shoulder till it looked as if it had a crutch beneath it.

"Because, with all due respects," Lionel suddenly blurted, " to my uncle . . . and to my mother . . . I can't believe that a modern court would sustain much of that. I mean the 'psychology' stuff..."

"Oh, no, no—we needn't worry about that," Salmson's glasses slid three circuits in one and ended on his nose, exact. "Indeed, no. That's—well—a wish, just a wish—but it might be that if somebody—er—mentioned in the will as possible—shall we say unofficial trustee—chose to exact fulfilment—of the clause relating to residence—as—er—opposed to sale—then—a situation would arise—in which—at least other opinion—might have." There was a sudden explosion of mauve silk from Mr. Salmson's left nipple and he disappeared behind a cloud in which he manipulated in such sort as to both excavate and anoint in a single movement, until one eye on Mrs. Spote gleamed and was hid again. Then he came out.

"Would have to be consulted."

"D'you mean if my mother insisted . . .?"

"I'm sure we needn't use words like that, Mr. Spote. This wording is flexible. I'm sure we all can be too. But it's true if someone—your son, for instance . . ."

"But I have no son."

"Ha, ha—very good. No. But say—if you had a son—or let us say just for sake of argument your mother—if she insisted that the words 'wish . . . expect' imposed a condition of acceptance, then it might be such a contention might have to be rebutted by you in a court of law, before sale could take place."

"But Mother," said Lionel, gazing at her, "would it occur to you . . . to . . ."

He did not trust himself to finish.

"I'm surprised Lionel it occurred to you to accept the inheritance without honouring your uncle's wishes."

After some time of being alone, utterly alone with himself

153

in their combined presence, he said, " Well. All right. Perhaps I'd better *not* accept it . . ."

And yet why *should* they . . . get away with . . .

" Mr. Spote," said Salmson exuding oil, " the words ' compatible with your business interests ' offer you enormous latitude. Quite enormous. *Carte blanche* almost."

Lionel froze him. " Mr. Salmson—land is a responsibility —like a train . . . or . . . or a cocoanut shy. If you own it—you can't just walk off and leave it. I get two weeks' holiday a year."

" But you can have a factor," said his mother wearily.

He had never meant to have this discussion. They had trapped him. So he got hysterical.

" I don't *approve* of owning property you never go near."

Really. He might have been twelve. The lawyer concealed the thought in another dry ablution—but his mother revealed and underlined it with a certain way of clearing her throat.

He was livid—even with himself for engaging with them. " Mother——" he said. " Just tell me. Will you oppose the sale of this land ? "

" Yes, dear," she said looking away, " you heard what your uncle said—it's my duty."

" And you heard what he said about old age . . .? He was *old when he wrote that will.*"

" Yes—*and* when he wrote the bit about old age. So where are you? No, no, Lionel—when you've lived as long as I have—you feel a *responsibility* to the young—to *slow them up.* Give them time to think. That's what I want to do with you—and—and this madcap scheme to sell—just because a German woman filled your head with stuff and nonsense about relations."

Dialogue with his mother had always been impossible.

He must remember this coolly. He exhaled, blew away the futile preparations for reply.

Silence.

It would be perfectly simple. It just meant time.

"Mr. Salmson," he said at last, "I should be very glad if you would take the other advice you mentioned—or allow me to—and put in writing exactly what chances I should have of rebutting—in a court—any objections to sale—which anyone might make. I am already in touch with auctioneers. I haven't the slightest wish to make another expedition here later. Do you think I—or you, *should you wish to try*, could get a ruling quickly which would leave no doubt as to the issue of a court action between my mother and myself?"

He judged the bluntness perfectly—so as to constitute the whole speech a rocket—and a warning.

Salmson stole a fast look of interrogation at Mrs. Spote.

Lionel said, "Could you?"

"Why, yes—I think we can do that quite easily."

Silence. Mr. Salmson waited for Mrs. Spote. But she told her beads.

Silence.

The meeting broke up. Lionel was cheerfully polite to his mother. But it cost dear.

She too was confident enough to be cheerful. A fact which reduced Lionel soon to pulp. He snarled through tea like a senile rheumatic—and afterwards said to Elizabeth with aggressive apartness:

"Elizabeth—before they come—the neighbours," (would they prove a *coup de grâce?*) "shall we disenturbulate a little? My uncle's records?"

"Hun—you know what music is to me—but I'll sit with you if it would help."

"It would," he said. "It would."

"Lizz and I thought we'd have a little music in the other room," he said to his mother and Mr. Salmson. "Will you be all right here?"

"Perhaps Mr. Salmson likes music," said Mrs. Spote.

"Mr. Salmson," said Lionel with urgent solicitude, "Won't you join us then?"

He eeled out of it—ha, ha—he liked music but he liked Mrs. Spote's talk of old days and the chair he was sitting in.

Before withdrawing Lionel looked at his mother as though they were strangers in a hotel and he was tired of her accosting him. Was it conceivable, his manner now implied, that after revealing her intentions *vis à vis* the will —she would still remain under the same roof—and ask for the jam to be passed as though nothing had happened? and even now, make suggestions with a critical slant. She was simply trading on the certainty that he hadn't got it in him to have her removed by a policeman.

On verra—he conveyed in one long gaze, straight into those twin TV screens of her stomach—her eyes.

"Just because I open my mouth, Lionel, don't at once look old-fashioned. You're not the only person who likes music even though you'd sometimes like to think so."

She was always trying to engage him on levels he *excluded*—simply excluded—he smiled slightly—making the tone of her voice unimportant or her whole self a joke they could all be fond of. "Good, then," he said, "Good."

And at the door he broke into a trombone rendering of a Rimsky-Korsakov air which in some simple way put him on top and all else under control, like a sledge hammer hitting stakes.

*   *   *

He said to Lizz, " You don't know how glad I am you're here." And he meant it—but the more he meant it on one level, the guiltier he felt on another.

It was like when he breathed the clean air. Determination to enjoy it, find it " nectar "—so now for Lizz.

She studied him.

" I think," he said, " Smiley—will be the answer to Salmson, and Lavinia Fleight can talk to my mother about blue babies, you can discuss the Zeitgeist with Other Fleight."

" Thanks." In deference to his entry she had pushed the *Daily Express* very slightly away from her. She never made big movements, or variations in vocal tone, but sprawled in positions that should have been relaxed, being so unorthodox on carpets and across chair arms, but which were in fact taut. She had only to look at a fire or a face for the atmosphere to be charged with the sickness of seeing things intellectually. Lionel wanted to get some wire-cutters that could get at just one strand behind those eyes and sever it—and because he couldn't and because she sometimes looked at him as though he might be able to, and so help, and because she had pushed the *Express* away, he remained bowed long over his uncle's radiogram which was an arquebus of electrical evolution.

" My uncle acquired the Tchaikovsky Piano Concerto No. 1 during the war," he said. " Would you object to it ? "

During the slow movement he told her about the will. Elizabeth couldn't engage—or if she could only politically and psycho-analytically—with Salmson and Mrs Spote. It was like collecting cigarette cards: she'd got those two already. They'd been almost the first she'd started with.

" I feel Salmson is where we came in," she said.

157

"But he's still here."

"Not really."

Lionel looked at her. She was the silt of something; an essence left over—of Virginia Woolf, smelling high now. Indeed the kind of alleged objectivity in her eyes—was beautiful and right somewhere—but where? His eyes widened as the association clicked—on a corpse.

"Lizz," he insisted, "We're going to get drunk to-night."

But he did not, so to speak, get this remark published in her attention, which was nothing if not selective.

And while he played more music she looked sideways into the fire, slowly revolving some hair-tips around one finger, round and round, as though it were the wheels of the train which had brought her so far, after getting his telegram— to this sofa and that peat fire which, she was sorry, was only just there, only just.

And in the face of this he closed his eyes admitting he was jamming her wavelength, which he had invited. Jamming it with music. Saying nothing to her.

Nothing . . . he was still thinking, miserably, minutes later. Absolutely nothing.

*   *   *

The dervish's wife looked extremely pretty in a yellow thing down to the floor, but came in with gorgeous self-consciousness which modified Lionel's appreciation.

The dervish himself followed in a frayed dinner jacket and walking shoes. He seemed assured to the point of disdain and undermined to the verge of twitch.

"Have a really stiff drink," Lionel said.

Fleight had this effect on him. Really, the man's eyes were the eyes of a Belsen stoker—a thorough lampshader.

Somebody had sat next to the Duke of Edinburgh. Fleight particularly relished the man's fitness for "filling the bill." He leant forward with glowing eyes and a smile of irony which overlapped into contempt.

Lizz said, "But of course they might as well wrap it up."

Lionel said, "No, Elizabeth. It's extremely important."

"As a 'symbol', hun?"

"Yes. If you like. As a symbol."

"What of?"

"Lizz—have you ever *been* in a crowd—when royalty was passing?"

"Or Greta Garbo," said Elizabeth.

He would not be red-herringed.

She said, "Once they had a purpose. The best bed, The best escritoire. The most horsemen. Top of a pyramid. Now . . . they're a sort of coloured balloon attached by a string which anyone can jerk—from the earth below. They're civil servants."

Fleight said, "That may be the facts—but it's not the emotion. And why do the remains of the upper class go to hideous lengths to get them to stay. Is it *merely* snobbery?"

Lizz said, "They want to get in on the piece of string. Otherwise they're just smaller balloons without the piece of string."

Lionel looked from one to the other. He said, "Isn't it a good thing to have *one* emotion a Canadian postmistress or a Durham miner can share with an old Etonian?"

"Uniting the Commonwealth," Elizabeth abbreviated, jaded, "and all classes. I can think of simpler emotions."

"The death-wish?" said Fleight sarcastically. He had read part of her last book.

She showed no sign of having heard.

159

Lionel said, "I rule that below the belt."

Fleight insisted, "Do tell me, Miss Craik, about the death-wish. What does it feel like? I mean, I was most interested in the Sartre quotation you chose for your flyleaf. 'I do not choose to choose but I should like it to be understood that that in itself is a choice.' Don't you ever get it funny? Or ill? I mean even the movement of blood in the veins is probably, in the last resort, a matter of choice. If you stop choosing, the blood will stop."

Lionel felt nervous. This could all end in boredom or hysteria. Fleight was leaning forward as though at last here was a chance of being psychologically sick. His eyes burnt with a soft and sensuous light.

Elizabeth began to look half somewhere else.

" Shall we talk about *your* novel," she said dryly.

" Happily," Fleight said.

Salmson said, "What was it called? I never get time to read."

"We certainly won't," Lionel said, who had found it in the house and read a page, then quickly, desperately smiling. " By which I mean merely . . ."

Salmson laughed.

" I can guess what you mean," Other said.

Insufferable creature.

Smiley said, curiously and simply, " Was it yer autobiography? Other? "

Salmson laughed.

Lionel then liking Fleight better because Smiley had addressed him naturally, insisted, " I am the host. I declare this conversation finished."

Salmson said, " Do you write under your own name? "

Lionel rose for the wine which stood by the fire and as he bent at Elizabeth's side he said, for solidarity, " Londoners

like Lizz and I take time to get used to the ' lunatic fringes '
... Ha, ha." The agreeable laugh—came too late—and
failed. But the dervish had planted it on him. Lionel
resented him more. But this was infantile. It must stop.
With great penitence and humility he looked at Fleight.

" Mr. Fleight—would you prefer whisky? " meaning
" let's be sensible. Forgive me."

Suddenly Lavinia Fleight pounced.

" Lunatic indeed. A ballot in the village about who was
the latest lunatic might surprise you."

Her husband lowered his eyes. And so did Lionel. Smiley
laughed, an open laugh. " Who's that, Lavinia? " he said
genially without preconception: such vast latitude of
possibility.

Lionel blessed him. Oh, dear. So old, so old—all of
them so old and grown up. God save us from fanatics.
But he mustn't bury it. He must face it.

So he turned to Mrs. Fleight, " I'm sorry," he said, " I
asked for it." Then to her husband, who was really to
blame for the whole atmosphere:

" Mr. Fleight—isn't it very difficult to keep in touch with
the world enough—up here—to write books about it? "

" Be *engagé*? " Fleight smiled slowly, provocatively at
Elizabeth.

 * Oh the jealousy of authors.

Lionel said, " Well, if you like—*yes, engagé*."

" *Engagé* with what? "

" No man is an island," said Lionel feeling the cardboard
of its usedness, but accepting it, believing in it.

" Could you rough out for me, then—some mainland—
in Europe—with which I might deeply coalesce? Except,
of course—the great lump of decomposition: France ...

and nearer. They say in a corpse—the brain turns smelly first. And certainly in Europe intellectuals and the intellectual country of Europe, France—seems to bear that out."

He really was far gone. Furtively Lionel glanced to see if there were foam at his mouth's edge. Instead he saw quite a normal smile—at Smiley.

Smiley shook his head at his plate. Search him.

"Fluach will do, won't it John?" Fleight said. "The act of sex isn't associated here with the noise of waste running out. There's quite a hot glee in the post van on the shortest night of the year."

They laughed. Some private allusion. But "waste running out"—had been a quotation from Elizabeth's last novel. Lionel had subbed it himself. It really was intolerable.

"Don't you respect suffering?—even French—or intellectual suffering?" Lionel said sternly to the dervish— and then wished he hadn't for the man repeated the question, at once, quietly. "Do I respect suffering . . ."

He must have a temperature, the way he now stared. There was silence. Had they all come to interview him for the *Spiritualist Times*? Was he a dog dreaming?

Like a prayer he said, "It's out of my respect for suffering that I *detest*—the cerebral left-wing intellectuals who are merely sick with addled liberalism—vacuums, separated from Communism only by mileage. To-day only the apocalyptic are cheerful."

Lampshades. Pure lampshades. Silence. In true curiosity Lionel said, "Are you cheerful, Mr. Fleight?"

"Yes," said Smiley. "He's always cheerful—except when you get talking like this."

Fleight said, "I'm cheerful."

Lionel turned to the company. "Well. Now we all

know. And what could be easier. All our troubles are over. We can look forward to a really nice cobalt bomb —say during the rush-hour, one thousand yards above Piccadilly Circus."

And Lionel looked round to unpack another subject but suddenly switched back and in his most couch manner said,

" But is it right for you to wish annihilation on the world merely because the world has suddenly turned inclement for you, Other Fleight? "

Fortunately few saw how personal a remark this might be to Fleight, who smiled as a cricket fan might smile at a foreseen change of bowler.

Fleight said " Does this line of Tagore mean anything to you ' Let only that little be left of me by which I name Thee my all '? "

" I have to have notice of these questions," said Lionel, keeping a loophole open just in case. " But yes—I think it could mean something. It would depend who said it to me. And how."

" If you read it. In the original context."

" Yes—it might."

" Then mightn't the converse mean something to you: let nothing be left of anything that rules out my All?"

Lionel's eyes narrowed.

" The trouble is," he muttered, almost to himself, " There are millions like you . . ."

" And in a little while—when things are a little worse —you'll be one of them—or will you get alopecia and follow Burgess and McLean before admitting it?".

" Haw haw," said Salmson.

" I think he might," said Gwendoline.

Calm and untroubled Lionel fixed young Fleight with

163

objective eyes. "And what I wonder," he said, "will you get?"

"I'm up to the tits in this," Elizabeth said wearily and from Gwendoline's and Salmson's silent reaction to this remark a certain neutralisation resulted.

Fleight said coolly, "I hear you're after April Gunter-Sykes' bracken."

On his own ground now Lionel decided to freeze this flow of familiarity.

"Did you?" and he turned to Smiley.

"Doctor Smiley . . ."

Fleight said, "Ten miles north she's selling better shooting ground. And there's nothing on that Fluach face. Not even woodcock. They don't like it."

"Who don't like it?"

"Woodcock."

Lionel frowned: Woodcock. *Tiens.*

"April Gunter-Sykes," Smiley reflected aloud.

"April," Lavinia said gluttonously.

Fleight didn't seem to like it when his wife uttered a word. He almost abandoned the conversation.

"She's selling everywhere," he conceded.

"She's selling Clashmannoch," Smiley said dully.

"She's selling everywhere except the Fluach face—her worst bit," Fleight said.

What was all this? Lionel looked at his guest with round, unamused eyes. Did anyone mind their own business in this place?

Fleight said, "So there it is. The only landowner that stays here more than two months a year does so only to breed Communists."

Smiley looked glum. He didn't like Communists—or April.

164

Mrs. Spote who had been listening to Fleight with um-
bilical approval said, "April's more *stupid* than bad."

Fleight looked long at Lionel. "The hope of the side,"
he said simply—and ironically.

"Yes," said Lavinia as though they had been talking
about it.

Their confidence bordered arrogance. *Bordered?* He
stared with new eyes: their second nature *was* arrogance.
He saw now—the Brahmin spot between their eyes. A
red dot in each case.

Yet Smiley—and the Fleights; Mrs. O'Shea and the
Fleights . . . The ease. And why did they look *well*?
"I *so* agree, Mr. Fleight," his mother said. Lionel closed
his eyes. They were all round him.

Elizabeth said, "With what?"

"All Mr. Fleight was saying."

Elizabeth said, "What was he saying? I never quite
could get around to having a clue what he was saying."

"I thought it was quite clear," Lavinia said, flaming.
"Not that it was anything much."

"Agreed," Elizabeth grated, not facing the bosomy
young mother, "but signatures were going down. I
wanted to know what for."

Lionel smiled sweetly at Lizz. With immense irony he
said to the company, "We could try horticulture—or
bee-keeping as a topic. But let's leave this one, Other!"
he said, trying the man's Christian name to see if that
helped. "I'm about at the fourteenth round with April.
I must warn you: you're backseat driving," he frowned
with mock severity. "So. Please . . ."

*　　　*　　　*

The party which Lionel had so looked forward to, left

him less disenturbulated than ever. Salmson's continual unrelated laugh haunted him all night; as did Other's eyes. Compassionate A-bomber . . .

You looked forward to a certain event as though life would be different afterwards. The coming of Salmson had merely petrified matters.

And Elizabeth . . .

★   ★   ★

Next day as usual he stood before a window and for a moment his attention was diverted by the sight of several children pushing the school car—to start it presumably—though when they disappeared still pushing, each of them an inverted L of effort, it occurred to him they might be pushing it all the way to the school.

* The Highlands. Adverse selection—even among cars.
* Colossal subsidies for unbelievable inefficiency.

The remote thudding of Elizabeth's typewriter—a short burst every five or ten minutes prodded him towards activity.

His mother said, "Darling, I thought we *had* to tell George Salmson to stay and fish as long as he liked."

Lionel said, "We?"

Why didn't he, Lionel, then do the going? Was it really a feeling of responsibility for this bracken scheme—into which he had put money? For the five unemployed of Fluach; for the whole skein of Fidge's seven-headed machinations?

Or for this property?

Then what . . .

Elizabeth found him turning listlessly the pages of a periodical. He looked up at once—from fickle concentra-

166

tion. " Elizabeth," he said, " you will go when you want to—won't you? "

" Go, hun? "

" Yes—get away."

"When are you going? "

" That's the point. I'm not."

His eyes were a little fevered. His mouth was tensely crooked. He smiled with such tender irony that she thought she detected a tear. Very seldom did she ever feel anything for a man.

" Not? " she said with care.

" No. My mother and I are going to stay here. Certainly for six years. Then the lawyer will come again. Sale will be forbidden. My uncle will appear to me at night. Blackmailing. I shall choose as my arms a Toad Craven—in a Hole, surmounted by a Mother rampant and Five Fluach peasants *poursuivant*." He almost dribbled with the bitterness of his facetiousness, the irk of impotence.

" Is it that? "

" What? "

" Which is keeping you."

" Then what else? Bracken? " he shouted.

" I wouldn't know, hun? "

She listened to you in a way which made you listen to yourself. His derisive shout came back to him off her, now, " Bracken "—he suddenly admitted, instead, turning away: Laura.

" Ha, ha." He laughed to put dust in her eyes. " Lizz. It was good of you to come. Oh God. I'm such a toad."

17

By EXAMINING him at his typewriter long enough Mrs. O'Shea eventually paralysed the movement of his hands and drew his eyes to the now familiar spectacle of herself in a trance of comparison.

"And hwat a lot of hwords," she said. "My, the knowledge and the learning you must have. I like Dickens."

"Good," he said conclusively.

"Mr. Spote," she said in an odd voice, beginning to slide a duster along a shelf in a soothing fashion as though it were a frightened horse, back and forth, "will ye be fetching the papers again before they arrive?"

Lately he had discovered that by driving to the village at six p.m. he could get the newspapers on the date which they bore, instead of the day after. Aware that Mrs. O'Shea satirised this haste in her heart, he paused for calculation and then said coldly and defiantly, "Yes, Mrs. O'Shea—I am."

"Well, won't you come in then—for a cup of tea—and a bit crack?" and she turned her eyes like beams of Yeatsey motherhood on him, in a stare that involved his genitals and ancestors, and melted the trappings of class and also (in a way that recalled the couch) any feeling he *must* this or *must* that. Yet, let him never forget even this would be angled.

"We—should—like—it," she said like a great actress, giving every word and every part of every word, definition, inflexion, and the pauses between each pure form.

And she won.

Self-wounded now to the quick with guilt for his suspicion, he now felt gratitude like a weakness of the loins. "Mrs. O'Shea—that's extremely kind of you. May I? Thank you very much."

"It's not only . . ." she seemed diverted by a bird, and had to soothe the shelf again. Now lower ". . . not only the pleasure we'd have of it. But I should say my cousin— is wanting to meet you . . . *there*," she said hypnotising him, "down at *our* place."

Trying desperately to translate—he waited, submissive, to her eyes.

"Not here," she murmured, pitying the place, and repeated, "Not here—isn't that right?"

He said, "Your *cousin* . . ."

"There's no *harm* in him," she said quietly as though she had been to God and found out, even smiling slightly at those who thought there was: at Lionel.

"Mrs. O'Shea—I've never even met him . . ."

*   *   *

Lionel was mistaken.

The cottage, one of a row, was fronted with primroses and a small rough square of grass. The little enamel number-plate contained the suggestion of a 2—and a black rusty gap, and the bell gurgled the other side of the wood. Mrs. O'Shea, as hostess, shone. The passageway was largely blocked by a mahogany hatstand studded with prongs and nobs strong enough for saddles. (Lionel put two of them to use) and bowing proceeded. The inner room had half shed its fisher-folk skin and half grown a *bourgeois* substitute. In a way it had the best of both worlds being humanly untidy, unpretentious and lived in, and yet, Lionel thanked God, not in any way *scabreuse*. Psyche flanked the upright grand on one side, Hope on the other and in the one arm-chair . . .

He froze, for there sat Major Mackay.

Marshal Hindenburg receiving a second-cousin teen-age candidate for the officer cadet corps, in an exclusive Berlin club, could not have insisted, more emphatically, by mere manner, on the discrepancy that here obtained.

It was no good, Mrs. O'Shea leaning forward whispering, " Look at his own self '" and then pouring verbally that which always overflowed from her eyes—the brotherhood or was it her own childless motherhood of man. Hindenburg merely creaked in his stays—or was it the chair and motioned Lionel to a seat.

" And while I'm fetching the tea," said Mrs. O'Shea, " You'll be tearing each other apart "—and she laughed, and then catching sight of Lionel's face she pleaded. " Mr. Spote, we're simple folk. Just ordinary. Nothing . . ." she judged the pause perfectly, " *special* " she whispered.

" Goo," a frog had formed. " Good, Mrs. O'Shea. Then we're all in the same boat," and he stared at her with some intensity, meaning wrong number, try April. Yet when he turned to the major he could not quite live up to his claim.

" Major Mackay—I had no idea you were related," he said pleasantly, perhaps too pleasantly.

The portly piper offered him a cigarette—as though a stopper for vapid small talk.

Lionel accepted.

When swathed in smoke which soon, owing to the low

ceiling, partly obscured them from each other, a voice came out of it, saying:

" So there's to be a plant for bracken."

Lionel, after a pause, said there was. The pipe major inhaled as though many plants had passed through his jurisdiction and some for bracken. He would ponder this latest, and perhaps allow it.

" And yer wanting ground for a road for it, is that right? "

" I understand we shall, *eventually* . . ."

" The Council's against it," he chipped fast taking some plunge—that Lionel did not recognise. " Half of them. Won't hear of it."

They smoked on. Lionel's eyes continually sought explanation from the major's face.

" Perhaps Sir Duncan Fidge will convince them. He's an extraordinary man, Major Mackay . . ."

" Half won't hear of it. Just half. No more. Or less . . . Unless it could be myself."

Lionel eyed him, pausing and construing, and then interpreting.

" You're a councillor, Major Mackay? I had no idea."

The major, feeling that perhaps he wasn't really a councillor after all, decided not to hear the remark. He puffed it up the ceiling slowly: an impertinence.

" Half," he said after some time. " Half exactly."

" That's the position I long for in Westminster. Then some vegetarian . . ." Lionel began.

" Half," interrupted the prime minister.

Lionel looked hopefully towards the back where there were noises of crockery. The little black eyes of the major wouldn't risk their integrity by an encounter, they left presence to the chest, the jut of the kilt.

" But," said the major, " I've an open mind. A councillor should have an open mind. Isn't that right? " Lionel treated the question as rhetorical.

The pipe major rose—and began to walk the room.

Piping after dinner in officers' messes had lent him some dexterity in the negotiation of furniture without looking at it. The pleats of his kilt rippled while the whole lilted like the fine mane it was for his bottom.

Stopping suddenly he said, " Did you get captain in the duration of the emergency, Mr. Spote? "

" Get?—was—yes, I was a captain, Major Mackay, for three weeks, I think."

" Three weeks," the march resumed. Lionel followed him politely with his eyes.

" And now you're wanting colonel? "

. . . " No," more firmly he added, " I'm not in the army, Major Mackay."

The major dealt with the red-herring as it deserved. By ignoring it. In a special dropped voice he said:

"Well, then—we could see eye to eye, is that right? " and he looked out of the window. For he had put the question, and couldn't watch its fate, but would have, instead, a fire down the road and everybody running.

Lionel, treating the question as general and political, said warmly, " I'm sure we could; indeed must."

For the major the issue now rested on the knife edge of Lionel's meaning. He would not disturb it. He would —maybe, add just a touch—in a voice like a note of a distant hymn heard in moonlight—say—while studying the fire down the road.

" You'll not take the cadets, then . . .? "

" No," said Lionel, grabbing at a solid, " I give you my word I shall not do that."

172

Colonel Mackay grew slacker in his clothes. He turned away and soon reappeared with whisky.

"To the New Road," he said, and Lionel taking this as political and general replied, "To the New Road."

"Oh, you men," said Mrs. O'Shea gushing in with the tea, "Haven't you finished?" and then she told them her husband was out and how she got married "one night" she said "and when I showed him to my mother she never said anything—no not a hword—she just luked and luked—and him there no bigger than a child—but all I could get—so I said, 'Come away John'—he's English—and she never spoke to him till she died, because among fishers a man was meant to be fine."

And Mrs. O'Shea said, "Look at that one with his whisky—he's that pleased. What have you said to him, Mr. Spote?"

She would take a drop herself though she never did—and it made her eyes so shine with love and everything that is under the counter also, that Lionel needed sunglasses.

"We're so harpy, Mr. Spote—you came. God bless you."

"God bless *you*, Mrs. O'Shea."

Her eyes overflowed but the little black ones of the pipe major examined the stuff of Lionel's tie. Thick as a curtain and dark with whole crowns. He looked up at the wall where there was no mirror—but his hand strayed, adjusting his tie, which suddenly had crowns on. Whole silver crowns, he thought. And a star or two beside.

18

As SOON as she heard the last syllable of the unbelievable statement April wheeled slowly upon her daughter and said throatily, " Laura—are you sure? "

"Well—you said yourself—all along—that *really—at heart*—he was anti-blood sports."

And virtually a conchie. That was so.

But this . . .

She had been on her way to the farm office but now she just stood.

She took four paces north—and stopped again.

" But what did he say? "

" I didn't hear it from *him*—at least not in so many words."

She took three paces south and faced a different arc of fire down the glen.

She knew law. Her teeth marked her lip. She was pale.

" I suppose you don't really care," she said measured, suddenly taking in her daughter's back.

" I care madly, Mother," and she turned a page. " But what can you do? "

April took four and a half paces east and put a bill with its kind in the arsenal of compartments bared by the roll-top. She touched her pearls. And felt vaguely, suddenly for her hair as though to fall back on her sex, once ascertained. But no. She stiffened again—and then detonated, went out fast, her legs moving athletically beneath her stiff thick skirt. " Stickett," she called—and went on through the house calling Stickett, Stickett, and then at sight of him, " Bring the Snipe round."

It seemed she had scarcely finished hauling on gauntlets before the gravel roared, and with one sharp squeak the immense Super-Snipe drew up.

Laura appeared. " Mother—where are you going? "

April walked through her daughter to the wheel. She let out the brake.

" Mother, what are you going to do? "

Through the window her mother said, " I can't do with a wet."

The Snipe churned the small stones like surf. April leant into the movement of the car and lowered her chin as though taking aim. She slipped fluently and in no time at all from first to top.

The rabbit grid made a brief crash. A prize Wyandot cockerel sacrificed four plumes of its glory to live. And then turned, appalled.

*   *   *

Lionel was reading the *Economist* leader—a moment for him which was paralleled by Buddhist contemplation. It had a position, a frame of mind—and it depended upon a preamble of peace, and certain material circumstances such as isolation, a pipe and the four freedoms, with one of his own added—freedom from his mother.

In prison, where most of these conditions had been impossible, he had sometimes contrived to imagine they obtained—and this to a certain extent, he had again succeeded in doing here, turning the subconscious picture of his mother washing upstairs—to the wall.

175

His expression and whole face would have done no discredit to any European prime minister of that moment —and to one at least would have been an undeserved and prodigious gift.

Every now and then he removed his pipe fractionally from his lips—as though the re-reading of a certain sentence and his reaction to and approving elaboration of it, stilled all physical processes, even the limp clinging of lips to a wet ebony teat; perhaps heart beat too.

He was the reader the writer had prayed for and surely he must have known it—just a bit. To smooth his hair he bent his head very slightly, into the curved cup of the palm.

Reason, the prerogative of man. His eyes were the two scales of the goddess of justice and his long nose the agate edge upon either side of which they depended.

And his shoulders were level.

Upstairs Elizabeth typed.

The gravel beyond the window erupted into one sustained swoosh so sudden he doubted the arrival of a car. No Doppler effect. Just silence before and silence after. His head which had swung with pipe removed into a frown fastidious as the shadow of smoke, returned to its pleasant chess.

". . . the task of M. Pflimlin, though no different in kind to that of his predecessors must be reckoned harder in degree, harder by the eighteen weeks without a government, the threatened show-down with the CGT, and the dissidence of the middle-of-the-road Catholics."

The frown came again—delicately knitting his brows, like a person who smells burning rubber at the wheel.

There were sharp, short, firm steps ranting up the passage.

The wrenching wrongly of the handle gave his face time to solidify in quite incredulous indignation—then in came April.

She came straight up to him, stopped short of his carpet slippers, mirrored him as a turd on a cushion—and rapped out one word, like spitting.

" CAD ! "

" I *beg* your . . . "

But she had gone. The door had banged. Another door had banged—and this time Lionel was ready for the glimpse of the great swerving saloon—and the swoosh of gravel.

As though his senses, not April, had taken leave down the drive he rose in some haste to catch a last sight of them. No. There she went.

And slowly—slowly his face taking it in, became corrugated—the laugh was not natural. She had been sick on him, actually left something on him. An archaism—and vomit.

*   *   *

The effect of this episode was, to a trained observer, evident in his manner, his very position at the breakfast table next morning. It drove him to unusual absorption in the *Northern Trumpet*, a four-page weekly, printed in Fluach.

One page was devoted to advertisements for second-hand bagpipes, drums, etc., and one to agony columns of verse on behalf of mothers long dead, inserted by their offspring, who gave their names. The third page was headed.

BRACKEN BOOM FOR NORTH
BY L. G. SPOTE

*   *   *

" The possible installation—in the near future "—Lionel read—" of the Brackenator—a machine for turning bracken into rope may mark the opening of a new era for the Highlands.

" It may on the other hand prove merely another minor though beneficial palliative to existing economic ills.

" In either case it is desirable that this new industry—whether on a small or large scale—should not fall into the hands of people whose main interest lie outside the Highlands; it is desirable that it should belong as far as possible to the people of this county.

" The directors have therefore wished to offer a number of two shilling shares in the hope that they will be widely subscribed. They had further decided to put the general public, if possible, in possession of sixty per cent of the total assets; themselves retaining 33 per cent, and Bloggs and Mende who provided the power unit—7 per cent.

" It is appreciated that many will be reluctant to invest even two shillings in an enterprise which may smack of the Arabian Nights until it has been seen at work.

" Therefore the shares will be kept open (in the possession of the directors) until after the machine has performed in public.

" Anybody, however, who wishes to obtain statistics of the Brackenator's performance in pamphlet form may do so from J. Lossie, 4 Shore Street; and if convinced they may obtain shares before inauguration from the same address.

" This space has been kindly allotted the directors by the editor not as an advertisement but as a means of bringing to the public's ears a piece of news, which, it is hoped, may be to the public's advantage."

Lionel approved. It had been with the greatest difficulty

he had persuaded Fidge to take this course; and it was with the greatest care that he himself had worded the announcement.

He had argued that it was morally right to make the machine as far as possible a " local baby "; and that to treat it in the press as a *fait accompli* would act as a lubricant for obstruction—whether by the Council or by April.

But how did it explain April's behaviour yesterday?

It didn't.

No. He closed his eyes, massaging his face. Laura was seldom far from his thoughts. Now she even invaded his official calculations. He had to admit that she must have done, with his permission, something probably fatal to the whole project, as well as in its own right morally leprous.

19

AFTER THE vote on the situation of the new school and the result which by a single voice, and after recount, still by a single voice, left unrequisitioned the land needed by the Fluach Brackenator Company—Pipe Major Hew Mackay walked out before the other business was finished and up to his stronghold, the Drill Hall, where seventeen children awaited a " Special " arranged for to-day in the Highland Dance.

He looked neither to right or left, self-consciousness being blinkers always but on this occasion more than ever because increased by guilt and triumph.

He had never yet made a speech in the council and to-day was no exception. His vote had been sensational by its unexpectedness—the simplicity of the single objection which didn't waste breath with words.

Members, like a naughty class, had stirred restlessly in their seats peering at the face of the Rev. Abigail, expecting him to do something as he always had in the past, when obstructed. And he did try. He tried to provoke the pipe major into a speech in order to have something to destroy—but the pipe major addressed himself to the convener: he had voted, he said, hadn't he.

The eager, ominous, trance of the minister's bulbous bleak eyes—like those of a fly-eating lizard—above stringy neck, had so sat upon the pipe major that for a minute it seemed conceivable a lightning tongue might dart twenty feet across institutional chairs—leaving one of them empty.

In such a hush the pipe major had at last been mesmerised into utterance. "Not at arl," he said smoothing his hair, and closing his eyes for more than a blink, reopening them calmer and firmer on the convener.

He had voted.

Now in the Drill Hall, facing his class, he received the hush of their disciplined line-up with such absent mind that a whisper developed. Yet no one was given a " drill " or " put in the report " for it.

He walked up and down—for now it came: his speech. Explaining his vote. Silent, in his head, the words.

At first in Gaelic, the overflooding for larger scope into a better known tongue—hadn't he heard with his own ears in the tailor's shop the plot to rig the issue? Well, he wouldn't do that. He didn't see eye to eye with Sir Duncan politically—as they all knew—but fair was fair. He wouldn't do that.

Suddenly the hinges of the central door wheezed slow to the world their long neglect—and then the broken spring allowed the crash which always announced an entry.

The Reverend Abigail Skene stood there. Black—except for the white surprise of his neck and face stemming awry from the white hole which led to his clothes.

The children turned.

"Now," said the pipe major officially to the class, "Are ye in yer groups? Well, move then, move, move. And *Geordie Mathieson* . . ."

His index finger accused—and all motion ceased.

A drill? A court-martial? Some necks craned.

" STANDSTILL EVERYONE."

" Geordie Mathieson—who comes in and who goes out —of thon door—d'ye hear me—has nothing to do with this cluss. Has nothing to do with you and nothing to do with me. Right?"

" Yes, sir."

" Now, then. Move to yer places for Jessie's Horn-pipe."

The minister approached up the east wall under the Boer uniforms. The pipe major retreated down the west wall under Queen Victoria. He adjusted two small shoulders till they touched.

The minister came round to the north following and it was now visible his knit hands behind him dragged a limp umbrella like a stiff tail.

By reaching the south end of the class the pipe major reached his box of pipes which to the amazement of the class he opened without any of the usual ceremony, like launching a battleship, and without measurable pause— there they were—shouldered and inflated.

" Get ready," he rapped and as the minister came down the west, the pipe major started to drone and turn livid going north. His little black eyes closed just at the moment his bag reached the consistency of his paunch and then the chanter declared itself sweetly: diddle-eddle-ow.

By the time he reached his original position in the north the class were in festive motion. As he swung to face them, the cruel pressure which had made his volume and coloured his face, eased into the relief of tune and prolific harmony.

Reaching *his* original position at the door the Rev. paused —stared black—trying to coat as with waste oil the wings

182

of that musician and then went. Then to the wheeze of the door was added a sudden inspiration on the chanter— a grace-note like the flatulence of Ariel.

Which continued after the crash.

★   ★   ★

"We could take the night train Friday," Lionel said walking to the window of Elizabeth's bedroom.

With hands deferred from the keys of her typewriter she watched him. "I'm easy, hun."

The epithet rebuked him. He frowned.

"There's not the slightest reason why I should stay."

"Not the slightest."

"It's not as easy as all that. Now I've committed myself to this bloody project—I suppose I shall have to attend the *confrontation* Fidge-April as interpreter.

"When she finds there's no gold—won't she sell?"

"No—she would lose face."

"But why need *you* be in on all this?"

He was silent until ready and then made the following address: "I have accepted a certain responsibility for the undertaking. My name—for my sins—is on the note-paper: Director: I do feel strongly, Elizabeth, that Directors should direct. Besides: I've encouraged local people to own this project themselves. Put their savings into it."

"O.K., then," she said. "O.K." And she disengaged.

Vast arrears of animosity brooded on his face. He went back to his window.

Silence.

Suddenly she said.

"Why don't you ring her up, hun?"

For a moment he appeared not to have heard. Then he

came back from the window and sat down. "I beg your pardon."

"Ring her up—she'll come off in your hand."

He considered it long. Whole minutes.

"Lizz. I'm *not* in love. We haven't a thing in common. Except possibly height," he said as though noticing the fact for the first time. "We're both tall. And have both left home, in the deepest sense."

* Perhaps that's it," he added vaguely.

"Both rich," Elizabeth added.

He disregarded her, and went on:

"Yet it might be—the match, I mean, for all I know— *happy*, in the pedantic sense—a happy chance—like a one-legged man finding a wooden leg."

"You being the man, from what you tell me of her."

"I being the wooden leg," he said, scientifically. "She has lost a husband she loved."

The great jackdaw's nest of projections which each person was . . . Lizz, dead-eyed, was tyrant, without feeling. She conceded no millimetre to his opinion: Laura was the wooden leg. Because even a little doubt, on this sort of valuation, would be the cliff . . . the bloody end. She had once met Laura—a fact she concealed from Lionel in order to be spared expressing an opinion.

So she looked at his feet. Falling in love—projection. Falling out of love into lust, if any—truth. She sawed with an old orange stick at a frayed finger which was a different age to her face. A child's chewed finger; yet she thought two people, who saw it her way, might have a really grown-up love affair.

Far away the telephone rang. He began moving at once. Then slowed—and at the door stopped.

184

"It's probably April," he said as though that would make her happy. And finally he went further, he smiled sweetly with raised brows, a smile which said—dear Lizz, I do sincerely authorise you to drop me as a toad. But even this he must *authorise*—or how else could it be controlled, kept neat, and within reason.

Lizz bent to her frayed finger.

"Don't apologise," she said.

But it wasn't April—or Laura.

A fruity far-off knew-your-father club voice said, "Oh, is that Captain Spote?"

"Lionel Spote," he corrected.

"This is the Territorial Army and Air Force Association here. Invercauldy. Jack Musker speaking. I expect you know your uncle was County Commandant for the Cadets, we wondered . . . if you'd care to take it on."

Lionel heard it out. The case was put to the tune of three lots of three telephone pips before he was allowed to say, "No—I'm sorry."

Silence:

"Hallo . . .?" Lionel inquired, thinking the line cut.

"No can do?"

After a parseing frown Lionel declined more elaborately and at last irritably.

*   *   *

"Was that April, dear? Why didn't you let *me* talk to her?"

"No, Mother—it wasn't."

"I've a good mind to go round to *her*. I'd sort her."

"You'd sort each other."

"She's going to apologise—if it's the last thing I make anyone do."

" Mother. Is George Salmson happy here? "

" Very. He was only saying so this morning."

" Good. *Good.* That's all that matters."

★   ★   ★

The days began to blend, or seem to, like compartments in an aquarium with Lizz, his mother, Salmson and himself suddenly looming into each other's faces, and, just missing each other, with a reflex jerk of fins, going on.

The telephone rang and far away that character of space-fiction Fidge, said:

" LIONEL SPOTE—weekisty."

" Sir Duncan—glad to hear your voice," Lionel said with relief. " Now, what's the latest? "

" Weekisty."

" Hallo—I think the line must be bad. Could you separate the words? "

" Lionel Spote—weekisty."

" Week . . ."

" WEEKISTY."

" Sir Duncan—I get you only very poorly."

" Weekisty—you have conquered. Latten."

Lionel waited.

" She's selling us—the Fluach face. Hallo . . . ? "

Lionel understood. He said " Excellent " and then, ekeing out a travesty of heartiness, " Well, that is excellent. How did you do it? "

" How did *I* do it?—You mean how did *you* do it." The voice dropped to the bottom F of respect. " Nice work, Lionel. Dark horse, eh? "

Lionel cleared his throat. " Sir Duncan . . ."

" I didn't like to suggest it. But now that you've done

186

it I can say—under the rose—of course: the ends sometimes justify the means."

Lionel wanted to *see* the man. At least he must have the evidence of his eyes when speaking to him. " Sir Duncan —where are you now?"

" Brussels. Lovely city. A great city."

" Brussels!"

" Clinching the Brackenator, Lionel. Packed. Shipped. See it over myself—but I've got a meeting. Loch Boisdale. Then south. Be a division Monday. Any good titles coming. Don't mind 'em in proof. Send them to the House. Well, Lionel Spote—put it there: Weekisty. What did she say about me?"

" Say about you!"

" I heard she said something to you about me. About my business . . . eh? Lionel . . . Never mind then. Now look, Lionel. What date for the opening?"

" Sir Duncan . . . will you arrange . . . everything . . . I mean: For you it *can all happen.*"

The flutes and oboes of compassion broke out low in the far, familiar timbre. " Overdoing it? Rest, Lionel, rest. Know what it is m'self. Only one thing. Chuck every-thing. That's what I do. Get right away. Take a whole week. Just take your secretary. Well, Lionel. Weekisty!"

And then—there was the black gadget, probably plastic, five by six inches, in two parts, on the edge of blotting paper.

As dead and inane as a ventriloquist's dummy slouched in a corner.

Weekisty!

So often his mother's voice succeeded a telephone call. It did now as she entered. " Lionel—I thought you'd like to know: Laura's fishing the Merry Madman now."

The Merry Madman was one of the best pools he shared with April. It lay immediately below the house and it was possible to identify anyone fishing it by spying with a telescope from the top east turret—or Camelot as Lionel muttered it. This was the fourth successive day his mother had brought to his notice that Laura was " on the river " which was odd, she said, because Laura didn't really like fishing.

The idea of his mother analysing the river through a stalking-glass and then coming down here and emphasising the word " now " in that prurient way gave immediate frostbite to a timid little blossom of desire to see Laura, and ask her what she had said to her mother; a desire, at least, to see her again.

He said, "I hope you have a rest for the telescope, Mother."

" I've used a towel-horse," she said.

" Good," he murmured wearily. " Mother—April has given in. She's selling."

Gwendoline focused him now: her depth stare. A grey ambivalent prism of self-interest and the understanding of self-interest, in which April was now caught and broken down into a long, varied spectrum of motives.

" Oh . . ." said Gwendoline, " and about time."

But she was intrigued. She pretended to do something with a flower, awry in a bowl, but she could not disguise her interest.

" Fidge never lets go." She tried it. But wasn't really satisfied. " Funny, I can't ever before remember April being persuaded," she said vaguely.

Weekisty? The word assumed ever more alarming proportions; and on its seven-headed, nine-legged scaley back rode Laura!

He massaged his eyelids with his fingertips.

He knew, of course, why she was there—under the house —fishing when she loathed it; he knew perfectly well. And he looked out of the window towards the sky about the Corgi.

She was fishing for him.

His jaw lowered slightly and a rather abject, hooked pitiful look came into his face—as though even now he was cruising apathetically, tiring fast, with April Iridescent hooked in the side of his mouth, and the shadow of the gaff wobbling on the surface above him.

Because now he began to understand Laura. The appointment . . .

He rose—slowly—and left his mother, consulting, as he did so, his locket-watch.

*   *   *

A toy. With character. Probably 19th century German. He had found it upstairs in a cupboard. Some relic of a visiting child. It still wound—and did a dance on its own attached musical box.

He carried it now, as he walked in his gent's gaberdine along the banks of the Corgi, under his arm—and as though to put beyond doubt its ridiculous juvenile nature and his intentions with it he assumed a particularly elderly and official air, and then, affected surprise when he came upon Laura, fishing.

" Oh, hallo," he said coolly.

" Hallo."

" Anything?"

" Nothing."

She gave up the rod with relief to the ghillie, and waded out.

"I brought this," he laughed, deprecating, "for your boy. Nobody ever told me his name."

"You know the sex. That's rather impressive."

"You mean from me," he said defensively.

"No . . . I didn't. I wasn't thinking personally. '

He looked at her ironically—as much as to say you really needn't bother to snub me. I was born snubbed. Permanent. And his eyebrows rose slightly—so go on, if you like.

She was flustered. By the look. So seldom people ever really *looked* at anybody else. Like a carpenter at wood or a gipsy at cards. Since Hilde Reisenthal, Lionel really looked at people.

As she should have looked at the gift?—his eyes said.

But she missed that. Perhaps because she was distrait.

* The hoggish insensitivity of riches.

"It winds, plays and the figure dances," he objected mildly.

"He'll love it."

He wished she would notice it. But no.

"I thought I might run into you," he said pompously, beginning to move. Then he stopped. "By the way—what did you say to your mother?"

He eyed her severely—only half joking.

She became oblique, tetchy with apprehension. Said? What had she said? Which made it easier to browbeat her facetiously, just once more.

"Because I hope you know," he said, "your mother assaulted me."

"Wait, I must get my coat."

"Why?" he said.

"Why 'Why '—you're like James."

"Then could you answer?"

" Need we go into it. You ought to thank me."

" But what did you tell her."

" I'll tell you one day."

" Why not now ? "

" Would you like to see where I caught my first salmon ? "

Normally she never mentioned herself. He had noticed with respect that she was rare in her class being free from narcissism. Most of her kind had made up for the notice which had been confiscated from them, by increased notice of themselves.

She blushed. And he perceived with dread that had she been merely flirting, she would have spoken merely flirtatiously.

" Your first salmon," he said with a strange and agreeable weakness in the pit.

As they set off he was reminded long ago of a moment when persuaded by someone else against his better judgment to take a ticket on the Whip at Olympia, he had experienced the first sluggish movement of his tin chariot, unwinding, now, towards predestined spinal sensation.

After a few steps he suddenly laughed, helplessly, his affected laugh. Meaning disorganisation. " Good. Your first salmon. Nothing I'd like better. Now I suppose you'll catch your next in the same place."

He really sighed for himself. Never leave a woman out in the open when she makes an advance. Cover her for her life's and your life's sake. Too late he tried to insist that he was in fact talking of fish.

" Lower down, isn't it," he said. " The best pool ? "

" Yes." She let him off and spoke so quietly and vulnerably, he repented. And loved her suddenly.

But his hands were deep in his pockets, and like those of a bad actor, they had their own separate lay identity.

They passed gorse with which the bank was stiffly cluttered.

"Lovely smell," she said.

It was. He hadn't noticed. Praising and to prove his admiration, impulsively he picked and experienced a sharp pain in his finger.

She laughed—too much, too gratefully for the opportunity.

He minded the pain more than he could conceal.

"It's bleeding," she said, with ill-concealed indifference, and peered over to quell her laughter as though he held a bright red lady-bird.

She stationed herself curiously close; a threat almost to his balance. The speck of blood apparently engrossed her.

"It's venous," she said, "not arterial."

The unfamiliar divinity of well-kept female hair crawled up his nostrils and slowly weakened his hams, and turned his lower stomach into craving. He was aware of a general floppiness which might at any moment collapse them like clothes slipping from two pegs.

"Blood," he said vacantly, because he had nearly said something else.

The bodies brushed into contact at several points and tended to stay, touching.

At last they kissed—without much change of position, change of anything.

"Good," he said loudly at last. The class had done well. Time. They could go. "There we are."

Then to atone for this astonishing summary he squeezed one of her hands tightly, and continued to do so, as they went on towards the spot where she had caught her first salmon.

20

ABOVE THE hill shaped like a German tin hat, which had served as discreet rendezvous for his eyes and Rupert's, there was a wide white radiance where the sun had disappeared.

Loch water which had mocked Mediterranean colours all day now turned black. Only here and there remote peaks and ridges of heather were amber and low wraiths of cloud still enjoyed pink day. In the higher ceiling, sudden shadows soared miles and reached out over the sea, and here where he walked a chill came reminding him of the lateness and of the people he had left behind. Of Lizz, that looking-glass with a flaw.

Am I in love Spote asked himself?

His gait as he took the flinty hill up to the lodge was changed. He did not march with chin tilted up, aggressively enjoying and savouring the country, but almost loitered.

The impossibility of planning, of being reasonable, at this moment, brought suddenly to his mind the circles, ellipses and dog.

Am I rather, he wondered, in love as much as it is given to me to be.

His dislike of personal questions and intimacies, was never more acute than when they came from—and for—himself. He stood still, frowning. " In love ": what did it *mean*. He found himself irritated with everyone who had ever used the phrase.

★　　　★　　　★

" Mother," he said with his fingers under his nose and scowling because she would smell on sight a case for curiosity. " Where's Elizabeth ? "

" She upped and went . . . I *thought* you didn't know. I said to her I'm quite sure Lionel isn't expecting you to go to-day. But she's so off-hand. Lionel, I don't like to say this—but I'm *glad* she's gone."

" Mother—I simply don't know what you're saying: *when* did she go ? "

" After tea. She condescended to have tea with us."

His mother was stitching at a tabouret and her upper half was etched against a green gap in the west.

" The most nat'ral conversation with me and George seemed labour for Miss Craik. If you ask me it's conceit. I eventually said to her: don't blame *us*—for Lionel goin' off gallivanting, and leaving you."

He turned.

There was an envelope by the drinks tray, addressed " Lionel."

At first he thought the contents blank. Then he per-perceived a single line of threadlike writing, written seemingly with an agate point dipped in shadow, flat against the top edge.

" Suddenly couldn't take it, hun."

Mrs. Spote said, " What has she got to say for herself ? "

He went up to her room. Crumpled paper lay under the table where she had typed. The bed-cover was disarranged.

A kind of fustiness, which belongs to many bed-sitters, lingered as witness to Lizz. Also three empty gin bottles.

He walked about restlessly. Some obscure cock in him seemed to have crowed, as usual, for the third time.

That night Lionel supped alone with his mother and Salmson.

All were in evening dress.

When he had spread his napkin on his knees he gazed from the vertical for some time into his soup like a man who has been told there is fish in that pond.

The sound of his mother cracking water biscuits and mixing them in energetically, then sucking with deafening discretion from the inclined near edge of her huge silver spoon, made him feel suddenly as if he was in the basket of a brown balloon with her and Salmson—millions of miles from the earth.

" Have you a long holiday, Mr. Salmson," he suggested.

Mrs. Spote chipped in as though alone with her son.

" Your father always thought Laura *most* attractive," and she crunched up another biscuit and cast the remains with one coarse gesture over the surface of her soup.

He picked up his spoon, remaining expectant to Salmson, who said:

" Every day stolen I'm afraid. Dread the reckoning."

" Did you have a cooked tea? " Mrs. Spote said, peering round at his apathy with the soup. Then, later, " You remember I said you'd find plenty to occupy you up here. Well, wasn't I right? You're not in such a hurry to get away now are you? I spoke to April on the telephone. I'm keeping for when we *meet* the names I'm going to call *her*. She was very friendly this evening, and so was I. She said Laura isn't going to London after all. Oh, I said, Why's that? "

" Mother—I shall almost certainly return to London this week. I think we should all plan to do the same."

Now—she was smiling—a smile of such complacent omniscience that he was struck dumb.

"Well?" he said quietly.

"Shall we wait and see?" she said.

Then she fixed him appraisingly—in order to get an even better leverage for the passion of knowing better, having known better all along, even during Hilde Reisenthal.

"Darling, a mother isn't blind," she sang. "You've never looked better. Never. You must allow me to know better sometimes, even though I've never been psychoanalysed. What you don't understand is you *never changed*. Not *one iota*," she crowed.

"*Mother*. You're in a draught there. I'm going to shut the window."

"It's not open."

"Yes, it is," he said walking soberly across the room and when corroborated by a sliding sound and a small bump he turned and smiled at her with formal sweetness, "at the top," he said and raising finger and thumb like the gap in the jaw of an adjustable spanner, he rendered invisible tangible form—pictorially as was *tout le rage*—for adult education—the distance suggested by the sound—and previously foretold by him, categorically.

"A little—even a very little—can mean all the difference in the world," he said.

"I don't call that open," she said.

21

THE FOLLOWING day was Sunday. Lionel had gone down
as usual to fetch the papers from a shop, half post office, half
haberdashery, run by two Arabs and a white woman. He
was standing hypnotised by the clock which he was sure
had stopped even though it told roughly the right time.
In some ominous way this suggested something personal,
like a dream. A woman had gone into the back room
saying " The Lodge, Ali," and had not come back, so leaving him with his clock, which soon jilted his intuition
with a perceptible jerk forward of its minute-hand. Then
he turned to a mass of posters which competed like a chorus
of governesses for his attention: " Have you got your
accident book ? "—" Men born between October 1926
and April 1927 should . . ."—" Have you read THIS. It
concerns YOU "—thinking of Laura and of Lizz who would
be getting in now. Her face close to the smutted pane of
the third class carriage would now be looking down into
the black catacombs of railside London—with relief. Oh,
City, City—the burnt-out ends of vacant days. Prufrock's
condition had even deteriorated, under the brilliance of
the apparent improvement. One couldn't even feel *that*
now. Lizz had never really explained—except by looking
like a boil that couldn't burst. Looking at *him*.
He faced a pictorial analysis of the national income but
saw instead her orange stick at work on her twelve-year-

old hands. Pity flooded the small sealed space in him which was still available for feeling. He thought of that purposeful mousiness. To be born a woman, cerebral, of no fixed address; unspiritual yet feeling her body like luggage; exiled from platitudes yet making hell out of the alternative; subsisting on pemmican of irony—and gin. Ah—Christ.

Lionel bent, to modify guilt for Lizz, scrutinised another poster.

> THE NATIONAL GARDEN SCHEME
> By kind permission of Mr. Lionel Spote the gardens at Rossiemurchat will be open to the public on SUNDAY, MAY 25TH from 12 a.m.
> The proceeds will be gifted to the Scottish Nursing Association.

Then he read it again.

Behind the P.O. half of the shop, which was shut, a miniature mahogany Palladian porch framed " TO-DAY'S DATE " May 23.

Then large as death, he read below:

FRIDAY.

" Your papers, mister." The Arab was sleek and weirdly unobsequious. " No *Observer*, mister."

He had particularly asked—but he never said a word. Not a word. He just went out into the street. Two women passed. One said " I saw where it said Sunday." " You never." They argued and went in. Their sudden silence was immense.

The car of his dead uncle struck him with the freshness of child sight.

It was twelve-fifteen.

A few seagulls were warming their rumps over the

chimneys of the low white houses. Some people in black were filtering downstreet towards him. He had seen a ten-inch pile of *Reveilles* waiting. They advanced with Sabbath faces.

★　　　　★　　　　★

The temptation to drive fast south for a long way was reversed into an equally extreme opposite: he drove fast north—a short way. Only, in fact a hundred yards, for turning a corner with a very slight protest, like a stepped-on dog, from the car's tyres he found himself bearing down on a black knot of people exchanging mutual recognition with an air of surprise as though Church had changed them.

The brakes when used severely imparted a bias to the car's direction. He was thus made more than ever conspicuous by halting at last slightly lofted on the gravelly pavement.

An incident in that street at any time was like the Pyramids in the desert. He met their eyes with a drawn determined indifference as though they were sheep huddled and hustled out of their wits, by rival silly fears.

Then he saw, was seen by—their shepherd—the Minister. To be quite so coated with such instant ocular mud was more than Lionel could stand. His perpetual weals of guilt now saw before them the Original Whip. His Mediterranean culture beheld two grey eyes like the wet-granite of a shut north pub. But he pretended to be unaffected.

The engine had stalled in protest against the handbrake.

He bowed to the button. Then he went on through them in first, his chin raised, peering to show deference, apology and caution—but only and adamantly to the extent he had infringed the Highway Code. Through the corner

199

of his eye he got a close-up of the Minister. "God" he then murmured. "My God"—like a soldier whose match, which he had been about to strike—had been lit by a sniper's bullet.

*   *   *

A craggy old woman who might have belonged to the betel-chewing nations but for the diamond terrier in her tweed cap, was congratulating his mother in the porch. Both of them held shallow baskets.

She came straight up to Lionel and said, "Put it there," extending a sallow hand wiry as a chimp's left over from thirty hill-station summers.

Lionel took it.

"I just want to say my husband and I were bucked to the core SOMEONE had the guts to do it. I'm going to spend more to-day than I've ever done before at any of these dreadful obligations. Perhaps that'll show 'em."

And she turned towards the garden, shouting "Bill" as for a recalcitrant dog. "Where's that silly old fool gone?" then fading out in savage tenderness, "he'll drown himself in the lily pond without me. *Ripping* lupins. BILL!"

"Mother," Lionel said coolly, "Did you know the garden was going to be opened to-day?"

She looked at him with her special post-his-analysis look —that is, in cricketing terms, with an eye for the bowler's hand.

She said, "So you think I'd let you offend ten thousand decent people who were perfectly *devoted* to your uncle— if I could have stopped you. I suppose you do. I suppose it fits in."

He passed by her—through her into the house where from a window on the first floor he could command a view

200

of the garden and the two drives. He might have spared himself. The truth was worse than apprehension.

His mother was calling up the stairs, " Lionel—I'm goin' out to receive. *Some*body must."

He let her repeat it, then said:

" I'm not stopping you, Mother."

And soon he saw her go down into the garden and greet people. He would join her. But first he must have a few minutes.

Regression—of the libido was always due to guilt. Desire to confess. Not something—but just to *confess*, i.e., *amalgamate*.

Sitting, he smoothed his hair rhythmically with his eyes closed and at last tilted his head back for some deep breaths. The irrationality of guilt . . . The supra-rationality of Communist confession. He felt iller. Oh, to have been born in a non-sleepwalking age.

There came a feathery breathing from close.

" Mrs. O'Shea! " he said his eyes starting wide on her. "What can I do for you? "

She stood " seeing " him—so that he felt loosened in his spatial socket, and altogether modified by another dimension.

She laid hand to her cheek as though she had tooth-ache. " And my," she said, " Mr. Spote, I said—shall I tell him? "

"What? " he said sharply.

" I was at the Kirk," she said. " And they were saying things. I said—Come from afar off and young, without his own people, set down here among strange customs—I said, shall I tell him what they are saying?

" They turned and looked at me, while the minister spoke, and I said to my sister shall I tell him?

201

" And he put words—hwaords you never heard—like a shadow between . . . hyou and the sun. I said I share the cold, the sudden cold.

" And this is why I've come, Mr. Spote: you're young and books, books so many books—but I said I'll be with him to . . . explain . . . and to be not like a book.

" For we must care what people think. We must care for what they care for."

He rose officially. " Mrs. O'Shea . . ." then he started again with frayed reciprocal warmth. " Mrs. O'Shea "— dumb again with inadequacy still he began again, this time taking her hand in his. " Mrs. O'Shea . . ." and found his clasped, requiring yet another start, but reduced to a whisper, warm and full of meaning.

" Mrs. O'Shea—you're a good woman."

" Be quiet," she hissed offended. " Indeed, don't be saying such a thing."

" Mrs. O'Shea. You know, I'm sure, it was an over-sight . . ."

He stopped because his gentle attempt to withdraw his hand from hers was resisted—and her eyes were drowning him—like drink.

" Mr. Spote," she whispered, " Go down to them and say to them—*please*—*go*."

The coincidence of his secret, cowed, inclination with this sudden ethical blurt from the local and therefore dominant collective subconscious, produced in him a painful stew of emotion.

Perhaps he *should*.

" Mrs. O'Shea—I should like to. But . . ." He smiled. Silence.

" Yes," she sighed, desisting. " I understand."

With warmest looks, skewered on an impracticable

202

affinity—agreeing by signs across a chasm—he went from her at last to face what had to be faced.

As he drew near the macrocarpa hedge which hid the trooping of the herbaceous border, he heard beyond it the sustained social shout of April Gunter-Sykes.

Presuming she could only have come *ex* some *officio* but would prefer a mutual cut on the lawn, Lionel was passing her with far focus when she rasped, " Hallo there."

And she was smiling.

He had no respect for elephants who never forgot, on the other hand to forget so quickly was worse than elephantine. He did not smile. He said, " Hallo."

" Well done. First class."

" Thank you," he said, without a clue.

" By the way—I've sold Fidge his blessed bracken."

" So I heard. I'm so glad, Mrs. Gunter-Sykes. It was extremely good of you." Let us Oh Lord, praise where we can. He commended her reluctantly, with his straight, straight stare.

She said, " So I conclude it'll be O.K.—hm?—ha ha— about the river. No R.S.P.C.A. grids. Ha ha. Fair's fair. Say no more, oh King."

Far, deep and loose he wandered in her face, smiling— cerebrating like a counting machine.

" Of course not," he flushed slightly for what might have happened. " Well . . ." he said walking backwards.

For some time Lionel walked about with one shoulder well up and his hands closed behind his back, his mouth a disassociated slot. When greeting or greeted—he bowed with immediate and warm connection and into the smallness of the subsequent talk injected a sincerity which at once threatened its life.

The sad, guileless stare of Dr. Smiley before a single

carrot which had perhaps lain low for years and then germinated between two rose trees, suddenly made him veer like a vehicle that has regained steerage.

"What a lonely vegetable," Lionel said gratefully for the true direct object of a sentence, so to speak, with a subject.

"It'll get First at Fluach," Smiley said glumly, "It's always there."

"What is it?"

"A carrot. He puts sand and ash and goats' piss for all I know and then puts it out there. My wife gets second. There's an awful lot of people here. I've never seen so many people at one of these things. It must be the Sunday," he said bleakly, scientifically, looking round. "What gave you the idea?"

"It was a mistake."

"All great discoveries are," and his disillusioned gaze continued to reckon and analyse.

"What interests me: there's fishers here. I've never seen fishers at one of these do's. Not even weekdays. I never thought they'd touch a Sunday."

"Perhaps it's rebellion," Lionel said weakly.

"No. It's not the church-goers here. It's the loafers. They've rebelled against a vacuum. Sunday shouldn't be a hole. I'm sure St. Pitter would be with me there, ye know. Well, congratulations. I'll be interested to see what happens to you. The Rev. Abigail will make a wax image of you to-night and he'll be off to Inverurie to-morra for more pins. And the women'll be helping him. Voluntirring with needles."

A delayed reaction to his own words caused a trace of a smile to dawn on Smiley's face—and he stared into the crowd with relish.

And Lionel noticed now for the first time the sharp, padded lines of some shoulders and the pale beige of several deep crepe-soled slotted bouncers.

A coarse voice yelled urgently, "Hey—Jock. C'm 'ere quick . . ." The cry had a looting note. Lionel frowned.

Smiley shook his head slowly. "Well, Mr. Spote, there's nothing like going the whole hog."

If there was a single virtue Lionel admired wholly it was moderation.

"Dr. Smiley," he said stiffly.

"Mr. Spote," the man countered dryly, "I've got a galloping cauliflower on a gall-bladder just coming up to Bechers Brook, and I must be off but let me know when you start getting pins and needles."

He was going, looking cheered, when suddenly he repented. The lost, shock-from-birth look came into his round eyes. "No—seriously. I *would* be glad to hear what happens. It's quite a departure. Will I hear from you . . . ? "

This Lionel appreciated, slowly, was a real question.

"All right, Dr. Smiley, All right. I'll let you know."

    *   *   *

The sharp-shouldered boys grouped, arms about each other's necks—a head was thrown up with a hip-flask bottle of whisky tilted vertical. On the hill the shabby tradesman's van in which the Fleights travelled, rattled in; and above the brouhaha Lionel heard his mother's voice competing with April's. ". . . . but you can't get them now, for love of money." She was often saved, he reflected, from a cliché, by misremembering it.

"Mother," he said, going up to her.

Now she was on the base line and April was serving—using her height and reach. He could tell from his mother's set face she was cutting and lobbing for dear life.

"Well," shouted April, "if my Rupert had tried it on I'd've quite simply told him to take a pull. The young nowadays are too much wrapped in themselves. I'd have said *that*—too."

"Yes, but . . ." she saw Lionel and without any shock or modification of expression and tone went on, "even if he did grow tomatoes under glass there wouldn't be much sale for them here."

"Mother," said Lionel like a parent who has caught the children out of bed but isn't going to say anything, "If you don't mind I think I'll go now. Will you cope?"

"That's what she's been doing," April said "Haw haw."

Lionel frowned, ignoring. "Mother . . . ?"

"*Quite* able to, dear. I know what a lot you've got to do. Lionel has local *responsibilities*—as well as his usual work," she said, addressing it all to him. "This rope factory has meant a lot of work. Of course he doesn't tell *me* anything, but puttin' two and two together he's been held up by downright, wilful, stoopidity."

As he left he seemed to hear the crowd sigh as his mother pushed it into April with another ace down the centre, cheerfully: "Now, April, I *want all* the news about Laura and young Botton. You must be thrilled."

Suddenly Lionel went in and telephoned. "Laura," he said, "can I come and have tea with you?"

*   *   *

He drove fast while still in the built-up area of his own home. A man at a small table spreadeagled himself over the piles of tickets and small change to save them from his slip-stream; and two policemen were stirred from vacancy as though their presence might yet have a point.

The drive was a mile long. Couples of what might have once been parlour maids on their day off were still stepping up primly.

He found the way to her house as though a department of his brain had been secretly at work on her for days, filing every relevant fact.

It seemed at first a poor-looking farm—the sort of farm you could only find at this date, in the Highlands. Then rounding a byre corner he came face to face with a bright yellow door and some big, low Georgian windows with big panes. The top and side petered into stedding.

It might have been, he realised rather sourly, the sort of thing you see in " House and Garden ". " Pauline Jinks after making ' Zamitte ' had an idea for a barn . . ."

His face might have been that of a dyspeptic and browned-off milkman when he made use, for want of anything else, of the knocker. Instantly the door opened and a small boy in glasses franked him with fierce curiosity and then as he moved forward slammed the door in his face.

Then Laura opened it, blushing. She must be the last blusher, he thought and said, academically—yet with determination:

" I thought I'd come round."

" I'm so glad." She was often defensive, her nervous laugh, ready as a tourniquet for every statement—and her eyes blackly lit with a pertinent personal remark—if necessary.

" I must apologise for a really horrid little boy," she said loudly backwards. " Stephen—come and say you're sorry."

207

In the darker light of the hallway Lionel looked up into two burning eyes.

"And come and say thank you for that lovely musical box," she added.

"It was no a musical box. Zing! yer parralysed."

Lionel saw an implement with a bulb and louvres pointed down at him.

She made a show of sternness, tried to establish a private language and threat, in a look and manner. She touched a leg and there was a roar, "I'm not doing anything." She whispered up and he tore free so as not to hear. Then up he scrambled shouting, "I know: that's the man who got played by a salmon. I know—I know—I know" breaking into rhythm, he disappeared.

"I'm so sorry . . ." she said fumbling for what note to strike—and then giggled nervously, because here he was in her house, which for some reason extinguished her aplomb. "But what can you do? I hit him the other day and he said he'd 'soo' me. The teacher must have made some joke . . ." Fortunately for her standing in Lionel's eyes she made these remarks about her child with such obvious maternal emotion, at the mere idea of his mischief, that something happened to her voice. And she looked nervous as though she might be detected in it and blamed for it.

The room they entered reflected no personality or taste. Yet it was agreeable and lived-in. Even its lack of "taste" was relatively agreeable. It owed nothing to the glossy magazines. It was fortuitous as silt. There was a picture of her first husband—drinking tea from an army mug, half turned, laughing at the surprise of looking into a lens.

Lionel noticed nothing.

She said, "Won't you have some tea—or a drink? What about your coat?"

"I wasn't quite sure how long I'd come for."

Then with a great galvanisation he rose, shed and hung it, and came back, still noticing nothing.

For some time he said nothing; he just sat acclimatising himself to the result of his compulsive action.

"I forgot to cancel the garden opening . . ." he said at last.

"Someone told me. You must have done it on purpose."

"No one seemed to mind. The most extraordinary spectacle—I didn't know it could still happen. The minor sqaws of capitalism on their Highland reservation. Beer, lavatory seats, syrup, safes, cotton, tinned veg—all represented. My mother might have been reciting from a trade magazine. Or playing happy families. Have you got Mrs. Heinz the tinner? Have you seen Mrs. Boots the chemist?

"The atmosphere, when you get a real concentration of Leicestershire-Scottish . . ." his face puckered donnishly. "Somehow . . ." It was the liberal, academic dither for the right word. No word came.

He shook his head. "It was your mother—and some Celtic Teddy Boys—who finally finished me. I felt she only refrained from ordering them to be flogged—by not looking at them.

"I simply came away," he ended, with dazed reproach as though he had been kidnapped."

She laughed with the unmistakable difficulty of one who wishes to laugh both at and with—but the former imperceptibly.

The sofa they sat on could not comfortably have fitted

a third between them. They talked—but gradually the spoken word became lopsided with the unspoken, and the unacted. At last silenced.

The light faded. It was when she came back from closing a window—that he took her hand as it passed.

Lionel's desire was not a tiger. But an amenable tom. The wind had to be in the right direction; food and sleep exactly right. Partner passive as a concept.

Even then a tiny little Lionel watched from the door.

★   ★   ★

Long after—out of peace born of simple and moderate caresses, which were best when they were courteous and merely flippant (and repulsed) when they fringed for form's sake the extravagance of lust, he suggested marriage. The suggestion came as when at a kindergarten, a mistress writes on the board:

" 2×4 "—and then points a finger . . . who shall it be . . . Lionel Spote. Let's have him. 2×4 Lionel makes . . . ? "

Silence.

A great smothering hen of silence at last hatched the cracked egg of his voice.

"Laura—would you consider," (this initiative was for *her* sake, let that be clear. Without it she might have been obliged to have said it all herself.) "—would you consider becoming my wife? "

"Yes," she said, less romantically than he could have wished.

"Good. Good, Laura. Then that's settled."

He was awed by the executive and prompt ring of her affirmative, but when he sealed the contract with a kiss, he found in her body a readiness, a softness that made him feel guilty. His ear, not her voice, had been at fault.

He held her hand, repenting. She would have appreciated a little follow-through. Perhaps it would come; he might grow younger, more spontaneous.

But what would they talk about, when they were alone together?

It was dark now and the curtains were undrawn.

"What's that glow in the sky," he said. "I've often noticed it from Rossiemurchat. Is it the Northern Lights?"

She laughed peacefully. "My mother's batteries."

"Her *batteries* . . . ?"

For a single instant the possibility of her mother being powered by batteries found reality in Lionel's suggestible eyes.

"Hens."

He frowned, picturing them floodlit. Laying against the clock.

The trouble was: no single item of information ever helped him to feel younger; more fluent and confident of life to come.

22

MAJOR MACKAY, suddenly appointed Storeman-Clerk of the suddenly revived Home Guard, at seven pounds a week, sat with his little black-dot eyes gummed up in what seemed, blood and brimming tears. Ungrateful, he would have called it, not to celebrate fantastic manna—but that apart, he had needed the comfort of the spirit to sustain him in this rigid vigil, till 12 o'clock, when Gordon Mackay, his cousin, a clerk at Territorial Army H.Q., Inverurie, would let him know for sure if the nephew had stood firm to his part of the bargain and if his own letter which he had spent the week wording, had been favourably entertained, getting him at last, Colonel-Commandant.

Glen, by massing chairs on top of tables had reached a height and position that might have earned him a drill or two on another morning, but the pipe major's face was continually taut and wordful as that of a man in public. Occasionally he even made a little self-conscious gesture with his hands—pocketing them—or playing with a pencil, or folding his arms in lesser attention and greater ease—as though he were the most conspicuous of many men meeting. Even the harmless blank daylight suddenly tweaked his attention like too much coughing in a crowded hall, and he looked out over it with distant warning—reminder of its relative anonymity.

Till he saw . . .

" *Glen!* Come off of there *at once.* No. Don't you dare move. D'you hear me? " His index finger trembled. " Yer for the C.O. if you move. Is that right? " he said, coming catlike to at least a catching position—with relief. Then he got hold of an ankle—and a wrist. " *You.* Look at you. If I hadn't happened to hear him," he said sighing sideways, " he'd 'ave broken his neck on me. And I in the passage not knowing he was even anywhere but with his own mother."

He shook the boy. " Is it jankers yer wanting? " and he kept his huge square head down by the little mouth.

Silence.

"Well, then. Beehave."

The telephone rang.

" Doing this to me," his voice sank craven, " on a day like this."

He paused. " D'ye want to come here again? "

" Yes," said the child like a leaf moving.

" Good boy, then," he said gratefully.

The telephone rang again—a long, long ring designed to alert the P.S.I. who would cross the road and fetch the major from the bar—or, failing that, seep through at last to the wily sober ear of the barman, through two walls, and a road.

The major straightened himself, and hardened, to the boy.

" But—I can't deal with you myself, though I should like to. You'll be ree-manded—*for the colonel.* Is that clear? "

The leaf stirred again.

" See what *he* says," said the pipe major approaching the great pendulous ear-trumpet with condescension; and nipping it off said in an interrupted but patient voice:

"Well, Gordon boy, what is it? Oh, that," he said, reminded. " Well, how's it to be? "

After a moment his square face with its purple undulations, its two little squashy lochs, and cairn of a nose flagrant with rowan and bilberry . . . went sunless and blank.

He put back the receiver and sat down.

The child still stood to attention waiting joyful promotion to higher punishment. The pipe major turned from him looking out into the street. He'd had a cold lately and now mopped it. Now mopped it more generally and blew, limbered up his face this way and that, blew again—the cold. But at last he leant forward and let the sensation take its own course. "Allameen," he whispered, "and nights up to the Kreevie Hall like a doctor in winter."

And he sobbed.

At last the knowledge of the child's trained attitude, obliged him to look up and out into the street and say backwards:

"Stand at ease, StnDeasy."

Then the child came close to him—with timid fascination. And remained close and timidly fascinated for about ten minutes, which obliged the pipe major to examine the road and roofs for the same amount of time.

He wasn't to get colonel.

*　　　*　　　*

Lionel suspected feeling. For him it led into a fog full of people who roared their arse was their elbow, and vice versa. He even feared it, because for him feeling usually meant dislike, or worse—a trivial irritation that spread.

But he had learnt, and recently even occasionally *felt*: that's wrong.

* We must feel.
* We must have positive feeling—without alcohol.

His way of looking into the eyes of strangers was one exercise he had set himself to make this possible. Know thy neighbour, he had decided, was the illness you must get before you could love him. And know thyself preliminary to either . . .

Hence, in the feeling days that followed he appeared above all else to be surprised . . . surprised to be feeling so feeling so frequently, and so undecipherably, and never with irritation, though with anxiety.

He woke up surprised and went to bed looking forward to the surprise of to-morrow. A queer sensation of being in tow—not only behind a particular person, but also behind a phenomenon, led him sometimes to look at people—Mrs. O'Shea, even his mother—with ironic apprehension as though they had noticed he was wearing a pair of knickers on his head.

But for some reason they did not notice—or if they did, were not surprised.

What exactly *did* he feel?

Perhaps merely the egg, he thought, just as Samuel Butler said—the egg struggling to get out.

If so then in his case the egg had no arms and no legs. It just sat at the window, making trouble.

He did look strange holding her hand by the river, at first courteously, and lightly while frowning at the blaze of gorse and broom, as though it had suddenly become something which could be lost; and asking her what she was thinking. But he permitted more naturally, as the days passed, a greater surface of her body to be in contact with his, as they walked, or sat or made love.

It was all like the aura of an anæsthetic—an increase of anonymous solidity with a decrease of control and definition. He had moments that were without thought.

Several times he began speeches as though to reveal to her the murder he was committing before it was too late. " I think you ought to know that I'm probably quite unfitted to marry *any*one . . ."

" You've never tried."

Sometimes the astrigence of her tone presented him with the fear that he was merely getting another good job. After all she would have great property . . . And he was clearly steady, decent, sober and politically pliant.

When, driven by theory, conscience and convention (in view of the future agreed on), to tell her he loved her, the words came out as a joke to protect themselves, and had to be atoned for by eyes that said, or wished they could say —more.

In this, however, her tidal and most undifferentiated self, did break into a small white-horse. Did he, she said, did he really.

After an extraordinary session of cerebration, in full committee, a voice, so to speak, not of the managing director, but heard from a radiator suddenly said with ghostly authority—" Yes, Laura—as a matter of fact, I do " —and the managerial voices of reason, which he trusted impotently, adjourned making him feel a little ill, because the ramifications of the precedent might give him a tic in a week.

And then, of course—(he might have guessed it)—she took it, for once, as the truth, *the* truth—this blurt of the boardroom central heating pipes.

" You do," she said weakly. " I believe you do."

He closed his eyes on the sunny bank and the river

gurgled by. But let it go, that statement. Let it go. He gave in to the solidity—of the moment. The solid blank of a feeling.

And then suddenly into the deserted boardroom flooded back the directors to endorse with one cry the motion of the radiator.

He squeezed her hand and said firmly, " Laura, I love you."

He was moved, and afterwards spoke very little.

Such moments were rare. They involved a Lionel who was a stranger to himself. There were others quite different, more typical, which he would not let her criticise: such as when Dr. Smiley had him in for a cantata and a glass of sherry and he stayed for the whole Matthew Passion and dinner without telephoning.

" But my dear Laura," he said getting heated, " I said I *might* come round. If I had said I *would* come round, then I *would* have."

She rang off without another word. And afterwards, he noticed, she tried never to give him claustrophobia—by touching him—or even expecting the smallest considera-tion, because if ever she did he became a crabbed pedant who briefly abused her breath or waist before fleeing lopsided.

Nevertheless, they were in love. His eye-whites were abnormally clear; he sang a lot and drew a picture of Milosh's inferiority complex on the flyleaf of a proof copy. Sixteen legs it had and giant mandibles.

*   *   *

" So," she said, one afternoon by the river—rather incredulously—perhaps even suspiciously and insecurely, " You still haven't told your mother ? "

217

" Not yet."

" But why, I mean . . ."

" Well? " She did not know what she meant. " I can't see how it matters—one way or the other—so *much*."

At which he became slowly, somebody she had so far only seen the fringe of.

" May I ask," he said, turning with ludicrous solemnity, " why I may not be allowed to tell my mother in my own time? "

She managed only to laugh a little, managed to freeze into a smile, at last even to apologise lightly. " Of course," and because she could not trust her voice she changed the subject by raising a seedy spire of summer grass till it touched the end of his formidable nose, which was almost *down* her.

He said, " And may *I repeat:* would you please *also* tell no one—until we agree to tell everyone."

" Agree . . . ? " she laughed a little nervously: the word seemed so inapposite.

" Yes," he said. " Agree. When the Brackenator has been opened—we can prepare a hand-out—for our mothers," and he repeated with scientific dispassion, " Our mothers. And then leave."

" Leave? You make it sound like for ever."

" Well . . ." he said, turning again, " Well . . . ? "

She plucked at grass for a bit.

" You're still going to sell Rossiemurchat, then? "

" But, of course," he whispered, fixing her in astonishment.

She laughed—without much confidence.

" Why hurry? " she said at last and failed to make the words sound casual.

" Why not? "

He could see her organising. When her voice came it was gentle bedrock. This, too, was an introduction.

" I want somewhere to live. Children like the country. You want children, don't you? "

Her face had even darkened as she organised. She had spoken with the early edge of the determined, vulnerable and limited arguer.

" You want to live in the Pole near your mother? " he said with difficulty.

" Not near my mother and not *all* the time—but I don't particularly mind. I can cope with her by now. I just want somewhere to live. Besides, I like the country: I know the people here. I like them. Besides . . ."

" Besides *what* . . . ?"

She was withholding.

" *What*," he repeated.

His face slowly corrugated with the implications of the collision—at this juncture. Then at last far, far away he must look. And take time to get the next word right. . .

But she said, " Besides you can't tell what may not happen. Soon. Particularly in the towns."

She planned, he knew, in decades. Even so he would not allow this sort of talk. And it was a digression: it was not what she had been about to say.

" Laura," he said at last, concessional, " shall we wait? Decide later."

" Yes, let's," she said fast, laughing—but with the shine of almost tears in her eyes. And there he was, on a limb in his infinity of compromise. Her " Yes." had been like the snap of a trap. Presumably he was inside. He turned pained eyes on her but now she wouldn't look at him. Let her say something more; in the name of civilised relationships, let her.

219

" I wonder who Fidge'll get for the opening," she said, pulling some grass.

He stared at her, with his nose almost down her again.

" I'm beginning to wonder something else," he said at last.

And because she knew, roughly, what—she raised the grass seed to the very slight flare of his long nostrils.

" I implore you for both our sakes," he said intensely, " not to do that again. To be back at school is my worst nightmare."

" My Pussie," she said, and giggled; which kept his eyes on her, unrelenting, sterner and sterner, a man who brought down £2,000 a year, and was related into the bargain. This threatened her self-control so severely that soon she had to do, say something:

" My Puss-wuss-wussy," she said.

His vexation lingered because he had smelt deception. She was concealing something.

" Sneeze," she said.

23

In a lodge up the Corgi hung a gong—shaped like a Swiss cow-bell, but different physically by forty tons and metaphysically by an alleged curse. The gong depended, in a specially constructed recess, on a vertical oak stanchions girdled with iron rising to an oak cross-piece that was really a girder geared to the house foundations. The gong surface, inner and outer, was covered with Chinese characters and had been planted by the shipping magnate who had built the lodge in 1892. Although his successor had wished to remove it, to make way for a gong of his own, local contractors had advised against, for, they said, the house " depended on it."

May be, of course, they advised this because they *couldn't* move it; but perhaps, also, because of the curse. Hadn't the gong been the property of prehistoric Chinese priests? The metal contained the carbonised remains of their victims who got a moment's devastating parole only when the thing was struck—thus accounting for the noise which was like wave after wave of scalded basso profundo pursuing each other into the mountains.

Highland imagination took easily to the tale, and several housemaids—in days when they were numerous and without fur-lined bootees—had left after eliciting a growl with one mistaken flip of a duster. Now a Mrs. Palmer had " thon place with a gong."

Only Sir Duncan Fidge could have dreamt of borrowing it, seized upon it as a suitable symbol with which to waft away the bad, barren superstitious past and inaugurate a great new mechanical triumph with one crashing bang from what, after all, was merely a great old mechanical triumph.

And only Sir Duncan Fidge would have attempted to poo-poo genially, oh genially, the crusty objections of local plumbers and contractors and tell them to their face they couldn't hump an old gong a mile—and that, too, in the age of the atomic bomb—and " and atomic *boom* too John Sutherland. *I've* seen your bulldozers at the back."

So—the gong was brought to the Seaforth Arms under straw, and let in by the back wall—with its whole cradle of girder and oak—but not hoisted on its black gyves but . . .

But that was to be the surprise.

★ ★ ★

Sir Duncan flew in from Tromsoe the day of the event with the Secretary of State for Scotland, whom he had persuaded to attend the second " Our Northern Heritage " International, at Spitzbergen, for no other reason than to have him at Fluach on the way back.

The party landed at Wick and from there boarded Jessie for Fluach where they arrived at about eleven o'clock. Fidge was snapped by the *Trumpet's* editor—with a small Kodak—as he got out.

" LIONEL SPOTE," he confirmed by telephone, speaking within a mile of the Brackenator's tarpaulin-shrouded shape " weekisty "—and after scarcely any embellishment rang off and busied himself with his agent, a man who like Lady Fidge, seemed to be sleep-walking and sleep-talking —and unlike her—worried by it.

Two children had been provided to hold up the first

length of rope excreted by the great cacophanous digester.

"Good lookers, Jim?" Fidge asked intensely. The agent began to explain his difficulty. "I know, I know—best you could find." Then close and intense again, "Anyhow, it won't be their faces which'll break the cameras."

The agent, slightly relaxed by his chief's joke at his own expense, had begun to laugh when Sir Duncan leant across again and whispered confidentially, "It'll be yours Jim, yours."

★   ★   ★

With one of his dead uncle's spy-glasses Lionel was able to make out the shape of the Brackenator on the edge of the Ardstruie land, above Fluach, like some final vengeful incarnation of the Industrial Revolution which had tracked April to her last retreat and had but a few miles more to eat before it ate her.

He folded up the glass with a succulent smack and with one last askance look at the possible implications of the new light industry of which he had been the unwitting, he might say impotent seed bearer—he turned inwards towards his mother who was already in dark purple, sequionous cowl and diamonds for the opening.

Seven days had passed since his engagement, and seven days he had relished her ignorance of it. She thought he spent his many absent hours playing LP records with that Smiley who had treated her husband's last gravel with a month's radiant-heat; and indeed he had spent a few—a few more than most lovers would have.

Music had been one of his earliest pretexts for avoiding a female next of kin. "You don't really enjoy it," his mother had told him ages ago. "You just *want* to enjoy it."

Even then—he had been about fourteen—(of course he had really always been eighty) he had said, " What's wrong with *that*? "

So she had accepted his absence as further confirmation of her favourite theory that people don't really change— and can't be changed—except in so far as their glands change as they get older. Some genes were stones and some sandstones—but environment was always just the wind and could only do a little with the sandstones. She knew Lionel like the inside of her bag—and when he read those articles in the *Economist* he was just the same as he used to be on his pot—couldn't *bear* to be disturbed. Yet if you had the courage to face his screams when you moved him— and potted him in a different place then he was often happier than ever. And so it would be here when he got settled in. The smallest novelty made him feel insecure. That's why he liked all this psychology: by inviting these weird monkey-gods into his garden—he could pat them on their polysyllabic heads and feel secure from them. Id indeed—three letters were missing if you asked her.

" Well, Fidge'll get his name in the papers again," she said.

" Yes, Mother."

" If he weren't quite so *vulgar*, though I suppose we should be glad of him."

" Some of us should thank God for him every night."

" I know you're getting at me, Lionel. But I'll tell you this. If you and I were on the street—who d'you think would survive? "

" Mother, nowadays everybody ' on the street ' survives."

She wouldn't be shaken off. " Who d'you think would *prosper?* "

" Mother," he leant forward for the opportunity, " please never suppose for a moment that I doubt your capacity to prosper. I know perfectly well that your sinus trouble— is merely overheating in a vacuum—real, genuine energy and ability—*addled*."

" Rubbish. Really, Lionel, what you forget is that *we* used to talk like that—*forty years ago*—but only when we were seventeen."

" Well, I shall talk like that when I'm seventy."

" You've always been seventy."

" Why d'you think that is? "

" That's not the sort of thing one knows."

" Mightn't a mature and truly parental attitude be developed even at birth if an infant sensed itself in the hands of ageing children? "

" I've only one word for what you're saying and . . ."

" Freud had two: reversal of the generations."

" It's about time you had one word for Freud. Really, Lionel. I read Freud before you were born. As a matter of fact I read him when I was expecting you. In Albemarle Street."

A nuance here stayed Lionel's tongue in mid-movement.

After a sober, ironic look athwart his pipe tip he reflected again with satisfaction how she didn't know he was engaged—how, in essence, totally shed she was; pathetic, hanging on to a legal quibble with the blind confidence of desperation, believing it might still be possible to have him under her roof, and wear him down by the sheer vitality of her lived, negative impulses.

But having thus dismissed her—did he then enter into himself and find Laura?

And peace?

On the contrary, he felt facing backwards on a toboggan.

And at the tail end, facing him, was his mother. He sat staring at her. Suddenly he said:

" Mother, will you come with me in the train to-morrow —or will you . . . stay for a few days more? "

She was astonished. " It's the first *I* heard of anyone going."

" Mother—I was only remaining up here till the Brackenator was opened. You surely understood that . . ."

" What about the estate? "

He looked at her with imperious kindness. She was, since she insisted, his guest; and his friend as long as she behaved. But let her be warned—she was nothing more. " Mother—as soon as I get word that no court will sustain legal objection to my selling the estate—I shall start selling. You know that has always been my intention."

The statement sounded dead, settled by Laura, but it still had one green shoot on it—for his mother. It was true, still, for her.

" Your *intention*. And what about your uncle's *wishes*? "

" My uncle wished the best for Rossiemurchat. And so do I. That is why I shall sell it, if possible to someone who will live and farm here."

" Farm!—all you want is a good grieve . . ."

" Mother. There's really no point in continuing. Besides," he couldn't resist it, at this point, " the future is not so crystal-clear: I'm engaged."

" So is everyone else," she snapped, " but they find time to rest and—enjoy themselves in the country. You get liberal holidays. Besides land's an excellent investment. You get off 30 per cent at death."

" Mother—I meant I'm engaged to be married."

To be surprised was to be at a disadvantage—a plight in which Gwendoline would never dawdle.

"Who to?" she said tersely—and then, "Laura."

It was no good, she still was pinioned—by surprise, but softening all the time with satisfaction.

"So Manchester's had it has he," she said, beginning to smile—then she suddenly put down her knitting and looked at her son. "My dear Lionel—I'm so glad."

He winced. He was getting his colours for soccer. Never before—he realised—had she addressed him in quite that tone. If the poor used to smell—then the rich still did—and his mother didn't miss the lovely aroma—even from afar.

Or was he unjust?

"*So* glad," she repeated in a grey soft reverie of calculation, her brain the mere beam of her stomach, playing on him.

"Yes—I think that's a very good thing," she said, averting her eyes, perhaps because her last thought had come as a shock even to herself. "Perfectly capital. When did you hear?"

He frowned.

She laid a hand to her brow—the self rebuke for dawning madness. "I mean when did you *decide*."

"Yesterday——" he discovered, was his reply.

She knitted away, levelly, hoisted more wool free—and in complete silence knitted, knitted it in.

Stop it he wanted to say, just stop it—it's not going to be anything like that.

*   *   *

A dais had been erected in the vicinity of the Brackenator. The small arc of dicky chairs was almost displaced by the wind until finally steadied by the weight of the two

directors, Lady Fidge, the Secretary for Scotland, April
and the two Fluach children whose fathers had died in
some far corner, Sir Duncan said, of a foreign field, thus
fitting them to press the Brackenator starter and then hold
up the first length of rope.

Lionel's gaberdine lacked a button low down and so a
flap chivvied him the whole time into contortions such as
women are supposed to make with their skirts when a
mouse is reported present. Sir Duncan's kilt, it would have
been supposed, raised as it was higher than eye-level, should
surely have neutralised one hand throughout—but for
some reason it scarcely stirred. Lionel suspected weights
in the lining, as for Communists in the capes of French
policemen.

Two people who were as tall almost as April sprouted
out of the dun level of the crowd. One was Laura, gaily
painted in a dowdy mackintosh, the other was the
Rev. Skene, who stared at the transaction of the rostrum
like a desert hermit suddenly vexed with a mirage of
such carnal frisking as he had never known he knew
happened.

Meanwhile, Sir Duncan's testing of the microphone
must have dismayed his bitterest political opponents with
the knowledge that if he lost his seat he'd be back with the
circus.

" Aloalloallo, ALLO, pish, bzz," he boomed—and then
as though it had nothing to do with real communication
he peered round the side of it and shouted, well clear and
more audibly, " Was that all right?—Hallo there, SYDNEY
TAWSE. Hallo, MRS. TAWSE."

The ommission of the Christian name drew many eyes
to her face and then sharply away again—as though her
mouth had all but got them. In the past Fidge must have

lost a bit of antennæ in that same gin-trap or he would have put her in headline capitals.

"Well, now, ladies and gentlemen . . ." and away he went, pausing only to address the television team. "Hallo there, Henry. Now say if the angle's too flat. Want a table? Want two tables?"

Soon he was in his most familiar position holding in front of him two people by the upper arm, thrusting them into deserved publicity—even though they were children.

"Henry Lot and Giuseppina (hey where do you come from) McAughtrie will now . . . START" he began shouting now to people in the hills behind "START . . . this NEW INVENTION . . . BROUGHT TO . . . US BY THE PERSEVER-ANCE . . ."

Lionel was just behind him, the dark shaven part of his jowl mingling imperceptibly with his cheek purple with cold, his lower lip caught in the teeth of endurance and hanging on, so to speak, only by his eyelids to the purport of the M.P.s words, one out of three being the most he ever heard.

He was therefore startled when a hand in brilliant pigskin strayed back leaving one of the children free—and grasped his upper arm.

"LIONEL SPOTE . . ."

He was raised. To his astonishment the crowd roared and clapped. He grinned, weeping from the wind and at the idea of his being cheered—and subsided into an even more contracted and attentive shape than before.

"Without whom—let it be written in fire—neither the bracken—nor the road to the oil well—would have become available."

"AND MRS. GUNTER-SYKES . . . er" said Sir Duncan

229

already fluting into the next word but pointing back to the outside left chair where April inclined with terrible geniality towards the mutter of clapping "and to the wonderful technicians" Sir Duncan suddenly hissed, angry, bumping his fist down on the air "the *MEN*"—he was still angry "THE WORKERS—who made this *superb* invention AND" his hand was up, hark! "YOU—the investors. Small investors. You've already responded *magnificently* with *Faith*—the sort of faith the Highlands need." And then . . .

"Monsieur Savette—PAUL SAVETTE—who I knew in Flanders—IN 1918—who let me have it—BEFORE THE AMERICANS—for pounds—not for dollars—but for pounds. FLUACH POUNDS" he yelled, staring into the faces, "who said Bodger, mon ammy—prennez la—which means take it . . ."

"Or leave it," somebody shouted. But the crowd didn't approve. They wanted more. So Fidge never heard.

He went on and on.

The wind blew. He told the story of the Brackenator. A man had escaped from prison by making a rope of bracken stalks. Later he met Paul Savette. There had been failure, and failure—and failure. "But about then I happened to run into Paul on the Golden Arrow—I said, Paul —go on." Fidge's voice dropped an emotional mile. He opened to the crowd, via his wide eyes, his whole heart and the ear which he got cauliflowered on their behalf. Quietly, firmly, he said,

"Two years later I got my reward. He said, Bodger— take it."

The applause was prolonged. Lionel noticed it contained a curious mixture of his own feelings for Sir Duncan. A certain hysterical hilarity—as though the next number was a dance—yet also tribute, yes tribute for like a gaudy floating casino he was yet preferable to the only visible alternative—the sea.

Then the Secretary of State for Scotland. He was much that was deplorable but none of what was vicious in the Conservative Party. Oh, my God, my God—thought Lionel, he's nice. As nice as me—hoo-hoo—and he caught his nose-tip hard—to make it all more distant.

The suave, diffident voice had collected some shadow of assertion in office. "... how extraordinarily *lucky* we are to have Sir *Duncan* ..." Public school prefect—speeches in Latin—and then tea in his room, then back to the deck chairs—and the movement of the slim white figures. The sharp crack of bat and ball—and the two running across each other—and the one running far out, alone ...

Lionel now was really hurting his nose. Lord Lord Lord Lord. He murmured, " Oh pity for the fated fur-collar."

" The energy of Sir Duncan ... champion of Highland development." In thanking him Fidge shouted, " Why didn't you applaud him properly. He's come a long way."

But he was clearly delighted they hadn't.

Then the rush to the Brackenator—Lady Fidge holding the little girl's hand with both of hers against harm, against the close bedlam of the thing's rhythmic flatulence and jug-a-jug jug-a-jug. Sir Duncan still shouting ... had both the children now. Moloch—was he going to pop them in? Their eyes suggested it. He was taking them to the rear, stooping, instructing them in front of the polished steel sphincter where soon ... ah ... now ... the crowd's

eagerness showed like a breeze across leaves—there—the
rope—slowly—like a conjurer's climax—inch by inch—
the rope.

Lionel found himself by Laura. " *On s'enmerde, pro-
gressivement,*" he yelled.

" What ? "

" I told Gwendoline," he shouted.

" And I told mummy—what a coincidence," she shouted
defiantly. " Did you ? " he said, not pleased. Their hands
locked in the crush. Who was this barring their movement ?
That minister. The Rev. Skene.

" Excuse me," Lionel said.

" I will not."

" Good afternoon, Mr. Skene," Laura said.

" I'm glad you think so, Mrs. Childe," he said with
selective affability—to her.

Lionel said, " May we pass, please. I don't quite . . ."

Mr. Skene's eyes were now only for Lionel, and at last
for his hand, holding Laura's. He didn't budge. At Lionel's
instigation they moved past. He rotated, watching them all
the time. Lionel murmured " Certifiable " and some yards
on turned to look back. The minister still stood, staring
at him.

" That man," Lionel said, " affects me physically. Quite
a lot, too. Himmler's id was in long clothes compared to
his."

Laura laughed. And *was it possible* . . . not entirely on
his, her fiancé's behalf . . . ?

★ ★ ★

The cars moved in procession from the Brackenator to
the Seaforth Arms. Salmson sat talking, alone in a Hillman
van. He was not driving yet it sped along.

April sat grey beside Gwendoline who was voluble.

In a coffee-coloured Rolls Lady Fidge clasped the children who had put in the symbolic length of rope. When ever flash bulbs popped her sleep-walking face became sudden, powdered death—smiling.

But Fidge was ebullient. He clasped many arms to prevent their owners talking, moving or even fluttering. When her flow faltered, or if he changed verbal gear, he gripped arms harder, to prevent the gap being turned into another's opportunity.

The Seaforth Arms looked over a last tee towards the Baltic. The windows were smeared with brine.

To-day the pin-flags stood out stiff and flatulent in the wind. Gulls looked affronted when they had to take little steps, among the white feathers and sheep dung, to keep balance.

Already in the Arms Car Park the main body had been preceded by the official vehicles of the Milk Marketing Board, County Roads Surveyor, the Hydro Board and District Nurse.

A piper was tuning up, in the sun lounge, like a lost donkey.

*   *   *

In the crush Lionel could see stuffed brown trout in glass cases. A man as high as his navel and broad and deep as three of him, took his hand and repeated " Meester Spoot . . . Meester Spoot . . . Meester Spoot . . ."

Drunk, promiscuously warmhearted, pityful or grateful . . . ? Lionel did not know. He devoted his whole person to reciprocal incoherence, with emphasis on warmth.

Then, there was Rupert—his brother-in-law-to be.

" I really am glad, Lionel," Rupert said tonelessly.

There was no hill like a German tin hat on which their

eyes could converge at a safe distance. Lionel was able to peer over people's heads in a grimace against the emotion he felt—and Rupert looked vaguely backwards through a gap to the door.

Then Lionel bent swiftly and with his fingers pinched for exactly the right quantity of snuff he snarled tenderly and ironically at his friend.

" I think it might add up—don't you? "

" It adds up for me."

" *Rupert!* " Lionel said as though *they* were engaged, and then, because no tongue, it seemed, could say more, " Are you up here for long? "

" Two days."

" Any change . . ." he said, meaning the farm.

If Lionel seemed sometimes a cross between eighteen and eighty, Rupert was a cross between eight and ninety. He lifted child's eyes to his friend and announced blankly, " I've taken on the cadets."

Lionel misheard—was corrected.

Now he said, blankly, " You've taken on the cadets? "

" Your uncle had them. A chap called Musker, Inverurie rang me up. I said I'd have to think it over. Then Mother rang—he must have got on to her. They can't get anyone else."

" But you live in London . . . ? "

" Yes—but they can't get anyone else. You see your retired colonel of yesteryear is bursting his heart growing commercial raspberries, to pay his milk bill. And raspberries don't do here. So—no colonels."

" But Rupert—from Tite Street——"

" I pointed that out. But this Musker man said there was no one else. He said I had a good No. 2—Mackay— at the Drill Hall. As a matter of fact he's U/S."

In friendship you took nothing for granted: Rupert, perhaps, was pleased. Lionel faced him seriously. "Well —congratulations, Rupert."

But Rupert invited comment. He said tentatively:

"They must be pushed . . .?"

Suddenly Lionel decided.

"You know—I'm sorry. But I don't think you can. Rupert, I'm afraid you've got to ring up—now. And resign."

"Just like that?"

"Have you got small change? Let me give it to you." Lionel was harried. "It's really more important than you know . . . speak in the most categorical terms." He began to usher Rupert to a gap.

It was a relief to see that grave and elderly mouse disappear into the glass box. Lionel turned back to the crowd feeling better.

"Hallo."

To be hailed with tolerant ennui by Other Fleight was not delightful.

"Hallo," Lionel said coolly. Fleight's kilt was torn and he looked dirty as well as soft-hearted and fanatical.

"Congratulations."

"On what?"

"I understood from Rupert you were engaged to Laura."

"It appears to have been broadcast."

"You're right. Once *I* knew—it had."

This was not right. Perhaps he had started it. Lionel frowned, smiling. "Anyhow thank you—very much."

"Are you going to live up here?" Fleight said more calmly.

"No."

"I'm sorry."

Lionel was mollified. It sounded meant. He said:

" By the way I've been meaning to ask you—if ever you have anything for publication we should be extremely . . ."

" I seem to have heard all this before, somewhere."

" Yes . . . I suppose it's the drill. Anyhow . . ."

" I'll remember."

" *Anything*. Apocalyptic foam—or a disenturbulator for the train."

" A what? "

" A disenturbulator. You might try one." Lionel felt apprehensive—as when passing the rear end of a horse. He must explain more. " See things thetawise. By themselves. Not Part of Something."

" Well, aren't they? "

Lionel began to edge away. " No," he smiled uneasily: he had known a German prison orderly who had looked like Other was looking now. " No," he repeated, " For God's sake, no. That's the point. Think about it "—and then there he was free in the crowd again, thankful and again a healer. Related.

★   ★   ★

" What've ye bin doing to Pipe Major Hew Mackay? " said a voice.

" Dr. Smiley, I never saw you."

" Well, what've ye bin doin' t'm—that's what I want to know. He's called you things I've never heard of. Broadened my education just listening to him."

" I'm afraid I don't understand."

" And he's written ' Mr. Spote go home' all over the urinal at the local. He's lying with a handkerchief in his mouth. He's dangerous."

News of this kind was always vaguely expected but he

could never understand the joy people took in breaking it.

"But Dr. Smiley—if you hadn't told me I'd never have known. And I don't really see why I *need* have known. Because I've had no dealings with him of any kind."

Yet Lionel's face, as he spoke, was a picture of responsibility.

"Well, at dinner the other night, you were talking about being reletted. I thought I'd relet you to Pipe Major Hew Mackay, who's going to use yer belly skin to make a haggis of yer heart."

"If he's the man I now think you mean my impression of him was: a hysteric."

"Ai," said Smiley wearily, "yer right: he's blubbing."

He looked away moodily and Lionel felt an alien painbearer.

"Though what *I've* got to do——"

People were looking round at them as at whisperers in a cinema.

"Sydney Tawse," Fidge was saying, "I have much pleasure in presenting you—the first stoker on the Brackenator—with this clock."

Sir Duncan's agent using both hands, transferred to Sir Duncan an outsize, sloping, polished clock, made in England, which Sir Duncan pressed into the strong arms of Sydney Tawse, looking up as he did so into the magnesium flashes.

Outside the pipes played *Crinan*.

"And now," said Sir Duncan, flinging an arm towards a dust sheet at the far end of the room, "we shall smite such a boom—for the Highlands, Sydney, for the Highlands —as shall never be put out. Dick—where are you, Dick— right: show us what with."

Two or three twitches on a tape—and there!—the legendary Gong was revealed suspended—as everybody by then blasély expected, by two slender lengths of bracken rope.

Lionel edged politely to Laura. Without looking at him her face showed knowledge of his arrival—and of the time she had waited for it.

" This should be good," he said.

" I don't know why you make so much fuss about your mother," she whispered. " We got on like a house on fire."

Lionel, frowning slightly, switched thought to the gong. It was, he perceived, a sort of igloo in cast iron . . . he hoped he would never have to live in that house on fire and the man who was going to strike it as in Gaumont British—a " house on fire " indeed; so what!—for five intitial minutes about what church, whether white or not, bridesmaids . . . yet

suppose they *did*

really

get on

like a *house on fire* . . .

*   *   *

The THUD—pause—shimmering disintegrating expanding annihilating humming which was also a pounding at minute intervals of ear-drums, yet also *sur le plan majeur*, part of one stunning total crash—was the sort of lark Lionel deplored with one wince of his raped reason and outraged sensibility.

His eyes remained shut—while goats in series across Scotland cocked a sudden ear and with eye of vital stupidity paused to speculate.

Lionel was about to open his eyes when he heard another

238

even more formidable THUD—not again he thought and his whole being winced on the brink of another ear-bursting chime in this high noon of madness.

But nothing came.

He heard a hum like disturbed flies.

Laura's hand suddenly bit into his flesh. "Look," she said with rabid, incredulous glee, "the gong. It's on the ground."

And so it was—beneath two frayed tails of bracken rope.

Whisper turned to mutter, mutter to agitation. Fidge was seen making his way to it—then his hands were up high fluttering towards the faces for silence.

"Ladies and gentlemen—my friends: if you lift a battleship with a strand of cotton—for ten minutes—and it then breaks—there's a kind of person—there's a kind of person—which goes home—and says—SAYS "—he turned this way and that, "that's lousy cotton. That's horrible weak cotton."

There was a murmur of reluctant laughter.

Lionel turned. "I think I want to go home."

"Why?"

"I just do."

When he perceived he was fuel to her mirth he cocked one eyebrow—slightly—but enough to have made a related person feel small—and said:

"If you think it's funny to have indirectly persuaded poor people to put their money into . . ." he paused at a loss, ". . . *fudge*," he nailed it into her, "then I'm afraid you must split your sides alone."

24

LITTLE GLEN sat in the window.

"Gosh," he cried, "luik, there's Russian sodgers in the street—dozens of 'em. Quick, luik!"

Pipe Major Mackay looked up. His eyes had the squashy look of hangover and/or tears. His mouth had a dyspeptic falling away to one side—and the bulb of his nose was lonely, as though it had taken on at last, like the gorgeous canker on oak, a life of its own. But he sat very straight and distinctly convalescent. He had turned, clearly, some profound, obscure, corner—by the skin of his teeth.

Then he continued to write:

". . . in view of the honour you do me in pressing me to become secretary for the Lifeboat Association I cannot readily see my way to declining."

His lady's nib never scruffed a word—stunted one with speed; never mutilated a letter on behalf of brevity, or legibility. Sometimes in sheer exuberance he wrapped a letter—having finished it—in its own self—so that it looked out of its tail like a cat wasn't it. So:

"However I should early make it clear, Sir, that having regard to the nature of my several commitments

240

in this area will preclude my giving to your worthy cause as much time as I should like."

"Luik—they're shuittin' Mr. Macauley."
He raised his eyes again—his body twitched slightly—in the direction of the window, then he felt his chin. And continued:

"As concerning condition which I must put to acceptance—except to say it hurts me to make it. That is: when replying I'd be glad if you'd indemnify more fully what expenses are provided for travel in the matter of door to door collections, organisations of feats and the like.

With best wishes I remain yours faithfully,
HEW MACKAY"

He dipped his pen in—examined the amount of ink that globuled the blade—and then with a brisk whisk did a C like the very crescent moon on an Ottoman banner. More carefully, but as beautifully he finished:

-O-L-O-N-E-L.
"Luik—they've Mrs. Lindsay by the skirt . . ."
Torn for a moment by dilemma—he did neither the one nor the other—just sat staring up past the boy on the sill; but at last he read back—his lips thrusting out a little.
He modelled in a few commas like performing tadpoles, and underlined Colonel in wavy red.
Then—and only in his own time—not at all hurried—he went to the window, and with some apprehension peered round the angle, till he saw the whole street.
"Don't," he said gravely and scarcely audibly, "be saying such things"—and with a mind permitted at last to be only half present he strolled a little to and fro.

Once he stopped and announced, " Now, boy . . ."
But the emotion was too much. He had to walk some
more.

★   ★   ★

Laura came to stay at Rossiemurchat the following day.
Lionel never quite knew why. His mother said she had
heard " you arranged it together "; and he heard from
Laura his mother had conveyed an invitation at her son's
request. Finally he was given the impression that it had
been laid down in some Norn-spun fabric of female um-
bilibalence, which could be interpreted (if you wished
to waste the time) as you chose. Anyhow it happened.
The house was his and he was leaving it on Sunday night,
but she was to come and join Salmson, and his mother,
making in all three uninvited guests.

"Aren't you going to fetch her?" his mother said seeing him slanting into a room with the *Manchester Guardian* of three days ago and two MSS. in ripped registered
packages.

" Mother—I haven't the foggiest idea when she's
coming."

It was the nearest he had come to protesting—a fact
which was revealed in the bitter emphasis on " foggiest "
and in his parted updrawn lips as though his mother were
high.

Suddenly spotting him clinically, she said, " Are you
acid to-day? I've got some new stuff."

★   ★   ★

The post, which arrived shortly before Laura, contained
a fat letter from a friend, a lawyer, to whom Lionel had
put his problem.

242

It said, in scarcely more words: Sell.

Lionel flipped the thing clear of him—and stared out of the window. There wasn't anything in the world he was sure of. Indeed the universe marched under some such sign as that which this moment descended the drive for no reason—Huish's car in which it could only be assumed as a matter of faith, that there was a Huish, though long ago—it is true he had witnessed one.

To sell or not now seemed a small matter.

He had committed himself to marriage.

Perfectly, perfectly still—he stood like a cat that has seen a near bird.

Was it possible that he, a man of reason, should have taken such a decision—as though accepting a cup of tea—or to go out to dinner?

Since yesterday he had no confidence. He sat aghast in the psychological wilderness of reason. Committed. . . .

With a mean and querulous lop-sidedness to his large well laid out face he picked up the *Northern Trumpet* and turned to what he expected . . . Fidge lunged out of the print with burning, come-off it confidence, pugnacious bothered-for-you sincerity.

" *M.P. tells Bracken-rope stress equalled jet dive* "—said the huge headline—ENGINEERS' STATISTICS

" The unfortunate incident whch marred the opening of the Fluach Brackenator must serve finally, said Sir Duncan in Geneva to-day, to give publicity to the rope's extraordinary endurance.

" If the gong had been troops marching over a bridge the frequency of its ' footfall ' backed by its weight (the same as that of a Churchill tank) would have amounted to a stress of forty thousand foot-pounds, or the equivalent strain met by the leading edge of a Dart jet fighter diving at 752 m.p.h."

"No other rope in the world, said Sir Duncan, could have looked at it. But if shareholders wished to sell up he knew of two ready buyers—the directors, Mr. Lionel Spote and himself."

Lionel put the paper by. He felt much older lately. Much much older. Laura was coming up the drive. Only the smallest chill-thrill tweeked his inside—and he let her pass the window without moving, without even much change of expression. Here, he thought, is my train now.

★   ★   ★

At lunch he felt a gooseberry. Laura looking round said she could remember having tea here during the war on Sundays when she was a landgirl.

* I have never experienced nostalgia, Lionel thought.

It was slightly better in the afternoon. He and Laura went down to the river and walked along it, pleased to have no rods and no more decisions to make.

"In a way," he said, "I suppose when the time comes and the bills of sale go up, I shall be rather sad."

She looked at him—and as a result smiled, obliquely, shelvingly, "Nothing." She took his arm more firmly with both hers moulding her body to his.

Later, she said, "There's plenty of time—to make up our minds."

"Laura—we have two separate minds."

"I know: I said our—because it's shorter than 'my mind and your mind.'"

On Monday the office. They would get a flat. She would take the *Express* and *Mirror* and on Sundays the whole boiling. She would brood over them like a hen over addled eggs, vaguely alienated but still broody.

They would see the Parkinsons, the Richetts, the Forbes-Matchetts, the Tates and Pilkingtons, all within a mile of Chelsea town hall. It would be like playing patience on a raft.

She would be unaware of his desire for disenturbulation at the piano but in a way this would be an insurance against the sort of presumptions and familiarities which a half-cock sympathy with his mental life might have entailed.

And he—he began snarling—would no doubt be painfully inadequate in *les petits soins de l'amour*—if that meant licking her behind the knees, and praising her looks before a party. No. There would be order. Presents, kisses at certain agreed moments accompanied by a mooing noise of irony to keep the thing safe and whatever service was advised regularly by the makers. "*Tu l'as voulu*," he muttered.

"What?"

"Nothing."

"I thought you said something."

"I assure you I didn't," he said with feeling.

After a speculative silence she smiled. They went on.

"Do you remember this place?" she said.

"Ah," he said. "This is where you caught your first salmon."

They stopped. She peered for the webby waving shape of a fish. He glowered against the ennui of the country, insisting it had "a place." At last inhaling vigorously the pure air.

She said suddenly, fast "Whether you sell Rossiemurchat or not—may not make much odds. I never told you did I: my uncle's leaving me Dundane."

"And what, may I ask, is Dundane?"

"A place near here. About three hundred thousand acres."

She had turned to face him and as a result lost the confidence to continue.

"Just ' By the way . . .' " he said oddly "Just like that I mean?"

"It's true."

"Oh doubtless. And now the marriage is fixed—I suppose this is the moment to sketch yourself in; tell me casually that I've got to give up my profession . . ."

He might have guessed. The ubiquitous Selection Board hadn't finished emphasising the ramifications of his suitability: he was to be Prime Minister of Ruritania.

"Most people would be pleased."

"I'll tell you possibly in some weeks," he said judiciously, "what I feel about being a Duke in the age of collective avalanches."

And there he stood. His eyes shrunk, by apprehension, to the size of fulltops, remained upon her unqualified by sexual flow of any kind.

"You are an ass," she said, having considered him.

"All right I'm an ass: perhaps you'd care to withdraw your proposal of marriage . . .?"

She turned away, being a non-crier, and walked in a funny sort of hunch.

He took hold of her arm and squeezed it enough to hurt his own bloodiness. They went on.

She peered for a fish and in bending for a stick steadied herself by his arm, which like its mate, was plunged, rigid, into the gaberdine.

"What are you doing?" he said nervously—the battle being to believe one was where one was.

"What are you doing now?" he repeated.

"I'm going to throw a stick in."

She was going to throw a stick in. Relief.

And the spash soon laid the matter.

"It's floating," he cheered. Then something . . . the electric light in his hen-battery mind slowly dimmed. In the immense mollification of this gloaming he felt her body pressed to his.

They went on—her eyes downcast, the lamp of expectation shaded with disappointment. It would be often like this. But it was not romantically tragic. She too was self-contained. Financial self-sufficiency had engendered other kinds of self-sufficiency. And she had loved once in a different way.

*   *   *

"Isn't she the flower?" Mrs. O'Shea sighed inwards, ogling him close.

"Well, *I* think so, anyway," he managed.

"I'm telling you she is," she contradicted, suddenly severe.

"Good."

"And my, you'll have to be looking after her," she laughed, her eyes shining with fiddle music, bundling and bells tied to the bed springs. He couldn't endure it; he would insist she meant merely consideration.

"Mrs. O'Shea—I shall do my best."

"I never saw a bull that didn't," she reflected (he was quite cornered—in the passage) " but " (she leant forward and whispered conniving), " be gentle because you'll not be knowing—oh, I can see—but you mustn't mind me what I say. I'm just an old woman."

"As a matter of fact," he burst out, " I *do* rather mind

what you say. And I rather suspect, Mrs. O'Shea, all this vaunted Highland honesty could be called something else."

"There then," she sighed, focusing instantly a thousand yards deep into the carpet. "There—I'm sorry, Mr. Spote. Ai sorry."

"Well—let's forget it."

"I was speaking," Mrs. O'Shea now insisted, with a gesture to one side, touching, in the air, a vernacular he might know, "out of my place isn't it?"

"No, *no* . . ."

Why did this woman always involve him like some bad films in the most ludicrous tendency to cry?

"No, Mrs. O'Shea, no," and he, who avoided other skin with his, again pressed her hand. "And thank you —you have a contribution—a very real contribution—to all sorts of people, in fact almost everyone I know."

"But . . ."

It was a big "but." She couldn't have everything her own way all the time. She must answer one thing:

"But I should like to know one thing: why did you make me feel as if I had committed a crime the other day —when the gardens were opened on Sunday. As far as I can see people were delighted."

He had spoken sternly.

"Which people?" she said.

"Well, except the minister,—at the bracken opening."

"Ai—at the bracken opening."

"And even at the garden opening."

"Ai—at the garden opening, too. Just boys with bottles or folks from lodges wasn't it?"

"I don't think so, entirely," he said firmly.

She said nothing. Lionel's eyes narrowed on her. She looked away.

* Perhaps just a *really* stupid woman.

At last she sang low and quite on one note: " It's true—everything is changing. But," she made a slow pass in thin air, " there are still people who . . ."

During the perfectly judged pause before the word which was still to come, she raised her large eyes to his so that his whole aggression and superior mental mobility was held like a wasp in marmalade. He felt in that stare, sluggish with vicarious humility, defeated—whole seconds before she finally chimed the last word like a closing chord:

". . . *mind.*"

He could not speak. No word would come.

* The feeling-level. He never even had a pawn to help out.

" WELL—I'm sorry," he said at last. " And . . ."

" It's done," she interrupted firmly.

Feeling better (i.e. less inferior) at once for this merely triumphant ejaculation he said:

" Well, it will soon be forgotten, Mrs. O'Shea. Besides —the sabbath was made for God, not man for the sabbath."

He was not quite sure he had got it right—a doubt she at once doubled, saying: " Is that it."

" Now you must forgive me, Mrs. O'Shea . . ."

" Yes, she'll be waiting on you. And what's a clever man like you wasting time with a silly old woman for. Oh, but my, she'll sort you."

This last prophecy was delivered with a raddled chuckle in such sharp contrast to the previous prayer-tones that Lionel winced. To manage to feel twice in a minute was pain enough; to be made to feel, in opposite directions five times in half a minute was to be raped.

He withdrew, murmuring something to this effect, backwards, confident that he need never feel he was talking above her head, even supposing he knew where her head was.

*   *   *

His mother knitted towards, even *into* Laura. Her silky interrogation met with not the slightest resistance. Perhaps, Lionel thought, April had never asked Laura anything, perhaps Laura was marrying him to be asked endlessly about herself by a mother. Then she had made a brilliant match.

On his knees his thumb subsided, followed by his index finger, followed by his longest bloodless finger—so—three days.

" You just went for the *summer* holidays to Ardstruie, then ? " his mother purred.

He got up—collected some papers, a book. Where was that other book ? He pointed in dumb play to his movements an hour ago—from there to there—to there, no book. He held his chin with formal protest—and went out.

At the foot of the stairs he paused to hear if Mrs. O'Shea was on the move upstairs. Silence. Lightly he sprinted up.

Laura had the room opposite his—a provision of his mother's which was confirmation (about his mother) if any had been needed.

But—he thought pausing in fury—it is one thing to dot a girl's i—quite another to fence her out of her room with three towel horses like a child's puff-puff, draped with clammy underclothes.

He would say something, as he passed. He rather wanted to interrupt in a certain tone of voice the uterine cats'-cradle that was developing on the sofa.

250

"Mother," he said, putting his head in, "I think you might let Laura get in and out of her room."

The two heads stared round as though flummoxed by his words—and in a larger sense by him, too.

"I mean," he said louder, "the washing. Three horses of washing blocking her door—and making furthermore an intolerable humidity by the pipes in the passage. There are, you know, *two* drying rooms——" and he turned to Laura. "My mother's fetish. Washing knickers. You just have to accept it."

Laura said, "I'm afraid that must be me."

Mrs. Spote said with her pale hand at her grey throat.

"*I* haven't been washing."

"Not you," Lionel said.

"No——" Laura was blushing—he had spoken with such extraordinary—well the word didn't leap to the mind with him—but passion, yes, on this occasion, passion. "I'll move them," she said embarrassed suddenly, behaving like a guest, almost like a little girl, "I can move them at once."

He would not hear of it—nor could he be sufficiently, apologetic. But lightly, lightly. The whole had no importance. "Laura—quite unpardonable of me." He shut her in when she was half-way to the door—and then he began to sing—to sing Tre-laldarra—tralaldarra.

At last a door crashed.

Gwendoline Spote reversed a needle smiling and drew closer. There was such a lot to go into. She was *most* glad of this delightful opportunity—*most* glad . . .

"He gets notions . . ." she began coolly.

25

WAS SPOTE complacent? Did he pursue guilts and not they him, just because he had no innate or organised sense of Sin?

Such was his main concern, as he went down to St. James Street, with a paranoiac reply from Fidge in his wallet, all on the eve of marrying Laura.

The clock at the bottom said midday. Its legs were one, like those of a drowned fly, upside down. It must have stopped, pending some total overhaul.

His shoulders were level.

So Fidge had burst like Humpty Dumpty.

Hilde could be God-Mother to their first.

Everything was bright with sun. Cotton frocks shimmered like bunting down the crowded hill. The tar blocks smelt; the women smelt and upon one his eye, rested and not on her face till finally. He even noticed the suggested division of her lower limbs long before it could be called legs.

* New Life always comes from the muddy—and moves towards the pure.

Have I a green shoot, Spote asked himself. Because if I have I ought to make myself available, I ought to start something . . .

* A Group.

The gravity of his face, as he entertained this thought might, in certain circumstances, have resulted in him being arrested, offered a fee as a model, treated for *dementia praecox* or avoided by the young.

Instead, a small logical positivist, slavering with inferiority, came into his head and kicked his thoughts in the stomach and when they were already on the ground, in the teeth. Call it the seven thousand a year Group, said the Positivist.

One of Lionel's shoulders moved slightly upwards—but his thoughts got up and walked on. Without teeth.

* Inferiority is inferiority, he replied.

* Relativism, turned back and used against its shrillest advocates—the logical positivists—nearly always reveals a large measure of predatory vileness, despite the frequent camouflage of no style (in writing) and no " position " (in society). They are all *communisants*.

And in them feeling is repressed and infantile.

People like me could be a Considerable Force, he thought, if we got together. We could provide—not a new engine, for that is an extension of the nightmare—but a Parachute. And one that didn't alight on the bandwagon of collectivity, but upon . . .

Lionel had a flitting vision of a Movement, or better still a new Mood, based perhaps on Seaford Castle . . . weekends made up of Jungian Psychologists, Priests, Probation Officers, Trade Union Leaders and Managers. Pamphlets: " Automation humanised ", " Go to the Moon—but take your Self with you ", " Towards. And not Because ".

And like a deaf man walking down a railway line on a windy day, in front of a grey goods, he thought and felt free—and related . . .

* My dear friends, he felt suddenly.

He turned into the office. There sat the girl in front of the switchboard. She was further on with *Crime and Punishment.*

" Hallo, Daphne."

" Oh, hallo, Mr. Spote . . ."

But no, not to-day. He went up soberly.

Then Archie Mackintosh came out, his face bright and pregnant.

" Hallo, Archie."

" I say Lionel—congratulations."

" Why ? "

" Your engagement, it's in *The Times.*"

" Oh, yes," he remembered, " it might be."

They stood together—trying to pick up a thread. Lionel caught the end of his nose—where, where had they got to.

" Thank you, Archie, *thank you.*"

" You look better, if may say so. "

Lionel frowned.

" All settled—sold up ? "

" No . . . no. As a matter of fact we're thinking of keeping the place."

In Archie's slow, approving, but surprised reaction he read a question which he couldn't embark on. Instead he looked at him with his frank suggestible eyes, seeming to say: no doubt I have been digested into it, but that, Archie, is life.

And he smiled—with a sweetness that was uncommon by virtue of its attempt to equate his powerlessness with even that of the fly at present trifling by Archie's left ear.

Archie said, " I couldn't understand more, old boy." Then his voice dropped reverently. " By the way, don't you march with April Gunter-Sykes ? "

After a pause, in which he looked reflectively aside Lionel replied. " Yes . . ." but some bubbles had formed and he had to clear them before concluding: " Yes, Archie, I suppose really I do."

THE END

CPSIA information can be obtained
at www.ICGtesting.com
Printed in the USA
LVOW12s2108071217
559042LV00001B/66/P

9 780648 023326